"Not that the story need be long, but it
will take a long while to make it short."
— Henry David Thoreau

The Light in the Piazza

Elizabeth Spencer is acknowledged as one of today's outstanding fiction writers. Born in Carrollton, Mississippi, she
graduated from Belhaven College and Vanderbilt University. Her short stories — which have appeared regularly for
four decades in such magazines as *The New Yorker, The
Atlantic, The Southern Review*, and *McCall's* — were published
by Penguin in a single volume, *The Stories of Elizabeth Spencer*,
to unanimous acclaim. She is also the author of several
highly praised novels, including *Fire in the Morning, The Voice
at the Back Door, No Place for an Angel, The Snare*, and her most
recent novel, *The Salt Line*. She has received four O. Henry
Awards, the Rosenthal Award of the American Academy of
Arts and Letters, a Guggenheim Fellowship, and, most
recently, the American Academy of Arts and Letters Award
of Merit Medal for the Short Story. Ms Spencer and her husband make their home in Montreal.

THE LIGHT IN THE PIAZZA

Elizabeth Spencer

Penguin Books

Penguin Books Canada Limited, 2801 John Street,
Markham, Ontario, Canada L3R 1B4
Penguin Books Ltd., Harmondsworth, Middlesex, England
Penguin Books, 40 West 23rd Street, New York, New York 10010 U.S.A.
Penguin Books Australia Ltd., Ringwood, Victoria, Australia
Penguin Books (N.Z.) Ltd., Private Bag, Takapuna, Auckland 9,
New Zealand

First published by Penguin Books Canada Ltd. 1986

Copyright © Elizabeth Spencer, 1960, 1965, 1985, 1986

All rights reserved.

Typesetting by Jay Tee Graphics Ltd.
Manufactured in Canada

Canadian Cataloguing in Publication Data
Spencer, Elizabeth, 1921-
The light in the piazza

(Penguin short fiction)
Contents: The light in the piazza — Knights and
dragons — The cousins.
ISBN 0-14-008712-5

I. Title. II. Series.

PS3537.P44L53 1986   813'.54   C85-099713-5

To Gloria and Tom

In lunga amicizia e con tanti bei ricordi

Acknowledgements

''The Light in the Piazza'' copyright © 1960 by Elizabeth Spencer first appeared in somewhat different form in *The New Yorker*. The version used in this collection was published by McGraw-Hill Book Company.

''Knights and Dragons'' copyright © 1965 by Elizabeth Spencer, reprinted from *The Stories of Elizabeth Spencer* by permission of Doubleday & Company, Inc.

''The Cousins'' copyright © 1985 by Elizabeth Spencer first appeared in *The Southern Review*.

THE LIGHT IN THE PIAZZA

Contents

Introduction

Introduction

The first time I saw Italy was in August of 1949, and I was half-asleep. It was the third, final month of my first summer abroad, my first trip to Europe. I had undertaken the venture on the modest proceeds of my first novel and the invitation from a close friend to visit her in Germany, where she had been working for three years with the American occupation. Except for a happy time I had spent in Paris while waiting for my permit to enter Germany, I had had so far little to rejoice about. To my friend and her fiancé, who tried their best to see that I "had a good time," I must have seemed hopelessly uninitiated to the moral rigors of postwar Europe. To them I must have been like a chirpy sparrow, flitting by accident through the horrors of a Max Ernst painting. I can see that now. My country training, for instance, had made me view all visits as a little like house parties — a bad mistake. While they worked daily in their government offices, in cloudy Bad Nauheim, I hung around the empty apartment a friend of theirs had lent me, reading, or walked in the village, knowing scarcely a word of German. I shivered at the pool. What, besides the temperature, was the difference between this and a dull summer in some little Southern town? There, at least, friends might call and come. I took to riding horses at a local stable, and so met a young Viennese who began to ask me out. He, too, was at loose ends, waiting for a work permit. My friends rose up with disapproval and suspicion. Who was he? What did he want? Mississippi old maids a dozen years back had cut up this way. I had to give up a pleasant friendship. My friends had worked in Nuremberg during the trials, and in this and many other episodes, they must have been right, as my life so far, they pointed out, had not got me prepared for things there.

All miseries end. This one ended for us all three when my pass ran out. I had a month to spend somewhere. What to do? Drearily (Germany had got to me, too) I agreed that the best choice was Italy. There might at least, I thought, be some sun. I came down on the night train to Milan.

Sun.

In the predawn light, I crept by taxi through the kind of bombed-out area I had become used to seeing in German towns. I wondered, as I locked the door to my hotel room in a bare new structure that still smelled of fresh cement, if I shouldn't go back to Paris after a few days and see people there again before my return. It had been the one happy time, with little French restaurants to discover and the sights to see, picnics in the Bois de Fontainebleau and evenings at the Deux Magots. With this resolve, I slept and woke. Breakfast came up. Coffee such as I had never known before — rich, smooth and hot. Tender croissants. Gobs of butter and jam. I pulled a blind. Sun poured into the room. I opened a window. Singing came up from the streets. All this in a vanquished city whose horrors of so short a time ago must linger still! Still unbelieving, I went out, found my way to the cathedral, bought a guidebook, wandered, fed pigeons at a café in a piazza. I smiled and talked to beautiful, smiling people without knowing a word they said. Well, maybe a little. *"Americana?"* *"Sì."* That was easy.

As was much else. That entire month I never carried my own bag, or lacked for a guide. Waiters guessed what I might like and brought it; workmen stopped building new walls to show the way to galleries and palaces. Sitting in the sun at that happy day's end, I felt that life had begun once more. If my friends in Germany had been stationed in Italy, I wondered, would things have been different? So pondering, I walked around till a certain truth dawned. I could think whatever I liked about anybody or anything, but everywhere around me Italy was making its first great statement. If I have dwelt too much here on that unfortunate time in Germany, it was only as a preface to Italy, only to show that there was never a heart more ready for Italy to impress it. And the measure of what Italy could do was astounding, and simply cannot to this day be taken.

From Milan I went to Verona, to another hotel, breakfast and guidebook — but this time as I went about the streets of that softly lyrical town, I became at every step more aware of what beauty was being cast up at me, regular and almost as rhythmic as the waves of the sea, on every side, at every turning. And all in the open, outside! A small-town Southerner is not apt to be ignorant of architecture, but I had never before thought of statues and fountains as accepted ornaments of life — its daily dress — to be enjoyed by everyone from moment to moment, mingling with the talk and bargaining and breath of life, with sunshine. If you try hard enough, even after many years, the chances are that you can reconstruct a good deal of everything that has happened. (I still remember, for instance, the look of my room in Milan that first night, and the smell of recent cement work.) But I cannot reconstruct anything from my first day in Verona but my own dazed feelings. I can recall my wanderings of that day as a kind of drunkenness, all this on perhaps one glass of wine at a lunch I cannot remember eating. I do know that under orders from my old Baedeker, I trudged to the outskirts of the town to see that (starred and not to be missed) Church of S. Zeno. I remember walking across the harsh stones of the old square before the church, with its bare upcurving sweep of romanesque façade tawny in the fall of the strong afternoon sun, and how I realized that anyone would have to feel its nobility. I saw then that what had been kept from me by a too strict Protestant up-bringing was true — that art can express religious emotion more truly than any sermon. Much later I saw this very church in a beautiful English movie of *Romeo and Juliet*; if that story happened at all, it must have happened there.

Then Venice . . . Florence . . . Siena . . . Rome. . . . How to get it all down! It was all crammed, and not just with churches and palaces, galleries, piazzas, mosaics and fres-coes, but also with people, a montage of remembered faces. Florence especially had (in addition to Michelangelo, Botti-celli and all the rest) a free and lively feeling about it that year, an airiness that was all ease and rightness. In recent times I have been there, tourists seem about to carry it off, like trooping multitudes of ants methodically lifting whole the carcass of a wonderful beast. But not so in that early postwar year. Italians were glad to be alive in a life that was possible to live, and their gladness filled the air and reached out to all comers. All the dancing and romancing, the easy friendships and dates, meetings and partings, may seem frivolous to talk about — though there's not much wrong with frivolity, God knows — but it was more than that that one felt in France and Italy in those days. It had come up out of the inferno just endured; it was a resurrection. Maybe it never reached Germany at all. But it had taken up head-quarters in Italy.

In Rome, a young Canadian who often ate at the same restaurant as I, asked me to the opera in the Baths of Caracalla. It was Berlioz's *The Damnation of Faust*. Every bit as ignorant as my friends in Germany believed, I loved the spectacle with little knowledge of what was going on. It was drama beneath the stars with attendant ruins and cypresses against a velvet Roman sky. We walked back along the Via Appia at midnight, holding hands.

Time to *go!* Oh, NO!!!

Back to a few days in Paris, retellings of everything, running into friends from the boat, evenings at the Deux Magots. Germany was almost forgotten except for the countryside, fairylike with some dark magic about it that seemed not to have heard of the war. The friendship on which I had based so much hope faded. But instead I had Italy, and the resolve to go back there when and how I could.

Four years later, with another novel published and the warm recognition of a Guggenheim Fellowship, I had my chance. I would spend a year there, I told myself, and finish a novel I had begun. But I met my husband in Rome and the year stretched out to two, then with marriage, to five in all. Even after we moved to Canada, I continued to visualize Italy, to see, as it were, by Italian light. The story in this book which has drawn more readers to it than any other I have written is "The Light in the Piazza." I wrote it in Montreal during a snowstorm the first winter after we came. Many stories and novels have followed. "The Cousins" was written in 1984 during a stay at Bellagio, where I had been invited as a guest of the Rockefeller Foundation. I hope they go on and on recurring, these memories, never rendered as literal ones, but in the way of fiction emerging as threads for weaving into the lives of others, the characters who come along looking for an author, "*personaggi in cerca d'autore.*"

Not everything, of course, that came after that magic summer of 1949 was good or even pleasant. Italy is a poor country where life is hard. Not all Italians are helpful and charming. Not everything is a delight. Illusion is, for one thing, that which comes before disillusion.

But Italy, not being an illusion, remains. It is itself the true measure of whatever is said or done or written about it. One can hope to rise up against that measure, but, failing that, at least to be seen by that light.

Elizabeth Spencer
Montreal, Quebec
October, 1985

The Light in the Piazza

The Light in the Piazza

To John

1

On a June afternoon at sunset, an American woman and her daughter fended their way along a crowded street in Florence and entered with relief the spacious Piazza della Signoria. They were tired from a day of tramping about with a guidebook, often in the sun. The café that faced the Palazzo Vecchio was a favorite spot for them; without discussion they sank down at an empty table. The Florentines seemed to favor other gathering places at this hour. No cars were allowed here, though an occasional bicycle skimmed through, and a few people, passing, met in little knots of conversation, then dispersed. A couple of tired German tourists, all but harnessed in fine camera equipment, sat at the foot of Cellini's triumphant *Perseus*, slumped and staring at nothing.

Margaret Johnson, lighting a cigarette, relaxed over her aperitif and regarded the scene that she preferred before any other, anywhere. She never got enough of it, and now in the clear evening light that all the shadows had gone from — the sun being blocked away by the tight bulk of the city — she looked at the splendid old palace and forgot that her feet hurt. More than that: here she could almost lose the sorrow that for so many years had been a constant of her life. About the crenellated tower where the bells hung, a few swallows darted.

Margaret Johnson's daughter, Clara, looked up from the straw of her orangeade. She, too, seemed quieted from the fretful mood to which the long day had reduced her. "What happened here, Mother?"

"Well, the statue over there, the tall white boy, is by Michelangelo. You remember him. Then — though it isn't a very happy thought — there was a man burned to death right over there, a monk."

Any story attracted her. "Why was he burned?"

"Well, he was a preacher who told them they were wicked and they didn't like him for it. People were apt to be very cruel in those days. It all happened a long while ago. They must feel sorry about it, because they put down a marker to his memory."

Clara jumped up. "I want to see!" She was off before her mother could restrain her. For once Margaret Johnson thought, Why bother? In truth the space before them, so satisfyingly wide, like a pasture, might tempt any child to run across it. To Margaret Johnson, through long habit, it came naturally now to think like a child. Clara, she now saw, running with her head down to look for the marker, had bumped squarely into a young Italian. There went the straw hat she had bought in Fiesole. It sailed off prettily, its broad red ribbon a quick mark in the air. The young man was after it; he contrived to knock it still farther away, once and again, though the day was windless; his final success was heroic. Now he was returning, smiling, too graceful to be true; they were all too graceful to be true. Clara was talking to him. She pointed back toward her mother. Oh, Lord! He was coming back with Clara.

Margaret Johnson, confronted at close range by two such

radiant young faces, was careful not to produce a very cordial smile.

"We met him before, Mother. Don't you remember?"

She didn't. They all looked like carbon copies of one another.

He gave a suggestion of a bow. "My — store —" English was coming out. "It — is — near — Piazza della Repubblica — how do you say? The beeg square. Oh, yes, and on Sunday, *si fanno la musica*. Museek, bom, bom." He was a whole orchestra, though his gestures were small. "And the lady —" Now a busty Neapolitan soprano sprang to view, in pink lace, one hand clenched to her heart. Margaret Johnson could not help laughing. Clara was delighted.

Ah, he had pleased. He dropped the role at once. "My store — is there." A chair was vacant. "Please?" He sat. Here came the inevitable card. They were shoppers, after all, or would be. Well, it was better than compliments, offers to guide them, thought Mrs Johnson. She took the card. It was in English except for the unpronounceable name. " 'Via Strozzi 8,' " she read. " 'Ties. Borsalino Hats. Gloves. Handkerchiefs. Everything for the Gentlemens.' "

"Not for you. But for your husband," he said to Mrs Johnson. In these phrases he was perfectly at home.

"He isn't here, unfortunately."

"Ah, but you must take him presents. Excuse me." Now Clara was given a card. "And for your husband, also."

She giggled. "I don't have a husband!"

"Signorina! Ah! Forgive me." He touched his breast. Again the quick suggestion of a bow. "Fabrizio Naccarelli."

It sounded like a whole aria.

"I'm Clara Johnson," the girl said at once. Mrs Johnson closed her eyes.

"Jean — Jean —" He strained for it.

"No, *Johnson*."

"Ah! Van Johnson!"

"That's right!"

"He is — *cugino* — *parente* — *famiglia*?"

''No,'' said Mrs Johnson irritably. She prided herself on her tolerance and interest among foreigners, but she was tired, and Italians are so inquisitive. Given ten words of English they will invent a hundred questions from them. This one at least was sensitive. He withdrew at once. ''Clara,'' he said as if to himself. No trouble there. The girl gave him her innocent smile.

Indeed, she could be remarkably lovely when pleased. The somewhat long lines of her cheek and jaw drooped when she was downhearted, but happiness drew her up perfectly. Her dark-blue eyes grew serene and clear; her chestnut hair in its long girlish cut shadowed her smooth skin.

Due to an accident years ago, she had the mental age of a child of ten. But anyone on earth, meeting her for the first time, would have found this incredible. Mrs Johnson had managed in many tactful ways to explain her daughter to young men without wounding them. She could even keep them from feeling too sorry for herself. ''Every mother in some way wants a little girl who never grows up. Taken in that light, I do often feel fortunate. She is remarkably sweet, you see, and I find her a great satisfaction.'' She did not foresee any such necessity with an Italian out principally to sell everything for the ''gentlemens.'' No, he could not offer them anything else. No, he certainly could not pay the check. He had been very kind . . . very kind . . . yes, yes, very, very kind. . . .

2

But Fabrizio Naccarelli, whether Margaret Johnson had cared to master his name or not, was not one to be underestimated. He was very much at home in Florence, where he had been born and his father before him and so on straight back to the misty days before the Medici, and he had given, besides, some little attention to the ways of the *stranieri* who were always coming to his hometown. It seemed in the next few days that he showed up on every street corner. Surely he could not have counted so much on the tie they might decide to buy for Signor Johnson.

Clara invariably lighted up when they saw him, and he in turn communicated over and over his innocent pleasure in this happiest of coincidences. Mrs Johnson noted that at each encounter he managed to extract from them some new piece of information, foremost among them, how long would they remain? Caught between two necessities, that of lying to him and not lying to her daughter, she revealed that the date was uncertain, and saw the flicker of triumph in his eyes. And the next time they met — well, it was too much. By then they were friends. Could he offer them dinner that evening? He knew a place only for Florentines — good, good, very good. "Oh, yes!" said Clara. Mrs Johnson demurred. He was very kind, but in the evenings they were always too tired. She was drawing Clara away in a pretense of hurry. The museum might close at noon. At the mention of noon the city bells began clanging all around them. It was difficult to hear. "In the piazza," he cried in farewell, with a gesture toward the Piazza della Signoria, smiling at Clara, who waved her hand, though Mrs Johnson went on saying, "No, we can't," and shaking her head.

Late that afternoon, they were taking a cup of tea in the big casino near Piazzale Michelangelo, when Clara looked at her watch and said they must go.

"Oh, let's stay a little while longer and watch the sun set," her mother suggested.

"But we have to meet Fabrizio." The odd name came naturally to her tongue.

"Darling, Fabrizio will probably be busy until very late."

It was always hard for Mrs Johnson to face the troubling-over of her daughter's wide, imploring eyes. Perhaps she should make some pretense, though pretense was the very thing she had constantly to guard against. The doctors had been very firm with her here. As hard as it was to be the source of disappointment, such decisions had to be made.

They must be communicated, tactfully, patiently, reasonably. Clara must never feel that she had been deceived. Her whole personality might become confused. Mrs Johnson sighed, remembering all this, and began her task.

"Fabrizio will understand if we do not come, Clara, because I told him this morning we could not. You remember that I did? I told him that because I don't think we should make friends with him."

"Why?"

"Because he has his own life here and, he will stay here always. But we must go away. We have to go back home and see Daddy and Brother and Ronnie —" Ronnie was Clara's collie dog — "and Auntie and all the others. You know how hard it was to leave Ronnie even though you were coming back? Well, it would be very hard to like Fabrizio, wouldn't it, and leave him and never come back at all?"

"But I already like him," said Clara. "I could write him letters," she added wistfully.

"Things are often hard," said Mrs Johnson in her most cheery and encouraging tone.

It seemed a crucial evening. She did not trust Fabrizio not to call for them at their hotel, or doubt for a moment that he had informed himself exactly where they were staying. So she was careful before dinner to steer Clara to that other piazza — not the Signoria — once the closing hour for the shops had passed. Secure in the pushing crowds of Florentines, she chose one of the less fashionable cafés, settling at a corner table behind a green hedge that grew out of boxes and over the top of which there presently appeared the face of Fabrizio.

She saw him first in Clara's eyes. Next he was beaming upon them. There had been a mistake, of course. He had said only piazza piazza. How could they know? *Difficile*. He was so sorry. Pardon, pardon.

There was simply nothing to be gained by trying to stare him down. His great eyes showed concern, relief, gaiety as clearly as if the words had been written on them, but self-betrayal was unknown to him. Trying to surprise him at his game, one grew distracted and became aware how beautiful his eyes were. His dress gave him away if anything did. Nothing could be neater, cleaner, more carefully or sleekly tailored. His shirt was starched and white; his black hair still gleamed faintly damp at the edges; his close-cut, cuffless gray trousers ended in new black shoes of a pebbly leather with pointed toes. A faint whiff of cologne seemed to come from him. There was something too much here, and a little touching. Well, they would be leaving soon, thought Mrs Johnson. She decided to relax and enjoy the evening.

But more than this was in it.

When she finally sat back from her excellent meal, lighting a cigarette and setting down her little cup of coffee, she glanced from the distance of her age toward the two young people. It was an advantage that Clara knew no Italian. She smiled sweetly and laughed innocently, so how was Fabrizio to know her dreary secret? Now Clara had taken out all her store of coins, the aluminum five- and ten-lire pieces that amused her, and was setting them on the table in little groups, pyramids and squares and triangles. Fabrizio, his handsome cheek leaning against his palm, was helping her with the tip of one finger, setting now this one, now that one in place. They looked like two children, thought Mrs Johnson.

It was as if a curtain had lifted before her eyes. The life she had thought forever closed to her daughter spread out its great pastoral vista.

After all, she thought, why not?

3

But, of course, the whole idea was absurd. She remembered it at once when she awoke the next morning, and flinched. I must have had too much wine, she thought.

"I think we must leave for Rome in a day or two," said Mrs Johnson.

"Oh, Mother!" Clara's face fell.

It was a mistake to set her brooding on a bad day. The rain that had started with a rumble of thunder in the early morning hours was splashing down on the stone city. From their window a curtain of gray hung over the river, dimming the outlines of buildings on the opposite bank. The *carrozza* drivers huddled in chilly bird shapes under their great black umbrellas; the horses stood in crook-legged misery; and water streamed down all the statues. Mrs Johnson and Clara put on sweaters and went downstairs to the lobby, where Clara was persuaded to write postcards. Once started, the task absorbed her. The selection of which picture for whom, the careful printing of the short sentences. Even Ronnie must have the card picked especially for him, a statue of a Roman dog. Toward lunchtime the sun broke out beautifully. Clara knew the instant it did and startled her mother, who was looking through a magazine.

"It's quit raining!"

Mrs Johnson was quick. "Yes, and I think if it gets hot again in the afternoon we should go up to the big park and take a swim. You know how you love to swim, and I miss it, too. Wouldn't that be fun?"

She had her difficulties, but when they had walked a short way along streets that were misty from the drying rain, had eaten in a small restaurant but seen no sign of anyone they knew, Clara was persuaded.

Mrs Johnson enjoyed the afternoon. The park had been refreshed by the rain, and the sun sparkled hot and bright on the pool. They swam and bought ice cream on sticks from the vender, and everyone smiled at them, obviously acknowledging a good sight. Mrs Johnson, though blond, had the kind of skin that never quite lost the good tan she had once given it, and her figure retained its trim firmness. She showed what she was: the busy American housewife, mother, hostess, cook and civic leader who paid attention to her looks. She sat on a bench near the pool, drying in the sun, smoking, her smart beach bag open beside her, watching her daughter, who swam like a fish, flashing here and there in the pool. She plucked idly at the wet ends of her hair and wondered if she needed another rinse. She observed without the slightest surprise the head and shoulders of Fabrizio surfacing below the diving board, as though he had been swimming underwater the entire time since they had arrived.

Like most Italians he was proud of his body and, having made his appearance, lost no time in getting out of the water. He was in truth slightly bowlegged, but he concealed the flaw by standing in partial profile with one knee bent.

Well, thought Mrs Johnson, it was just too much for her. She watched them splash water in each other's faces, watched Clara push Fabrizio into the pool, Fabrizio pretend to push Clara into the pool, Clara chase Fabrizio out among the shrubs and down the fall of ground nearby. Endlessly energetic, they flitted like butterflies through the sunlight. Except that butterflies, thought Mrs Johnson, do not really think very much about sex. The final thing that had happened at home, that had really decided them on another trip abroad, was that Clara had run out one day and flung her arms around the grocery boy.

These problems had been faced; they had been reasoned out, patiently explained; it was understood what one did and didn't do to be good. But impulse is innocent about what is good or bad. A scar on the right side of her daughter's head, hidden by hair, lingered, shaped like the new moon. It was where her Shetland pony, cropping grass, had kicked in a temper at whatever was annoying him. Mrs Johnson had been looking through the window, and she still remembered the silence that had followed her daughter's sidelong fall, more heart numbing than any possible cry.

Things would certainly take care of themselves sooner or later, Mrs Johnson assured herself. She had seen the puzzled look commence on many a face, and had begun the weary maneuvering to see yet another person alone before the next meeting with Clara. Right now, for instance — Clara could never play for long without growing hysterical, screaming even. There, she had almost tripped Fabrizio; he had done an exaggerated flip in the air. She collapsed into laughter, gasping, her two hands thrust to her face in a spasm. Poor child, thought her mother. But then Fabrizio came to her and took her hands down. In one quick motion he stood her straight, and she grew quiet. Something turned over in Mrs Johnson's breast.

They stood before her, panting, their sun-dried skin like so much velvet. "Look," cried Clara, and parted her hair above her ear. "I have a scar over my ear!" She pointed. "A scar. See!"

Fabrizio struck down her hand and put her hair straight. *"No. Ma sono belli.* Your hair — is beautiful."

We must certainly leave for Rome tomorrow, Mrs. Johnson thought. She heard herself thinking it, at some distance, as though in a dream.

She entered thus from that day a conscious duality of existence, knowing what she should and must do and making no motion toward doing it. The Latin temperament may thrive on such subtleties and never find it necessary to conclude them, but to Mrs Johnson the experience was strange and new. It confused her. She believed, as most Anglo-Saxons do, that she always acted logically and to the best of her ability on whatever she knew to be true. And now she found this quality immobilized and all her actions taken over by the simple drift of the days.

She had, in fact, come face to face with Italy.

4

Something surely would arise to help her.

One had only to sit still while Fabrizio — he of the endless resource — outgeneraled himself and so caught on, or until he tired of them and dreamed of something else. One had only to make sure that Clara went nowhere alone with him. The girl had not a rebellious bone in her, and under her mother's eye she could be kept in tune.

But if Mrs Johnson had been consciously striving to make a match, she could not have discovered a better line to take. Fabrizio's father was Florentine, but his mother was a Neapolitan, who went regularly to mass and was suspicious of foreigners. She received with approval the news that the *piccola signorina americana* was not allowed to so much as mail a postcard without her mother along. *"Ma sono italiane?* Are they Italian?" She wanted to know. *"No, Mamma, non credo."* And though Fabrizio declaimed his grand impatience with the *signora americana*, in his heart he was pleased.

A few days later, to the immense surprise of Fabrizio, who was taking coffee with the ladies in the big piazza, they happened to be noticed by an Italian gentleman, rather broad in girth, with a high-bridged Florentine nose and a pair of close-set, keen, cold eyes. *"Ah, Papà!"* cried Fabrizio. *"Fortuna! Signora, signorina, permette.* My father."

Signor Naccarelli spoke English very well, indeed. Yes, it was a bit rusty, perhaps; he must apologize. He had known many Americans during the war, had done certain small things for them in liaison during the occupation. He had found them very *simpatici*, quite unlike the Germans, whom he detested.

This was a set speech. It gave him time. His face was not at all regular; the jaw went sideways from his high forehead, and his mouth, like Fabrizio's, was somewhat thin. But his eye was pale, and he and Mrs Johnson did not waste time in taking each other's measure. She sensed his intelligence at once. Now at last, she thought ruefully, between disappointment and relief, the game would be up.

Sitting sideways at the little table, his legs neatly crossed, Signor Naccarelli received his coffee, black as pitch. He downed it in one swallow. The general pleasantries about Florence were duly exchanged. And they were staying? At the Grand. Ah.

"Domani festa," he noted. "I say tomorrow is a holiday, a big one for us here. It is our saint's day, San Giovanni. You have perhaps seen in the Signoria, they are putting up the seats. Do you go?"

Well, she supposed they should really; it was a thing to watch. And the spectacle beforehand? She thought perhaps she could get tickets at the hotel. Signor Naccarelli was struck by an idea. He by chance had extra tickets and the seats were good. She must excuse it if his signora did not come; she was in mourning.

"Oh, I'm very sorry," said Mrs Johnson.

He waved his hand. No matter. Her family in Naples was a large one; somebody was always dying. He sometimes wore the black band, but then someone might ask him who was dead and if he could not really remember? *Che figura!* His humor and laugh came and were over as fast as something being broken. "And now — you will come?"

"Well —"

"Good! Then my son will arrange where we are to meet and the hour." He was so quickly on his feet. "Signora." He kissed her hand. "Signorina." Clara had learned to put out her hand quite prettily in the European fashion and she liked to do it. With a nod to Fabrizio he was gone.

So the next afternoon they were guided expertly through the packed, noisy streets of the *festa* by Fabrizio, who found them a choice point for watching the parade of the nobles. It seemed that twice a year, and that by coincidence during the tourist season, Florentine custom demanded that titled gentlement should wedge themselves into the family suit of armor, mount a horse and ride in procession, preceded by lesser men in striped knee breeches beating drums. Pennants were twirled as crowds cheered, and while it was doubtless not as thrilling a spectacle as the Palio in Siena, everyone agreed that it was in much better taste. Who in Florence would dream of bringing a horse into church? Afterward in the piazza, two teams in red and green jerseys would sweat their way through a free-for-all of kicking and running and knocking each other down. This was medieval *calcio*; the program explained that it was the ancestor of American footballs. Fabrizio, whose English was improving, managed to convey that his brother might have been entitled

to ride with the nobles, although it was true h
direct line for a title. Instead, his cousin, the Marc
Valle — there he went now, drooping along on tha
black horse that was not distinguished. "My bro
Giuseppe wish so much to ride today," said Fabrizio. "Al
he offer to my cousin the marchese much money." He
laughed.

Fabrizio wished his English were equal to relating what a
figure Giuseppe had made of himself. The marchese, who
was fat, slow-witted and greedy, certainly preferred twenty
thousand lire to being pinched black and blue by forty
pounds of steel embossed with unicorns. He giggled and
said, "*Va bene.* All right." He sat frankly admiring the tall,
swaying lines of Giuseppe's figure and planning what he
would do with the money. Giuseppe was carried away by a
glorious prevision of himself prancing about the streets amid
fluttering pennants, the beat of drums, the gasp of ladies.
He swaggered about the room describing his noble bearing
astride a horse of such mettle and spirit as would land his
cousin the marchese in the street in five minutes, clanging
like the gates of hell. He knew where to find it — just such
an animal! Nothing like that dull beast that the marchese
kept stalled out in the country all year round and that by this
time believed himself to be a cow. . . . Unfortunately the
mother of the marchese had been listening all the time
behind the door, and took that moment to break in upon
them. The whole plan was canceled in no time at all, and
Giuseppe was shown to the door. There was not a drop of
nobility in his blood, he was reminded, and no such
substitution would be tolerated by the council. As Giuseppe
had passed down the street, the marchese had flung open the
window and called down to him, "Mamma says you only
want to impress the American ladies." Everyone in the
street had laughed at him and he was furious.

Perhaps it was as well, Fabrizio reflected, not to be able to
relate all this to the Signora and Clara. What would they
think of his family? It was better not to tell too much.

pe had enjoyed many successes
loped elaborate theories of love,
detail, relating examples from his
h the same serious savor, as if for
ery much wiser not to speak too
American ladies.

in the piazza at this moment,"

son in the grandstand during the game, Signor Naccarelli dropped a significant remark or two. Her daughter was charming; his son could think of nothing else. It would be a sad day for Fabrizio when they went away. How nice to think that they would not go away at all, but would spend many months in Florence, perhaps take a small villa. Many outsiders did so. They wished never to leave.

Mrs Johnson explained her responsibilities at home — her house, her husband and family. And what did Signor Johnson do? A businessman. He owned part interest in a cigarette company and devoted his whole time to the firm. Cigarettes — ah. Signor Naccarelli rattled off all the name brands until he found the right one. Ah.

And her daughter — perhaps the signorina did not wish to leave Florence?

"It is clear that she doesn't," said Mrs Johnson. And then she thought, I must tell him now. It was the only sensible thing, and would end this ridiculous dragging on into deeper and deeper complications. She believed that he would understand, even help her to handle things in the right way. "You see —" she began, but just then the small medieval cannon that had fired a blank charge to announce the opening of the contest took a notion to fire again. Nobody ever seemed able to explain why. It was hard to believe that it had ever happened, for in the strong sun the flash of powder, which must have been considerable by another light, had been all but negated. All the players stopped and turned to look, and a man who had been standing between the cannon and the steps of the Palazzo Vecchio fell to the ground. People rushed in around him.

"Excuse me," said Signor Naccarelli. "I think I know him."

There followed a long series of discussions. Signor Naccarelli could be seen waving his hands as he talked. The game went on and everyone seemed to forget the man, who, every now and then, as the movement around him shifted, could be seen trying to get up. At last two of the drummers from the parade, still dressed in their knee breeches, edged through the crowd with a stretcher and took him away.

Signor Naccarelli returned as the crowds were dispersing. He had apparently been visiting all the time among his various friends and relatives and appeared to have forgotten the accident. He took off his hat to Mrs Johnson. "My wife and I invite you to tea with us. On Sunday at four. I have a little car and I will come to your hotel. You will come, no?"

5

Tea at the Naccarelli household revealed that they lived in a spacious apartment with marble floors and had more bad pictures than good furniture. They seemed comfortable, nonetheless, and a little maid in white gloves came and went seriously among them.

The Signora Naccarelli, constructed along ample Neapolitan lines, sat staring first at Clara and then at Mrs Johnson and smiling at the conversation without understanding a word. Fabrizio sat near her on a little stool, let her pat him occasionally on the shoulder and gazed tenderly at Clara. Clara sat with her hands folded and smiled at everyone. She had more and more nowadays a rapt air of not listening to anything.

Giuseppe came in, accompanied by his wife. Sealed dungeons doubtless could not have contained them. He said at once in an accent so middle western as to be absurd,

"How do you do? And how arrre you?" It was all he knew except "goodbye"; he had learned it the day before. Yet he gave the impression that he did not speak out of deference to his father, whose every word he followed attentively, making sure to laugh whenever Mrs Johnson smiled.

Giuseppe's wife was a slender girl with black hair cut short in the new fashion called simply "Italian." She had French blood, though not as much as she led one to believe. She smoked from a short ivory holder clamped at the side of her mouth, and pretended to regard Giuseppe's amours — of which he had been known to boast in front of her, to the distress of his mama — with a knowing sidelong glance. Sometimes she would remind him of one of his failures. Now she took a place near Fabrizio and chatted with him in a low voice, casting down on him past the cigarette holder the eye of someone old in the ways of love, amused by the eagerness of the young. She looked occasionally at Clara, who beamed at her.

Signor Naccarelli kept the conversation going nicely and seemed to include everybody in the general small talk. There was family anecdote to draw upon; a word or two in Italian sufficed to give the key to which one he was telling now. Some little mention was made of the family villa in a nearby *paese*, blown up unfortunately by the Allies during the war — the Americans, in fact — but it was indeed a necessary military objective and these things happen in all wars. *Pazienza.* Mrs Johnson remarked politely on the paintings, but he was quick to admit with a chuckle that they were no good whatsoever. Only one, perhaps; that one over there had been painted by Ghirlandaio — not the famous one in the guidebooks — on the occasion of some ancestor's wedding; he could not quite remember whose.

"In Florence we have too much history. In America you are so free, free — oh, it is wonderful! Here if we move a stone in the street, who comes? The commission on antiquities, the scholars of the middle ages, priests, professors, committees of everything, saying, 'Do not move it. No, you cannot move it.' And even if you say, 'But it has just this minute fallen on my foot,' they show you no pity. In Rome they are even worse. It reminds me, do you remember the man who fell down when the cannon decide to shoot? Well, he is not well. They say the blood has been poisoned by the infection. If someone had given him penicillin. But nobody did. I hear from my friend who is a doctor at the hospital.'' He turned to his wife. *''No, Mamma? Ti ricordi come ti ho detto. . . .''*

When they spoke of the painting, Clara admired it. It was of course a Madonna and Child, all light-blue and pink flesh tones. Clara had developed a great all-absorbing interest in these recurring ladies with little baby Jesus on their laps. She had a large collection of dolls at home and had often expressed her wish for a real live little baby brother. She did not see why her mother did not have one. The dolls cried only when she turned them over; they wet their pants only when you pushed something rubber, and so on through eye-closing and walking and saying, ''Mama.'' But a real one would do all these things whenever it wanted to. It certainly would, Mrs Johnson agreed. She was glad those days, at any rate, were over.

Now Clara stared on with parted lips at the painting on which the soft evening light was falling. She had gotten it into her little head recently that Fabrizio and babies were somehow connected. The Signora Naccarelli did not fail to notice the nature of her gaze. On impulse she got up and crossed to sit beside Mrs Johnson on the couch. She sat facing her and smiling with tears filling her eyes. She was all in black — black stockings, black crepe dress cut in a V at the neck, a small black crucifix on a chain. *''Mio Figlio,''* she pronounced slowly, *''è buono. Capisce?''*

Mrs Johnson nodded encouragingly. *''Si. Capisco.''*

''Non lui,'' said the signora, pointing at Giuseppe, who glanced up with a wicked grin — he was delighted to be bad. The signora shook her finger at him. Then she indicated Fabrizio. *''Ma lui. Si, è buono. Va in chiesa, capisce?''* She put her hands together as if in prayer.

''No, ma Mamma. Che roba!'' Fabrizio protested.

"*Si, è vero,*" the signora persisted solemnly; her voice fairly quivered. "*È buono. Capisce, signora?*"

"*Capisco,*" said Mrs Johnson.

Everyone complimented her on how well she spoke Italian.

6

"Galileo, Dante Alighieri, Boccaccio, Machiavelli, Michelangelo Buonarroti, Donatello, Amerigo Vespucci . . ." Clara chanted, reading the names off the rows of statues of illustrious Tuscans that flanked the street. Her Italian was sounding more clearly every day.

"Hush!" said Mrs Johnson.

"Leonardo da Vinci, Benvenuto Cellini, Petrarco . . . ." Clara went right on, like a little girl trailing a stick against the palings of a picket fence.

Relations between mother and daughter had deteriorated in recent days. In the full flush of pride at the subjugation of Fabrizio to her every whim, Clara, it is distressing to report, calculated that she could afford to stick out her tongue at her mother, and she did — at times, literally. She refused to pick up her clothes or be on time for any occasion that did not include Fabrizio. She was quarrelsome and she whined about what she didn't want to do, lying with her elbows on the crumpled satin bedspread, staring out of the window. Or she took her Parcheesi board out of the suitcase and sat cross-legged on the floor with her back to the rugged beauties of the sky line across the Arno, shaking the dice in the wooden cup, throwing for two sets of "men" and tapping out the moves. When called she did not hear or would not answer, and Mrs Johnson, smoking nervously in the adjoining room, thought the little sounds would drive her mad. She had never known Clara to show a mean or stubborn side. Yet the minute the girl fell beneath the eye of Fabrizio, her rapt, transported Madonna look came over her, and she sat still and gentle, docile as a saint, beautiful as an angel. Mrs Johnson had never beheld such hypocrisy. She had let things go too far, she realized, and whereas before she had been worried, now she was becoming afraid.

Whether she sought advice or whether her need was for somebody to talk things over with, she had gone one day directly after lunch to the American consulate, where she found, on the second floor of a palazzo whose marble halls echoed the click and clack of typing, one of those perpetually young American faces topped by a crew cut. The owner of it was sitting in a seersucker coat behind a standard American office desk in a richly paneled room cut to the noble proportions of the Florentine Renaissance. Memos, documents and correspondence were arranged in stacks before him, and he looked toward the window while twisting a rubber band repeatedly around his wrist. Mrs Johnson had no sooner got her first statement out — she was concerned about a courtship between her daughter and a young Italian — than he had cut her off. The consulate could give no advice in personal matters. A priest, perhaps, or a minister or doctor. There was a list of such as spoke English. "Gabriella!" An untidy Italian girl wearing glasses and a green crepe blouse came in from her typewriter in the outer office. "There's a services list in the top of that file cabinet. If you'll just find us a copy." All the while he continued looking out of the window and twisting and snapping the rubber band around his wrist. Mrs Johnson got the distinct impression that but for this activity he would have dozed right off to sleep. By the time she had descended to the courtyard, her disappointment had turned into resentment. We pay for people like him to come and live in a palace, she thought. It would have helped me just to talk, if he had only listened.

The sun's heat pierced the coarsely woven straw of her little hat and prickled sharply at her tears. The hot street was deserted. Feeling foreign, lonely and exposed, she walked past the barred shops.

The shadowy interior of an espresso bar attracted her.

Long aluminum chains in bright colors hung in the door and made a pleasant muted jingling behind her. She sat down at a small table and asked for a coffee. Presently, she opened the mimeographed sheets that the secretary had produced for her. There she found, as she had been told, along with a list of tourist services catering to Americans, rates for exchanging money and advice on what to do if your passport was lost, the names and addresses of several doctors and members of the clergy. Perhaps it was worth a try. She found a representative of her ancestral faith and noted the obscure address. With her American instinct for getting on with it, no matter what it was, she found her tears and hurt evaporating, drank her coffee and began fumbling through books and maps for the location of the street. She had never dared to use a telephone in Italy.

She went out into the sun. She had left Clara asleep in the hotel during the siesta hour. A lady professor whose card boasted of a number of university degrees would come and give Clara an Italian lesson at three. Before this was over, Mrs Johnson planned to have returned. She motioned to a *carrozza* and showed the address to the driver, who leaned far back from his seat, almost into her face, to read it. He needed a shave and reeked of garlic and wine. His whip was loud above the thin rump of the horse, and he plunged with a shout into the narrow, echoing streets so gathered-in at this hour as to make any noise seem rude.

After two minutes of this Mrs Johnson was jerked into a headache. He was going too fast — she had not said she was in a hurry — and taking corners like a madman. "*Attenzione!*" she called out twice. How did she say "slow down"? He looked back and laughed at her, not paying the slightest attention to the road ahead. The whip cracked like a pistol shot. The horse slid and, to keep his footing, changed from a trot to a desperate two-part gallop that seemed to be wrenching the shafts from the carriage. Mrs Johnson closed her eyes and held on. It was probably the driver's idea of a good time. Thank God the streets were empty. Now the wheels rumbled; they were crossing the river. They entered the quarter of Oltr'arno, the opposite bank, through a small piazza from which a half-dozen little streets branched out. The paving here was of small, rough-edged stones. Speeding toward one tiny slit of a street, the driver, either through mistake or a desire to show off, suddenly wheeled the horse toward another, almost at right angles to them. The beast plunged against the bit that had flung its head and shoulders practically into reverse, and with a great gasp in which its whole lungs seemed involved as in a bellows, it managed to bring its forelegs in line with the new direction. Mrs Johnson felt her head and neck jerked as cruelly as the horse's had been.

"Stop! STOP!"

At last she had communicated. Crying an order to the horse, hauling in great lengths of rein, the driver obeyed. The carriage stood swaying in the wake of its lost momentum, and Mrs Johnson alighted shakily in the narrow street. Heads had appeared at various windows above them. A woman came out of a doorway curtained in knotted cords and leaned in the entrance with folded arms. A group of young men, one of them rolling a motor scooter, emerged from a courtyard and stopped to watch.

Mrs Johnson's impulse was to walk away without a backward glance. She was mindful always, however, of a certain American responsibility. The driver was an idiot, but his family was probably as poor as his horse. She was drawing a five-hundred-lire note from her purse, when, having wrapped the reins to their post in the *carrozza*, the object of her charity bounded suddenly down before her face. She staggered back, clutching her purse to her. Her wallet had been half out; now his left hand was on it while his right held up two fingers. *"Due! Due mila!"* he demanded, forcing her back another step. The young men around the motor scooter were noticing everything. The woman in the doorway called a casual word to them and they answered.

"Due mila, signora!" repeated the driver, and thrusting his devil's face into hers, he all but danced.

The shocking thing — the thing that was paralyzing her,

making her hand close on the wallet as though it contained
something infinitely more precious than twenty or thirty
dollars in lire — was the overturn of all her values. He was
not ashamed to be seen extorting an unjust sum from a lone
woman, a stranger, obviously a lady; he was priding himself
rather on showing off how ugly about it he could get. And
the others, the onlookers, those average people so depended
on by an American to adhere to what is good? She did not
deceive herself. Nobody was coming to her aid. Nobody was
even going to think, It isn't fair.

She thrust two thousand-lire notes into his hand, and
folding her purse closely beneath her arm in ridiculous
parody of everything Europeans said about Americans, she
hastened away. The driver reared back before his audience.
He shook in the air the two notes she had given him. "*Mancia! Mancia!*" No tip! Turning aside to mount his carriage,
he thrust the money into his inner breast pocket, slanting
after her a word that makes Anglo-Saxon curses sound like
nursery rhymes. She did not understand what it meant, but
she felt the meaning; the foul, cold, rat's foot of it ran after
her down the street. As soon as she turned a corner, she
stopped and stood shuddering against a wall.

Imagine her then, not ten minutes later, sitting on a sofa
covered with comfortably faded chintz, steadying her nerves
over a cup of tea and talking to a lively old gentleman with a
trace of the Scottish highlands in his voice. It had not occurred to her that a Presbyterian minister would be anything
but American, but now that she thought of it she supposed
that the faith of her fathers was not only Scottish but also
French. A memory returned to her, something she had not
thought of in years. One Christmas or Thanksgiving as a little girl she had been taken to her grandfather's house in
Tennessee. She could reconstruct only a glimpse of something that had happened. She saw herself in the corner of a
room with a fire burning and a bay window overlooking an
uneven shoulder of side yard partially covered with a light
fall of snow. She was meddling with a black book on a little

table and an old man with wisps of white hair about his brow was leaning over her: "It's a Bible in Gaelic. Look, I'll show you." And putting on a pair of gold-rimmed glasses he translated strange broken-looking print, moving his horny finger across a tattered page. In this unattractive roughness of things, it was impossible to escape the suggestion of character.

It came to her now in every detail about the man before her. Even the hairs of his gray brows, thick as wire, had each its own almost contrary notion about where to be, and underneath lived his sharp blue eyes, at once humorous and wry. Far from being disinterested in his unexpected visitor, who so obviously had something on her mind, he managed to make Mrs Johnson feel even more uncomfortable than the specimen of American diplomacy had done. He was, in fact, too interested, alert as a new flame. She had a feeling that compromise was unknown to him, and really, come right down to it, wasn't compromise the thing she kept looking for?

Touching her tea-moistened lip with a small Florentine embroidered handkerchief, she told him her dilemma in quite other terms than the ones that troubled her. She put it to him that her daughter was being wooed by a young Italian of the nicest sort, but naturally a Roman Catholic. This led them along the well-worn paths of theology. The venerable minister, surprisingly, showed little zeal for the workout. An old war-horse, he wearied to hurl himself into so trifling a skirmish. He wished to be tolerant . . . his appointment here after retirement had been a joy to him . . . he had come to love Italy, *but* — one could not help observing. . . . For a moment the sparks flew. Well.

Mrs Johnson took her leave at the door that opened into a narrow dark stair dropping down to the street.

"Ye'll have written to her faither?"

"Why, no," she admitted. His eyelids drooped ever so slightly. Americans . . . divorce; she could see the suspected pattern. "It's a wonderful idea! I'll do it tonight."

Her enthusiasm did not flatter him. "If your daughter's religion means anything to her," he said, "I urge ye both to make very careful use of your brains."

Well, thought Mrs Johnson, walking away down the street, what did Clara's religion mean to her? She had liked to cut out and color things in Sunday school, but she had got too big for that department, and no pretense about churchgoing was kept up any longer. She wanted every year, however, to be an angel in the Christmas pageant. She had been, over the course of the years, every imaginable size of angel. Once, long ago, in a breathless burst of adoration, she had reached into the Winston-Salem First Presbyterian Church Ladies' Auxiliary's idea of a manger, a flimsy trough-shaped affair, knocked together out of a Sunkist orange crate, painted gray and stuffed with excelsior. She was looking for the little Lord Jesus, but all she found was a flashlight. Her teacher explained to her, as she stood cheated and tearful, holding this unromantic object in her hands, that it would be sacrilegious to represent the Son of God with a doll. Mrs Johnson rather sided with Clara; a doll seemed more appropriate than a flashlight.

Now what am I doing? Mrs Johnson asked herself. Wasn't she employing the old gentleman's warning to reason herself into thinking that Clara's romance was quite all right? More than all right — the very thing? As for writing to Clara's father, why Noel Johnson would be on the transatlantic phone within five minutes after any such suggestion reached him. No, she was alone, really alone.

She sank down on a stone bench in a poor plain piazza with a rough stone paving, a single fountain, a single tree, a bare church façade, a glare of sun, the sound of some dirty little black-headed waifs playing with a ball. Careful use of your brains. She pressed her hand to her head. Outside the interest of conversation, her headache was returning and the shock of that terrible carriage ride. She did not any longer seem to possess her brains, but to stand apart from them as from everything else in Italy. She had got past the guidebooks and still she was standing and looking. And her own mind was only one more thing among the things she was looking at, and what was going on in it was like the ringing of so many different bells. Five to four. Oh, my God! She began to hasten away through the labyrinth, the chill stench of the narrow streets.

She must have taken the wrong turning somewhere, because she emerged too far up the river — in fact, just short of the Ponte Vecchio, which she hastened to cross to reach at any rate the more familiar bank. A swirl of tourists hampered her; they were inching along from one show window to the next of the tiny shops that lined the bridge on both sides, staring at the myriads of baubles, bracelets, watches and gems displayed there. As she emerged into the street, a handsome policeman who, dressed in a snow-white uniform, was directing traffic as though it were a symphony orchestra, smiled into the crowd that was approaching along the Lungarno and brought everything to a dramatic halt.

There, with a nod to him, came Clara! He bowed; she smiled. Why, she looked like an Italian!

Item at a time, mother and daughter had seen things in the shops they could not resist. Mrs Johnson with her positive, clipped American figure found it difficult to wear the clothes, and had purchased mainly bags, scarves and other accessories. But Clara could wear almost everything she admired. Stepping along now in her hand-woven Italian skirt and sleeveless cotton blouse, with leather sandals, smart straw bag, dark glasses and the glint of earrings against her cheek, she would fool any tourist into thinking her a native; and Mrs Johnson, who felt she was being fooled by Clara in a far graver way, found in her daughter's very attractiveness an added sense of displeasure, almost of disgust.

"Where do you think you're going?" she demanded.

Clara, who was still absorbed in being adored by the policeman, could not credit her misfortune at having run into her mother. Mrs Johnson took her arm and marched her straight back across the street. Crowds were thronging

against them from every direction. A vender shook a fistful
of cheap leather bags before them; there seemed no escaping
him. Mrs Johnson veered to the right, entering a quiet street
where there were no shops and where Fabrizio would not be
likely to pass, returning to work after siesta.

"Where were you going, Clara?"

"To get some ice cream," Clara pouted.

"There's ice cream all around the hotel. Now you know
we never tell each other stories, Clara."

"I was looking for you," said Clara.

"But how did you know where I was?" asked Mrs
Johnson.

They had entered the street of the illustrious Tuscans.
"Galileo, Dante Alighieri, Boccaccio, Machiavelli, Michelangelo . . ." chanted Clara.

This is not my day, sighed Mrs Johnson to herself.

She was right about this; alighting from her taxi with
Clara before the Grand Hotel, she heard a cry behind her.

"Why, Mar-gar-et John-son!"

Two ladies from Winston-Salem stood laughing before
her. They were sisters — Meg Kirby and Henrietta Mulver-
hill — a chatty, plumpish pair whose husbands had
presented them both with a summer abroad.

Now they were terribly excited. They had no idea she
would be here still. They had heard she was in Rome by
now. What a coincidence! They simply couldn't get over it!
Wasn't it wonderful what you could buy here? Linens!
Leather-lined bags! So cheap! If only she could see what just
this morning —! And how was Clara?

Constrained to go over to the Excelsior — their hotel, just
across the street — for tea, Margaret Johnson sat like a
creature in a net and felt her strength ebb from her. The
handsome salon echoed with Winston-Salem news, gossip,
exact quotations, laughter, and during it all, Clara became
again her old familiar little lost self, oblivious, searching
through her purse, leafing for pictures in the guidebooks on
the tea table, only looking up to say, "Yes, ma'am," and
"No, ma'am."

"Well, it's just so difficult to pick out a hat for Noel without him here to try it on," said Mrs Johnson. "I tried it once in Washington, and —" I've been blinded, she thought, the image of her daughter constant in the corner of her vision. Blinded — by what? By beauty, art, strangeness, freedom. By romance, by sun — yes, by hope itself.

By the time she had shaken the ladies, making excuses about dinner but with a promise to call by for them tomorrow, and had reached at long last her hotel room, her headache had grown steadily worse. She yearned to shed her street clothes, take aspirin and soak in a long bath. Clara passed sulking ahead of her through the anteroom, through the larger bedroom, the bath and into her own small room. Mrs Johnson tossed her bag and hat on the bed and, slipping out of her shoes, stepped into a pair of scuffs. A rap at the outer door revealed a servant with a long florist's box. Carrying the box, Mrs Johnson crossed the bath to her daughter's room.

Through the weeks that they had dallied here, Clara's room had gradually filled with gifts from Fabrizio. A baby elephant of green china, its howdah enlarged to contain brightly wrapped sweets, grinned from a tabletop. A stuffed dog, Fabrizio's idea of Ronnie, sat near Clara's pillow. On her wrist a charm bracelet was slowly filling with golden miniature animals and tiny musical instruments. She did not have to be told that another gift had arrived, but observed from a glance at the label, as her mother had not, that the flowers were for both of them. Then she filled a tall vase with water. Chores of this sort fell to her at home.

Mrs Johnson sat down on the bed.

Clara happily read the small card. "It says, 'Naccarelli,' " she announced.

Then she began to arrange the flowers in the vase. They were rather remarkable flowers, Mrs Johnson thought — a species of lily apparently highly regarded here, though with their enormous naked stamens, based in a back-curling, waxen petal, they had always struck her as being rather blatantly phallic. Observing some in a shop window soon

after they had arrived in Florence, it had come to her to
wonder then if Italians took sex so much for granted that
they hardly thought about it at all, as separate, that is, from
anything else in life. Time had passed, and the question,
more personal now, still stood unanswered.

The Latin mind — how did it work? What did it think?
She did not know, but as Clara stood arranging the flowers
one at a time in the vase (there seemed to be a great number
of them — far more than a dozen — in the box and all very
large), the bad taste of the choice seemed, in any language,
inescapable. The cold eye of Signor Naccarelli had selected
this gift, she felt certain, not Fabrizio, and that thought, no
less than the flowers themselves, was remarkably effective in
short-circuiting romance. Could she be wrong in perceiving
a kind of Latin logic at work — its basic quality factual,
hard, direct? Even if nobody ever *put* it that way, it was
there. And no matter what *she* might think, it was, like the
carrozza driver, not in the least ashamed. A demand was
closer to being made than she liked to suppose. Exactly
where, it seemed to say, did she think all this was leading?
She looked at the stuffed dog, at the baby elephant who carried sweets so coyly, at the charm bracelet dancing on
Clara's wrist as her hand moved, setting in place one after
another the stalks with their sensual bloom.

It's simply that they are facing what I am hiding from, she
thought.

"Come here, darling."

She held out her hands to Clara and drew her down to the
edge of the bed beside her. Unable to think of anything else
to do, she lied wildly.

"Clara, I have just been to the doctor. That is where I
went. I didn't tell you — you've been having such a good
time — but I'm not feeling well at all. The doctor says the
air is very bad for me here and that I must leave. We will
come back, of course. As soon as I feel better. I'm going to
call for reservations and start packing at once. We will leave
for Rome tonight."

Later she nervously penned a note to the ladies at the Excelsior. Clara was not feeling well, she explained, and the doctor had advised their leaving. They would leave their address at American Express in Rome, though there was a chance they might have to go to the lakes for cooler weather.

7

To the traveler coming down from Florence to Rome in the summertime, the larger, more ancient city is bound to be a disappointment. It is bunglesome; nothing is orderly or planned; there is a tangle of electric wires and tramlines, a ceaseless clamor of traffic. The distances are long; the sun is hot. And if, in addition, the heart has been left behind as positively as a piece of baggage, the tourist is apt to suffer more than tourists generally do. Mrs Johnson saw this clearly in her daughter's face. To make things worse, Clara never mentioned Florence or Fabrizio. Mrs Johnson had only to think of those flowers to keep herself from mentioning either. They had come to see Rome, hadn't they? Very well, Rome would be seen.

At night, after dinner, Mrs Johnson assembled her guidebooks and mapped out strenuous tours. Cool cloisters opened before them, and the gleaming halls of the Vatican galleries. They were photographed in the spray of fountains and trailed by pairs of male prostitutes in the park. At Tivoli, Clara had a sunstroke in the ruin of a Roman villa. A goatherd came and helped her to the shade, fanned her with his hat and brought her some water. Mrs Johnson was afraid for her to drink it. At dusk they walked out the hotel door and saw the whole city in the sunset from the top of the Spanish Steps. Couples stood linked and murmuring together, leaning against the parapets.

"When are we going back, Mother?" Clara asked in the dark.

"Back where?" said Mrs Johnson vaguely.

"Back to Florence."

"You want to go back?" said Mrs Johnson, more vaguely still.

Clara did not reply. To a child, a promise is a promise, a sacred thing, the measure of love. "We will come back," her mother had said. She had told Fabrizio so when he came to the station, called unexpectedly out of his shop with this thunderbolt tearing across his heart, clutching a demure mass of wild chrysanthemums and a tin of caramelle. While the train stood open-doored in the station, he had drawn Clara behind a post and kissed her. "We are coming back," said Clara, and threw her arms around him. When he forced down her arms, he was crying, and there stood her mother.

Day by day, Clara followed after Mrs Johnson's decisive heels, always at the same silent distance, like a good little dog. In the Roman Forum, urged on by the guidebook, Mrs Johnson sought out the ruins of "an ancient basilica containing the earliest known Christian frescoes." They may have been the earliest, but to Mrs Johnson they looked no better than the smeary pictures of Clara's Sunday-school days. She studied them one at a time, consulting her book. When she looked up, Clara was gone. She called once or twice and hastened out into the sun. The ruins before her offered many a convenient hiding place. She ran about in a maze of paths and ancient pavings, until finally, there before her, not really very far away, she saw her daughter sitting on a fallen block of marble with her back turned. She was bent forward and weeping. The angle of her head and shoulders, her gathered limbs, though pained was not pitiful. And arrested by this, Mrs Johnson did not call again, but stood observing how something of a warm, classic dignity had come to this girl, and no matter whether she could do long division or not, she was a woman.

To Mrs Johnson's credit she waited quietly while Clara straightened herself and dried her eyes. Then the two walked together through the ruin of an open court with a quiet rectangular pool. They went out of the Forum and crossed a busy street to a sidewalk café, where they both had coffee. In all the crash and clang of the tramlines and the hurry of the crowds there was no chance to speak.

A boy came by, a beggar, scrawny, in clothing deliberately oversized and poor, the trousers held up by a cord, rolled at the cuffs, the bare feet splayed and filthy. A jut of black hair set his swart face in a frame, and the eyes, large, abject, imploring, did not meet now, perhaps had never met, another's. He mumbled some ritualistic phrases and put out a hand that seemed permanently shriveled into the wrist; the tension, the smear and fear that money was, was in it. In Italy, especially in Rome, Mrs Johnson had gone through many states of mind about beggars, all the way from, Poor things, why doesn't the church do something? to, How revolting, why don't they ever let us alone? So she had been known to give them as much as a thousand lire or spurn them like dogs. But something inside her had tired. Clara hardly noticed the child at all; exactly like an Italian, she took a ten-lire piece out of the change on the table and dropped it in his palm. And Mrs Johnson, in the same way that people crossed themselves with a dabble of holy water in the churches, found herself doing the same thing. He passed on, table by table, and then entered the ceaseless weaving of the crowd, hidden, reappearing, vanishing, lost.

She closed her eyes and, with a sigh that was both qualm and relief, she surrendered.

A lull fell in the traffic. "Clara," she said, "we will go back to Florence tomorrow."

8

It wasn't that simple, of course. Nobody with a dream should come to Italy. No matter how dead and buried the dream is thought to be, in Italy it will rise and walk again. Margaret Johnson had a dream, though she thought reality had long ago destroyed it. The dream was that Clara would one day be perfectly well. It was here that Italy had attacked her, and it was this that her surrender involved.

Then "surrender" is the wrong word, too. Women like Margaret Johnson do not surrender; they simply take up another line of campaign. She would go poised into combat, for she knew already that the person who undertakes to believe in a dream pursues a course that is dangerous and lonely. She knew because she had done it before.

The truth was that when Clara was fourteen and had been removed from school two years previously, Mrs Johnson had decided to believe that there was not anything the matter with her. It was September, and Noel Johnson was away on a business trip and conference that would last a month. Their son was already away at college. The opportunity was too good to be missed. She chose a school in an entirely new section of town; she told a charming pack of lies and got Clara enrolled there under most favorable conditions. The next two weeks were probably the happiest of her life. With other mothers, she sat waiting in her car at the curb until the bright crowd came breasting across the campus: Clara's new red tam was the sign to watch for. At night the two of them got supper in the kitchen while Clara told all her stories. Later they did homework, sitting on the sofa under the lamp.

Three teachers came to call at different times. They were puzzled, but were persuaded to be patient. Two days before Noel Johnson was due to come home, Mrs Johnson was invited to see the principal. Some inquiries, he said, had been felt necessary. He had wished to be understanding, and rather than take the evidence from other reports had done some careful testing of his own under the most favorable circumstances: the child had suspected nothing.

He paused. "I understand that your husband is away." She nodded. "So you have undertaken this — ah — experiment entirely on your own." She nodded again, dumbly. Her throat had tightened. The word "experiment" was damning; she had thought of it herself. No one, of course, should experiment with any human being, much less one's own daughter. But wasn't the alternative, to accept things as they were, even worse? It was all too large, too difficult to explain.

The principal stared down at his desk in an embarrassed way. "These realities are often hard for us to face," he said. "Yet from all I have been able to learn, you did know. It had all been explained to you, along with the best techniques, the limits of her capabilities —"

"Yes," she faltered, "I did know. But I know so much else besides. I know that in so many ways she is as well as you and I. I know that the doctors have said that no final answers have been arrived at in these things." She was more confident now. Impressive names could be quoted; statements, if need be, could be found in writing. "Our mental life is not wholly understood as yet. Since no one knows the extent to which a child may be retarded, so no one can say positively that Clara's case is a hopeless one. We know that she is not one bit affected physically. She will continue to grow up just like any other girl. Even if marriage were ever possible to her, the doctors say that her children would be perfectly all right. Everyone sees that she behaves normally most of the time. Do I have to let the few ways she is slow stand in the way of all the others to keep her from being a whole person, from having a whole life?" She could not go on.

"But those 'few ways,' " he said, consenting, it was obvious, to use her term, "are the main ones we are concerned with here. Don't you see that?"

She agreed. She did see. And yet . . .

At the same moment, in another part of the building, trivial, painful things were happening to Clara — no one could possibly want to hear about them.

The serene fall afternoon, as she left the school, was as disjointed as if hurricane and earthquake had been at it. Toward nightfall, Mrs Johnson telephoned to Noel to come home. At the airport, with Clara waiting crumpled like a

bundle of clothes on the backseat of the car, she confessed
everything to him. When he said little, she realized he
thought she had gone out of her mind. Clara was sent to the
country to visit an aunt and uncle, and Mrs Johnson spent a
month in Bermuda. Strolling around the picture-postcard
landscape of the resort, she said to herself, I was out of my
mind, insane. As impersonal as advertising slogans, or sky-
writing, the words seemed to move out from her, into the
golden air.

Courage, she thought now, in a still more foreign landscape, riding the train back to Florence. *Coraggio*. The
Italian word came easily to mind. Mrs Johnson belonged to
various clubs, and campaigns to clean up this or raise the
standards of that were frequently turned over to committees
headed by her. She believed that women in their way could
accomplish a great deal. What was the best way to handle
Noel? How much did the Naccarellis know? As the train
drew into the station, she felt her blood race, her whole
being straighten and poise to the fine alertness of a drawn
bow. Whether Florence knew it or not, she invaded it.

As for how much the Naccarelli family knew or didn't
know or cared or didn't care, no one not Italian had better
undertake to say. It was never clear. Fabrizio threatened
suicide when Clara left. The mother of Clara had scorned
him because he was Italian. No other reason. Everyone had
something to say. The household reeled until nightfall, when
Fabrizio plunged toward the central open window of the
salotto. The serious little maid, who had been in love with
him for years, leaped in front of him with a shriek, her arms
thrown wide. Deflected, he rushed out of the house and went
tearing away through the streets. The Signora Naccarelli
collapsed in tears and refused to eat. She retired to her
room, where she kept a holy image that she placed a great
store by. Signor Naccarelli alone enjoyed his meal. He said
that Fabrizio would not commit suicide and that the ladies
would probably be back. He had seen Americans take fright
before; no one could ever explain why. But in the end, like

everyone else, they would serve their own best interests. If he did not have some quiet, he would certainly go out and seek it elsewhere.

He spent the pleasantest sort of afternoon locked in conversation with Mrs Johnson a few days after her return. It was all an affair for juggling, circling, balancing, very much to his liking. He could not really say she had made a conquest of him: American women were too confident and brisk. But he could not deny that encounters with her had a certain flavor.

The lady had consented to go with him on a drive up to San Miniato, stopping at the casino for a cup of tea and a pastry. Signor Naccarelli managed to get in a drive to Bello Sguardo, as well, and many a remark about young love and many a glance at his companion's attractive legs and figure. Margaret Johnson achieved a cool but not unfriendly position while folding herself into and out of a car no bigger than an enclosed motorcycle. The management of her skirt alone was enough to occupy her entire attention.

"They are in the time of life," Signor Naccarelli said, darting the car through a narrow space between two motor scooters, "when each touch, each look, each sigh arises from the heart, the heart alone." He removed his hands from the wheel to do his idea homage, flung back his head and closed his eyes. Then he snapped to and shifted gears. "For them love is without thought, as to draw breath, to sleep, to walk. You and I — we have come to another stage. We have known all this before — we think of the hour, of some business — so we lose our purity, who knows how? It is sad, but there is nothing to do. But we can see our children. I do not say for Fabrizio, of course — it would be hard to find a young Florentine who has had no experience. I myself at a younger age, at a much younger age — do you know my first love was a peasant girl? It was at the villa where I had gone out with my father. A *contadina*. The spring was far along. My father stayed too long with the animals. I became, how shall I say — bored, yes, but something more also. She was very beautiful. I still can dream of her, only her — I never succeed to dream of others. I do not know if your daughter will be for Fabrizio the first, or will not be. I would say not, but still — he is *figlio di mamma*, a good boy — I do not know." He frowned. They turned suddenly and shot up a hill. When they gained the crest, he came to a dead stop and turned to Mrs Johnson. "But for her he has the feeling of the first woman! I am Italian and I tell you this. It is unmistakable! That, *cara signora*, is what I mean to say." Starting forward again, the car wound narrowly between tawny walls richly draped with vines. They emerged on a view and stopped again. Cypress, river, hill and city like a natural growth among them — they looked down on Tuscany. The air was fresher here, but undoubtedly very hot below. There was a slight haze, just enough to tone away the glare, but even on the distant blue hills outlines of a tree or a tower were distinct to the last degree — one had the sense of being able to see everything exactly as it was.

"There is no question with Clara," Mrs Johnson murmured. "She has been very carefully brought up."

"Not like other American girls, eh? In Italy we hear strange things. Not only hear. *Cara signora*, we *see* strange things, also. You can imagine. Never mind. The signorina is another thing entirely. My wife has noticed it at once. Her innocence." His eyes kept returning to Mrs Johnson's knee, which in the narrow silk skirt of her dress it was difficult not to expose. Her legs were crossed and her stocking whitened the flesh.

"She is very innocent," said Mrs Johnson.

"And her father? How does he feel? An Italian for his daughter? Well, perhaps in America you, too, hear some strange words about us. We are no different from others, except we are more — well, you see me here — we are here together — it is not unpleasant — I look to you like any other man. And yet perhaps I feel a greater — how shall I say? You will think I play the Italian when I say there is a greater . . ."

She did think just that. She had been seriously informed on several occasions recently that Anglo-Saxons knew very little about passion, and now Signor Naccarelli, for whom she had a real liking, was about to work up to the same idea. She pulled down her skirt with a jerk. "There are plenty of American men who appreciate women just as much as you do," she told him.

He burst out laughing. "Of course! We make such a lot of foolishness, signora. But on such an afternoon —" His gesture took in the landscape. "I spoke of your husband. I think to myself, He is in cigarettes, after all. A very American thing. When you get off the boat, what do you say? 'Where is Clara?' says Signor Johnson. 'Where is my leetle girl?' 'Clara, ah!' you say. 'She is back in Italy. She has married with an Italian. I forgot to write you — I was so busy.' "

"But I write to him constantly!" cried Mrs Johnson. "He knows everything. I have told him about you, about Fabrizio, the signora, Florence, all these things."

"But first of all you have considered your daughter's heart. For yourself, you could have left us, gone, gone. Forever. Not even a postcard." He chuckled. Suddenly he took a notion to start the car. It backed at once, as if a child had it on a string, then leaping forward, fairly toppled over the crest of a steep run of hill down into the city, speeding as fast as a roller skate. Mrs Johnson clutched her hat. "When my son was married," she cried, "my husband wrote out a check for five thousand dollars. I have reason to think he will do the same for Clara."

"*Ma che generoso!*" cried Signor Naccarelli, and it seemed he had hardly said it before he was jerking the hand brake to prevent their entering the hotel lobby.

She asked him in for an aperitif. He leaned flirtatiously at her over a small round marble-topped table. The plush decor of the Grand Hotel, with its gilt and scroll-edged mirrors that gave back wavy reflections, reminded Mrs Johnson of middle-aged adultery, one party only being titled. But neither she nor Signor Naccarelli was titled. It was a relief to know that sin was not expected of them. If she were thinking along such lines, heaven only knew what was running in Signor Naccarelli's head. Almost giggling, he drank down a red, bitter potion from a fluted glass.

"So you ran away," he said, "upset. You could not bear the thought. You think and you think. You see the signorina's unhappy face. You could not bear her tears. You return. It is wise. There should be a time for thought. This I have said to my wife, to my son. But when you come back, they say to me, 'But if she leaves again?' But I say, 'The signora is a woman who is without caprice. She will not leave again.' "

"I do not intend to leave again," said Mrs Johnson, "until Clara and Fabrizio are married."

As if on signal, at the mention of his name, Fabrizio himself stepped before her eyes, but at some distance away, outside the archway of the salon, which he had evidently had the intention of entering if something had not distracted him. His moment of distraction itself was pure grace, as if a creature in nature, gentle to one word only, had heard that word. There was no need to see that Clara was somewhere within his gaze.

Signor Naccarelli and Mrs Johnson rose and approached the door. They were soon able to see Clara above stairs — she had promised to go no farther — leaning over, her hair falling softly past her happy face. "*Ciao*," she said finally, "*come stai?*"

"*Bene. E tu?*"

"*Bene.*"

Fabrizio stood looking up at her for so long a moment that Mrs Johnson's heart had time almost to break. Gilt, wavy mirrors and plush decor seemed washed clean, and all the wrong, hurt years of her daughter's affliction were not proof against the miracle she saw now.

Fabrizio was made aware of the two in the doorway. He had seen his father's car and stopped by. A cousin kept his shop for him almost constantly nowadays. It was such a little shop, while he — he wished to be everywhere at once. Signor Naccarelli turned back to Mrs Johnson before he followed his son from the lobby. There were tears in her eyes; she thought perhaps she observed something of the same in his own. At any rate, he was moved. He grasped her hand tightly, and his kiss upon it as he left her said to her more plainly than words, she believed, that they had shared together a beautiful and touching moment.

9

Letters, indeed, had been flying; the air above the Atlantic was thick with them. Margaret Johnson sat up nights over them. A shawl drawn round her, she worked at her desk near the window overlooking the Arno, her low night-light glowing on the tablet of thin airmail stationery. High diplomacy in the olden days perhaps proceeded thus, through long cramped hours of weighing one word against another, striving for just the measure of language that would sway, persuade, convince.

She did not underestimate her task. In a forest of question marks, the largest one was her husband. With painstaking care, she tried to consider everything in choosing her tone: Noel's humor, the season, their distance apart, how busy he was, how loudly she would have to speak to be heard.

Frankly, she recalled the time she had forced Clara into school; she admitted her grave error. Point at a time, she contrasted that disastrous sequence with Clara's present happiness. One had been a plan, deliberately contrived, she made clear; whereas here in Florence, events had happened of their own accord.

"The thing that impresses me most, Noel," she wrote, "is that nothing beyond Clara ever seems to be required of her here. I do wonder if anything beyond her would ever be required of her. Young married girls her age, with one or two children, always seem to have a nurse for them; a maid does all the cooking. There are mothers and mothers-in-law competing to keep the little ones at odd hours. I doubt if these young wives ever plan a single meal.

"Clara is able to pass every day here, as she does at home, doing simple things that please her. But the difference is that here, instead of being always alone or with the family, she has all of Florence for company, and seems no different from the rest. Every afternoon she dresses in her pretty clothes and we walk to an outdoor café to meet with some young friends of the Naccarellis. You would be amazed how like them she has become. She looks more Italian every day. They prattle. About what? Well, as far as I can follow — Clara's Italian is so much better than mine — about movie stars, pet dogs, some kind of car called Alfa Romeo and what man is handsomer than what other man.

"I understand that usually in the summer all these people go to the sea, where they spend every day for a month or two swimming and lying in the sun. They would all be there now if Fabrizio's courtship had not so greatly engaged their interest. Courtship is the only word for it. If you could see how he adores Clara and how often he mentions the very same things that we love in her: her gentleness, her sweetness and goodness. I had expected things to come to some conclusion long before now, but nothing of the sort seems to occur, and now the thought of separating the two of them begins to seem more and more wrong to me, every day. . . ."

This letter provoked a transatlantic phone call. Mrs Johnson went to the lobby to talk so Clara wouldn't hear her. She knew what the first words would be. To Noel Johnson, the world was made of brass tacks, and coming down to them was his specialty.

"Margaret, are you thinking that Clara should marry this boy?"

"I'm only trying to let things take their natural course."

"*Natural* course!" Even at such a distance, he could make her jump.

"I'm with her constantly, Noel. I don't mean they're left

to themselves. I only mean to say I can't wrench her away from him now. I tried it. Honestly I did. It was too much for her. I saw that.''

"But surely you've talked to these people, Margaret. You must have told them all about her. Don't any of them speak English?" It would seem unbelievable to Noel Johnson that she or anyone related to him in any way would have learned to communicate in any language but English. He would be sure they had got everything wrong.

"I've tried to explain everything fully," she assured him. Well, hadn't she? Was it her fault a cannon had gone off just when she meant to explain?

Across the thousands of miles she heard his breath and read its quality: he had hesitated. Her heart gave a leap.

"Would I encourage anything that would put an ocean between Clara and me?"

She had scored again. Mrs Johnson's deepest rebellion against her husband had occurred when he had wanted to put Clara in a sort of "school" for "people like her." The rift between them on that occasion had been a serious one, and though it was smoothed over in time and never mentioned subsequently, Noel Johnson might still not be averse to putting distances between his daughter and him.

"They're just after her money, Margaret."

"No, Noel — I wrote you about that. They *have* money." She shut her eyes tightly. "And nobody wants to come to America, either."

When she put down the phone a few minutes later, Mrs Johnson had won a concession. Things should proceed along their natural course, very well. But she was to make no permanent decision until Noel himself could be with her. His coming, at the moment, was next to impossible. Business was pressing. One of the entertainers employed to advertise the world's finest smoke on a national network had been called up by the Un-American Activities Committee. The finest brains in the company were being exercised far into the night. It would not do for the American public to conclude they were inhaling Communism with every puff on a well-known brand. This could happen; it could ruin them. Noel would go to Washington in the coming week. It would be three weeks at least until he could be with her. Then — well, she could leave the decision up to him. If it involved bringing Clara home with them, he would take the responsibility of it on himself.

Noel and Margaret Johnson gravely wished each other good luck over the transatlantic wire, and each resumed the burden of his separate enterprise.

"Where'd you go, Mother?" Clara wanted to know as soon as Mrs Johnson returned.

"You'll never guess. I've been talking with Daddy on the long-distance phone!"

"Oh!" Clara looked up. She had been sitting on a footstool shoved back against the wall of her mother's room, writing in her diary. "Why didn't you tell me?"

"I didn't know that's who it was," she lied.

"But I wanted to talk to him, too!"

"What would you have said?"

"I would have said . . . " She hesitated, thinking hard, staring past her mother into the opposite wall, her young brow contracting faintly. "I would have said, '*Ciao. Come stai?*' "

"Would Daddy have understood?"

"I would have told him," Clara said faithfully.

After that she said nothing more but leaned her head against the wall, and forgetful of father, mother and diary, she stared before her with parted lips, dreaming.

Oh, my God, Margaret Johnson thought. How glad I am that Noel is coming to get me out of this!

10

After her husband's telephone call, Margaret Johnson went to bed in as dutiful and obedient a frame of mind as any husband of whatever nationality could wish for. She awoke flaming with new anxiety, confronted by the simplest truth in the world.

If Noel Johnson came to Florence, he would spoil everything. She must have known that all along.

He might not mean to — she gave him the benefit of the doubt. But he would do it. Given a good three days, her dream would all lie in little bright bits on the floor like the remains of the biggest and most beautiful Christmas-tree ornament in the world.

For one thing, there was nothing in the entire Florentine day that would not seem especially designed to irritate Noel Johnson. From the coffee he would be asked to drink in the morning, right through the siesta, when every shop, including his prospective son-in-law's, shut up at the very hour when they could be making the most money, up through midnight, when mothers were still abroad with their babies in the garrulous streets — he would have no time whatsoever for this inefficient way of life. Was there any possible formation of stone and paint hereabout that would not remind him uncomfortably of the Catholic church? In what frame of mind would he be cast by Fabrizio's cuffless trousers, little pointed shoes and carefully dressed hair? No, three days was a generous estimate; he would send everything sky-high long before that. And though he might regret it, he would never be able to see what he had done that was wrong.

His wife understood him. She sat over her *caffe latte* at her by-now-beloved window above the Arno, and while she thought of him, a peculiarly tender and generous smile played about her face. "Clara," she called gently, "have you written to Daddy recently?" Clara was splashing happily in the bathtub and did not hear her.

Soon Mrs Johnson rose to get her cigarettes from the dresser, but stopped in the center of the room, where she stood with her hand to her brow for a long time, so enclosed in thought she could not have told where she was.

If she went back on her promise to Noel to do nothing until he came, the whole responsibility of action would be her own, and in the very moment of taking it, she would have to begin to lie. To lie in Winston-Salem was one thing, but to start lying to everybody in Italy — why, Italians were past masters at this sort of thing. Wouldn't they see through her at once? Perhaps they already had.

She could never quite get it out of her mind that perhaps, indeed, they already had. Her heart had occasionally quite melted to the idea — especially after a glass of wine — that the Italian nature was so warm, so immediate, so intensely personal, that they had all perceived at once that Clara was a child and had loved her anyway, for what she was. They had not, after all, gone the dreary round from doctor to doctor, expert to expert, in the dwindling hope of finding some way to make the girl "normal." They did not *think*, after all, in terms of IQ, "retarded mentality" and "adult capabilities." And why, oh, why, Mrs Johnson had often thought, since she, too, loved Clara for herself, should anyone think of another human being in the light of a set of terms?

But though she might warm to the thought — and since she never learned the answer she never wholly discarded it — she always came to the conclusion that she could not act upon it, and had to put it aside as being, for all practical purposes, useless. "Ridiculous," she could almost hear Noel Johnson say. Mrs Johnson came as near as she ever had in her life to wringing her hands. Oh, my God, she thought, if he comes here!

But she did not, that morning, seek out advice from any crew-cut diplomat or frosty-eyed Scot. At times she came flatly to the conclusion that she would stick to her promise to Noel because it was right to do so — she believed in doing right — and that since it was right, no harm could come of it. At other times, she wished she could believe this.

In the afternoon, she accompanied Clara to keep an appointment at a café with Giuseppe's wife, Franca, and another girl. She left the three of them enjoying pretty pastries and chattering happily of movie stars, dogs and the merits of the Alfa Romeo. Clara had learned so much Italian that Mrs Johnson could no longer understand her.

Walking distractedly, back of the hotel, away from the river, she soon left the tourist-ridden areas behind her. She went thinking, unmindful of the people who looked up with curiosity as she passed. Her thought all had one center: her husband.

Never before had it seemed so crucial that she see him clearly. What was the truth about him? It had to be noted first of all, she believed, that Noel Johnson was in his own and everybody else's opinion a good man. Meaning exactly what? Well, that he believed in his own goodness and the goodness of other people, and would have said, if asked, that there must be good people in Italy, Germany, Tasmania, even Russia. On these grounds he would reason correctly that the Naccarelli family might possibly be as nice as his wife said they were.

Still, he did not think — fundamentally, he doubted, and Margaret had often heard him express something of the sort — that Europeans really had as much sense as Americans. Intellect, education, art and all that sort of thing — well, maybe. But ordinary sense? Certainly he was in grave doubts here when it came to the Latin races. And come right down to it — in her thoughts she slipped easily into Noel's familiar phrasing — didn't his poor afflicted child have about as much sense already as any Italian? His first reaction would have been to answer right away: Probably she does.

Other resentments sprang easily to his mind when touched on this sensitive point. Americans had had to fight two awful wars to get Europeans out of their infernal messes. He had a right to some sensitivity, anyone must admit. In the first war he had risked his life; his son had been wounded in the second; and if that were not enough, he could always remember his income tax. But there was no use getting really worked up. Some humor would prevail here, and he was not really going to lose sleep over something he couldn't help.

But Clara, now — she could almost hear him saying — this thing of Clara. There Margaret Johnson could grieve for Noel almost more than for herself. Something had happened here that he was powerless to do anything about; a chance accident had turned into a persisting and delicate matter, affecting his own pretty little daughter in this final way. An ugly finality, and no decent way of disposing of it. A fact he had to live with, day after day. An abnormality; hence, to a man like himself, a source of horror. For wasn't he dedicated, in his very nature, to "doing something about" whatever was not right?

How, she wondered, had Noel spent yesterday afternoon after he had replaced the telephone in his study at home? She could tell almost to a T, no crystal-ball gazing required. He would have wandered, thinking, about the rooms for a time, unable to put his mind on the next morning's committee meeting. As important as it was that no Communist crooner should leave a pink smear on so American an outfit as their tobacco company, he would not have been able to concentrate. He likely would have entered the living room, only to find Clara's dog, Ronnie, lying under the piano, a spot he favored during the hot months. They would have looked at each other, the two of them, disputing something. Then he would presently have found himself before the icebox, making a ham sandwich, perhaps, snapping the cap from a cold bottle of beer. Tilting beer into his mouth with one hand, eating with the other, he might later appear strolling about the yard. It might occur to him — she hoped it had — that he needed to speak to the yardman about watering the grass twice a week so it wouldn't look like the Sahara Desert when they returned. When *they* returned! With Clara, or without her? Qualms swept her. Her heart went down like an elevator.

"*Signora! Attenzione!*"

The voice was from above. A window had been pushed wide and a woman was leaning out to shake a carpet into the street. Margaret Johnson stopped, stepping back a few paces. Dust flew down, then settled. An arm came out and closed the shutters. She went on.

And quite possibly Noel, then, as dusk fell, his mind being still unsettled, would have walked over three blocks and across the park to his sister Isabel's apartment. Didn't he, in personal matters, always turn to women? Isabel, yes, would be the first to hear the news from abroad. She would not be as satisfactory a listener as Margaret, for being both a divorcée and something of a businesswoman — she ran the hat department in Winston-Salem's largest department store — she was inclined to be entirely too casual about everybody's affairs except her own. She would be beautifully dressed in one of her elaborate lounging outfits, for nobody appreciates a Sunday evening at home quite so much as a working woman. She would turn off the television to accommodate Noel, and bring him a drink of the very best Scotch. When she had heard the entire story of the goings-on in Florence, she would as likely as not say, "Well, after all, why not?" Hadn't she always advanced the theory that Clara had as much sense as most of the women she sold hats to? "They're going to want a dowry," she might add.

Now mentioning a dowry that way would be all to the good. Noel would feel a great relief. He disliked being taken advantage of, and he was obviously uneasy that the Naccarellis were only after Clara's money. Wouldn't Margaret be staying in the best hotel, eating at the best restaurants, shopping in the best shops? The Italians had "caught on," of course, from the first that she was well off. But now, through Isabel, he would have a name for all this. Dowry. It was customary. "Of course, they're all Catholics," he would go on to complain. Isabel would not be of any use at all there. Religion was of no interest to her whatever. She could not see why it was of interest to anybody.

Later as they talked, Isabel would ask Noel about the Communist scare. She would be in doubt that the crooner was actually such a threat to the nation or the tobacco company that a song or two would ruin them all. And was all this trouble and upset necessary — trips to Washington, committee meetings, announcements of policy and what not? Noel would not be above reminding her that she liked her dividend checks well enough not to want them put in any jeopardy. He might not come right out and say this, but it would cross his mind. More and more in recent years, Noel's every experience found immediate reference in his business. Or had he always been this way, if, in his younger years, less obviously so? Yet Mrs Johnson remembered once on a summer vacation they had taken at Myrtle Beach during the Depression, Noel playing ball on the sand with the two children, when a wind had driven them inside their cottage and for a short time they had been afraid a hurricane was starting. How they had saved to make that trip! That was all Noel could recall about it in later years. But at the time he had remarked as the raw wind streamed sand against the thin tremulous walls — he was holding Clara in his lap, "Well, at least we're all together." The wind had soon dropped, and the sea had enjoyed a quiet green dusk; their fear had gone, too, but she could not forget the steadying effect of his words. When, at what subtle point, had money come to seem to him the very walls that kept out the storm? Or was the trouble simply that with Clara and her problem always before him at home, he had found business to be a thing he could at least handle successfully, as he could not, in common with all mankind (poor Noel!), ultimately "handle" life? And business was, after all, so "normal."

Whatever the answer to how it had happened — and perhaps the nature of the times had had a lot to do with it: depression, the New Deal, the war — the fact was that it had happened, and Margaret knew now that nothing on earth short of the news of the imminent death of her or Clara or both, could induce Noel Johnson to Florence until the business in hand was concluded to the entire satisfaction of the tobacco company, whose future must, at all personal cost, be secure. On the other hand, since she had already foreseen that if he came here he would spoil everything, wasn't this an advantage?

She had wandered, in this remote corner of the city, into a small, poor bar. She lighted a cigarette and asked for a coffee. Since there was no place to sit, she stood at the counter. Two young men were working back of the bar, and seeing that she only stared at her coffee without drinking it, they became extremely anxious to make her happy. They wondered whether the coffee was hot enough, if she wanted more sugar or some other thing perhaps. She shook her head, smiling her thanks, seeing as though from a distance their great dim eyes, their white teeth and their kindness. *"Simpatica,"* one said, more about her than to her. *"Si, simpatica,"* the other agreed. They had exchanged a nod. One had an inspiration. *"Americana?"* he asked.

"Si," said Mrs Johnson.

They stood back, continuing to smile like adults who watch a child, while she drank her coffee down. At this moment, she had the feeling that if she had requested their giant espresso machine, which seemed, besides a few cheap cups and saucers and a pastry stand, to be their only possession, they would have ripped it up bodily and given it to her. And perhaps, for a moment, this was true.

What is it, to reach a decision? It is like walking down a long Florentine street where, at the very end, a dim shape is waiting until you get there. When Mrs Johnson finally reached this street and saw what was ahead, she moved steadily forward to see it at long last up close. What was it? Well, nothing monstrous, it seemed, but human, with a face much like her own, that of a woman who loved her daughter and longed for her happiness.

"I'm going to do it," she thought. "Without Noel."

11

Signor Naccarelli was late coming home for lunch the next day; the water in the pasta pot had boiled away once and had to be replenished. He was not as late, however, as he had been many times before, or as late as he would have preferred to be that day. And though his news was good, his temper was short. Signora Johnson had talked with her husband on the telephone from America. Signor Johnson could not come to Italy from America. He could not leave his business. They were to proceed with the wedding without Signor Johnson. He neatly baled mouthfuls of spaghetti on his fork, mixed mineral water with a little wine and found ways of cutting off the effusive rejoicing his family was given to. The real fact was that he was displeased with the American signora. Why, after dressing herself in the new Italian costume of printed white silk, which must have cost at least 60,000 lire in the Via Tornabuoni — and with the chic little hat, too — should she give him her news and then leave him in the café after thirty minutes, saying "lunch" and "time to go" and "Clara"? American women were at the mercy of their children. It was shocking and disgusting. She had made the appointment with him, well and good. In the most fashionable café in Florence; they had been observed talking deeply together over an aperitif in the shadow of a great green umbrella. It would not be the first time he had been observed with this lady about the city. And then, after thirty minutes —! An Italian man would see to manners of this sort. This bread was stale. Were they all eating it, or was it saved from last week, especially for him?

Signora Naccarelli, meanwhile, from the mention of the word "wedding," had quietly taken over everything. She had been more or less waiting up to this time, neither impatient nor anxious, but, like a natural force, quite aware of how inevitable she was, while the others debated and decided superficial affairs. The heart of the matter in Signora Naccarelli's view was so overwhelmingly enormous that she did not have to decide to heed it, because there was nothing outside of it to make this decision. She simply *was* the heart — that great pulsing organ that could bleed with sorrow or make little fishlike leaps of joy and that always knew just what it knew. What it knew in Signora Naccarelli's case was very little and quite sufficient. Her son Fabrizio was handsome and good, and Clara, the little

American flower, so sweet and gentle, would bear children for him. The signora's arms had yearned for some time for Clara and were already beginning to yearn for her children, and this to the signora was exactly the same thing as saying that the arms of the Blessed Virgin yearned for Clara and for Clara's children, and this in turn was the same as saying that the Holy Mother Church yearned likewise. It was all very simple and true.

Informed with such certainties, Signora Naccarelli had not been inactive. A brother of a friend of her nephew's was a priest who had studied in England. She had fixed on him already, since he spoke English, as the very one for Clara's instruction. That same afternoon she set about arranging a time for them to meet. Within a few days, the priest was reporting to her that Clara had a real devotion to the Virgin. The signora had known all along that this was true. A distant cousin of Signor Naccarelli's was secretary to a *monsignore* at the Vatican, and through him special permission was obtained for Clara to be married in a full church ceremony. At this the signora's joy could not be contained, and she went so far as to telephone Mrs Johnson and explain these developments to her, a word at a time, in Italian, at the top of her voice, with tears.

"*Capisce, signora? In chiesa! Capisce?*"

Mrs Johnson did not *capisce*. She thought from the tears that something must have gone wrong.

But nothing had, or did, until the morning in the office of the *parroco*, where they gathered a little more than two weeks before the wedding to fill out the appropriate forms.

12

What had happened was not at all clear for some time; it was not even clear that anything had.

The four of them — Clara and Fabrizio, with Margaret Johnson and Signor Naccarelli for witnesses — were

assembled in the office of the *parroco*, a small dusty room
with a desk, a few chairs and several locked cabinets that
reached to the ceiling and one window looking down on a
cloister. In the center of the cloister was a hexagonal
medieval well. It was nearing noon. Whatever noise there
was seemed to gather itself together and drowse in the sun
on the stone pavings below, so that Mrs Johnson experienced the reassuring tranquillity of silence. Signor Naccarelli,
hat in hand, took a nervous turn or two around the office,
looked at a painting that was propped in the back corner
and, with a sour downturning of his mouth, said something
uncomplimentary about priests, which Mrs Johnson did not
quite catch. Fabrizio sat by Clara and twirled a clever straw
ornament attached to her bag. So much stone was all that
kept them cool. The chanting in the church below had stopped, but the priest did not come.

The hours ahead were planned: they would go to lunch to
join Giuseppe and Franca, his wife, and two or three other
friends. Of course, Mrs Johnson was explaining to herself,
this smell of candle smoke, stone dust and oil painting is to
them just what blackboards, chalk and old Sunday-school
literature are to us; there's probably no difference at all if
you stay open-minded. To be ready for the questions that
they were there to answer, she made sure that she had
brought her passport and Clara's. She drew them out of
their appropriate pocket in the enormous bag Winston-
Salem's best department store had advised for European
travel and held them ready.

Signor Naccarelli decided to amuse her. He sat down
beside her. Documents, he explained in a jaunty tone, were
the curse of Italy. You could not become a corpse in Italy
without having filled in the proper document. There were
people in offices in Rome still sorting documents filed there
before the war. What war? they would say if you told them.
But, Mrs Johnson assured him, all this kind of thing went on
in America, too. The files were more expensive, perhaps.
She got him to laugh. His quick hands picked up the pass-

ports. Clara and Fabrizio were whispering to each other.
Their voices, too, seemed to go out into the sun, like a neigh-
borhood sound. Signor Naccarelli glanced at Mrs Johnson's
passport picture — how terrible! She was much more
beautiful than this. Clara's next — this of the signorina was
better, somewhat. A page turned beneath his thumb.

A moment later, Signor Naccarelli had leaped up as
though stung by a bee. He hastened to Fabrizio, to whom he
spoke rapidly in Italian. Then he shot from the room.
Fabrizio leaped up, also. *"Ma Papà! Non possiamo fare nulla
—!"* The priest came, but it was too late. He and Fabrizio
entered into a long conversation. Clara retreated to her
mother's side. When Fabrizio turned to them at last, he
seemed to have forgotten all his English. "My father —
forget — remember — the appointments," he blundered.
Struck by an idea, he whirled back to the priest and embarked on a second conversation, which he finally summarized to
Clara and her mother, "Tomorrow."

At that, precisely as though he were a casual friend who
hoped to see them again sometime, he bowed over Mrs
Johnson's hand, made an appropriate motion to Clara and
turned away. They were left alone with the priest.

"Tomorrow" . . . *domani.* Mrs Johnson knew by now to
be the word in Italy most likely to signal the finish of everything. She felt, indeed, without the ghost of an idea how or
why it had happened, that everything was trembling, totter-
ing about her, had perhaps, without her knowledge, already
collapsed. She looked out on the priest like someone seen
across a gulf. As if to underscore the impression, he spread
his hands with a little helpless shrug and said, "No
Eeenglish."

Mrs Johnson zipped the passports back into place and
went out into the corridor, down the steps and into the sun.
"Domani," the priest said after them.

Holding Clara by the hand, she made her way back to the
hotel.

The instant she was alone she had the passports out,

searching through them. Would nothing give her a clue to what had struck Signor Naccarelli? She remembered stories: the purloined letter; the perfect crime, marred only by the murderer's driver's license left carelessly on the hotel dresser. What had she missed? She thought her nerves would fly apart in all directions.

Slowly, with poise and majesty, the beautiful afternoon went by. A black cloud crossed the city, flashed two or three fierce bolts, rumbled halfheartedly and passed on. The river glinted under the sun, and the boys and fishermen who had not been frightened inside shouted and laughed at the ones who had. Everything stood strongly exposed in sunlight and cast its appropriate shadow: in Italy there is the sense that everything is clear and visible, that nothing is withheld. Fabrizio, when Margaret Johnson had touched his arm to detain him in the office of the *parroco*, had drawn back like recoiling steel. When Clara had started forward with a cry, he had set her quickly back, and silent. If they were to be rejected, had they not at least the right to common courtesy? What were they being given to understand? In Florence, at four o'clock, everything seemed to take a step nearer, more distinctly, more totally to be seen.

When the cloud came up, Mrs Johnson and Clara clung together, pretending that was what they were afraid of. Later they got out one of Clara's favorite books: Nancy Drew, the lady detective, turned airline hostess to solve the murder of a famous explorer. Nancy Drew had so far been neglected. Clara was good and did as she was told about everything, but could not eat. Late in the evening, around ten, the telephone rang in their suite. A gentleman was waiting below for the signora.

Coming down alone, Mrs Johnson found Signor Naccarelli awaiting her, but how changed! If pleasant things had passed between them, he was not thinking of them now; one doubted that they had actually occurred. Grave, gestureless, as though wrapped in a black cape, he inclined to her deeply. Margaret Johnson had trouble keeping herself from giggling. Wasn't it all a comedy? If somebody would only laugh out loud with enough conviction, wouldn't it all crumble? But she recalled Clara, her eye feasting on Fabrizio's shoulder, her finger exploring the inspired juncture of his neck and spine, and so she composed herself and allowed herself to be escorted from the hotel.

She saw at once that his object was to talk and that he had no destination — they walked along the river. The heat had been terrible for a week, but a breeze was blowing off the water now, and she wished she had brought her shawl.

"I saw today," Signor Naccarelli began in measured tones, but when Mrs Johnson suddenly sneezed, "Why did not you tell me?" he burst out, turning on her. "What can you be thinking of?"

Stricken silent, she walked on beside him. Somehow, then, he had found out. Certain dreary, familiar feelings returned to her. Meeting Noel at the airport, Clara behind in the car, wronged again, poor little victim of her own or her mother's impulses. Well, if Signor Naccarelli was to be substituted for Noel, she thought with relief that anyway she could at last confess. Instead of Bermuda, they could go to the first boat sailing from Naples.

"It is too much," went on Signor Naccarelli. "Two, three years, where there is love, where there is agreement, I say it is all right. But, no, it is too much. It is to make the fantastic."

"Years?" she repeated.

"Can it be possible! But you must have understood! My son Fabrizio is twenty years old, no more. Whereas, your daughter, I see with my two eyes, written in the passport today in the office of the *parroco* — twenty-six! Six years difference! It cannot be. In that moment I ask myself, What must I say, what can I do? Soon it will be too late. What to do? I make the excuse, an appointment. I see often in the cinema this same excuse. It was not true. I have lied. I tell you frankly."

"I had not thought of her being older," said Mrs

Johnson. Weak with relief, she stopped walking. When she leaned her elbow against the parapet, she felt it trembling. "Believe me, Signor Naccarelli, they seemed so much the same age to me, it had not entered my mind that there was any difference."

"It cannot be," said Signor Naccarelli positively, scowling out toward the noble skyline of his native city. "I pass an afternoon of torment, an inferno. As I am a man, as I am a Florentine, as I am a father, as I long for my son's happiness, as —" Words failed him.

"But surely the difference between them is not as great as that," Mrs Johnson reasoned. "In America we have seen many, many happy marriages with an even greater difference. Clara — she has been very carefully brought up. She had a long illness some years ago. To me she seemed even younger than Fabrizio."

"A long illness." He whirled on her scornfully. "How am I to know that she is cured of it?"

"You see her," countered Mrs Johnson. "She is as healthy as she seems."

"It cannot be." He turned away.

"Don't you realize," Mrs Johnson pleaded, "that they are in love? Whatever their ages are, they are both young. This is a deep thing, a true thing. To try to stop what is between them now —"

"*Try* to stop? My dear lady, I will stop whatever I wish to stop."

"Fabrizio —" she began.

"Yes, yes. He will try to kill himself. It is only to grow up. I, also, have sworn to take my life — can you believe? With passion I shake like this — and here I am today. No, no. To talk is one thing, to do another. Do not make illusions. He will not."

"But Clara —" she began. Her voice faltered. She thought she would cry in spite of herself.

Signor Naccarelli scowled out toward the dark river. "It cannot be," he repeated.

Mrs Johnson looked at him and composure returned to her. Because whether this was comedy or tragedy, he had told her the truth. He could and would stop everything if he chose, and Fabrizio would not kill himself. If Mrs Johnson had thought it practical, she would have murdered Signor Naccarelli. Instead she suggested that they cross over to a small bar. She was feeling that perhaps a brandy . . .

The bar was a tourist trap, placed near to American Express and crowded during the day. At night few people wandered in. Only one table was occupied at present. In the far corner, what looked to Mrs Johnson exactly like a girl from Winston-Salem was conversing with an American boy who was growing a beard. Mrs Johnson chose a table at equidistance between the pair and the waiter. She gave her order and waited, saying nothing till the small glass on the saucer was set before her. It was her last chance and she knew it. It helped her timing considerably to know how much she detested Signor Naccarelli.

"This is all too bad," said Mrs Johnson softly. "I received a letter from my husband today. Instead of five thousand dollars, he wants to make Clara and Fabrizio a present of fifteen thousand dollars."

"That is nine million three hundred and seventy-five thousand lire," said Signor Naccarelli. "So now you will write and explain everything, and that this wedding cannot be."

"Yes," said Mrs Johnson, and sipped her brandy.

Presently Signor Naccarelli ordered a cup of coffee.

Later on they might have been observed in various places, strolling about quiet, less frequented streets. Their talk ran on many things. Signor Naccarelli recalled her sneeze and wondered if she was cold. Mrs Johnson was busily working out in the back of her mind how she was going to get fifteen thousand dollars without her husband, for the moment, knowing anything about it. It would take most of a family legacy, invested in her own name; and the solemn confidence of a lawyer, an old family friend; a long-distance request for him to trust her and cooperate; a promise that Noel would know everything anyway, within the month. Later, explaining to Noel, "In the U.S. you would undoubtedly have wanted to build a new house for your daughter and her husband. . . ." A good point.

"You must forgive me," said Signor Naccarelli, "if I ask a most personal thing of you. The Signorina Clara, she would like to have children, would she not? My wife can think of nothing else."

"Oh, Clara longs for children!" said Mrs Johnson.

Toward midnight they stopped in a bar for a final brandy. Signor Naccarelli insisted on paying, as always.

When she returned to her room, Margaret Johnson sat on her bed for a while. Then she stood at the window for a while and looked down on the river. With one finger, she touched her mouth where there lingered an Italian kiss.

How had she maneuvered herself out of further, more prolonged and more intimately staged embraces without giving the least impression that she hadn't enjoyed the one he had surprised her with? In the shadow of a handsome façade, before the stout, lion-mouth crested arch where he had beckoned her to stop — "Something here will interest you, perhaps" — how, oh, how, had she managed to manage it well? Out of practice in having to for, she shuddered to think, how many years. Nor could anything erase, remove from her the estimable flash of his eye, so near her own, so near.

"Mother!"

Why, I had forgotten *her*, thought Mrs Johnson.

"Yes, darling, I'm coming!" In Clara's room she switched on a dim Italian lamp. "There, now, it's all going to be all right. We're going to meet them tomorrow, just as we did today. But tomorrow it will be all right. Go to sleep now. You'll see."

It's true, she thought, smoothing Clara's covers, switching out the light. No doubt of it now. And to keep down the taste of success, she bit hard on her lip (so lately kissed). If he let me out so easily, it means he doesn't want to risk anything. It means he wants this wedding. He wants it, too.

13

In that afternoon's gentle decline, Fabrizio had found himself restless and irritable. Earlier he had deliberately ignored his promise to meet Giuseppe, who was doubtless burning to find out why the luncheon had not come off. That day he traveled unfamiliar paths, did not return home for lunch and spent the siesta hours sulking about the Boboli Gardens, where an unattractive American lady with a guidebook flattered herself that he was pursuing her. Every emotion seemed stronger than usual. If anyone he knew should see him here! He all but dashed out at the thought, entered narrow streets and, in a poor quarter, gnawed a workingman's sandwich — a hard loaf with a paper-thin slice of salami. When the black cloud blew up he waited in the door of a church he had never seen before.

About six he entered his own little shop, where he had been seldom seen of late and then always full of jokes and laughter. Now he asked for the books and, finding that some handkerchief boxes had got among the gloves, imagined that everything was in disorder and that the cousin was busy ruining his business and robbing him. The cousin, who had been robbing him, but only mildly — they both understood almost to the lira exactly how much — insisted that Fabrizio should pay him his wages at once and he would leave and never return voluntarily as long as he lived. They both became bored with the argument.

Fabrizio thought of Clara. When he thought of her thighs and breasts he sighed; weakness swept him; he grew almost ill. So he thought of her face instead. Gentle, beautiful, it rose before him. He saw it everywhere, that face. No lonely villa on a country hillside, yellow in the sun, oleanders on the terrace, but might have inside a chapel, closed off, unused for years, on the wall a fresco, work of some ancient name known in all the world, a lost work — Clara. He loved her. She looked up at him now out of the glass-enclosed counter for merchandise, but the face was only his, framed in socks.

At evening, at dark, he went the opposite way from home, down the Arno, walking sometimes along the streets, descending wherever he could to walk along the bank itself. He saw the sun set along the flow, and stopping in the dark at last he said aloud, "I could walk to Pisa." At another direction into the dark, he said, "Or Vallombrosa." Then he turned, ascended the bank to the road and walked back home. Possessed by an even deeper mood, the strangest he had ever known, he wandered about the city, listening to the echo of his own steps in familiar streets and looking at towering shapes of stone. The night seemed to be moving along secretly, but fast; the earth, bearing all burdens lightly, spinning, and racing ahead — just as a Florentine had said, so it did. The silent towers tilted toward the dawn.

He saw his father the next morning. "It is all right," said Signor Naccarelli. "I have talked a long time with the signora. We will go today as yesterday to the office of the *parroco*."

"But Papà!" Fabrizio spread all ten fingers wide and shook his hands violently before him. "You had me sick with worry. My heart almost stopped. Yesterday I was like a crazy person. I have never spent such a day."

"Yes, well. I am sorry. The signorina is a bit older than I thought. Not much, but — Did you know?"

"Of course I knew. I told you so. Long ago. Did you forget it?"

"Perhaps I did. Never mind. And you, my son. You are twenty-one years, *vero*?"

"Papà!" Here Fabrizio all but left the earth itself. "I am twenty-three! The sun has cooked your brain. I should be the one to act like this."

"All right, all right. I was mistaken. But my instinct was

right.'' He tapped his brow. ''It is always better to discuss everything in great detail. I felt that we were going too quickly. You cannot be too careful in these things. But my son —'' He caught the boy's shoulder. ''Remember to say nothing to the Americans. Do you want them to think we are crazy?''

''You are *innamorato* of the signora. I understand it all.''

14

At the wedding Margaret Johnson sat quietly while a dream unfolded before her. She watched closely and missed nothing.

She saw Clara emerge like a fresh flower out of the antique smell of candle smoke, incense and damp stone, and advance in white Venetian lace with so deep a look shadowing out the hollow of her cheek, she might have stood double for a Botticelli. As for Fabrizio, he who had such a gift for appearing did not fail them. His beauty was outshone only by his outrageous pride in himself; he saw to it that everybody saw him well. Like an angel appearing in a painting, he seemed to face outward to say, This is what I look like, see? But his innocence protected him like magic.

Clara lifted her veil like a good girl exactly when she had been told to. Fabrizio looked at her and love sprang up in his face. The priest went on intoning, and since it was twelve o'clock all the bells from over the river and nearby began to ring at slightly different intervals — the deep-throated ones and the sweet ones, muffled and clear — one could hear them all.

The Signora Naccarelli had come into her own that day. She obviously believed that she had had difficulties to overcome in bringing about this union, but having gotten the proper heavenly parties well informed, she had brought everything into line. Her bosom had sometimes been known to heave and her eye to dim, but that day she was serene.

She wore flowers and an enormous medallion of her dead
mother outlined in pearls. That unlikely specimen, a
middle-class Neapolitan, she now seemed both peasant and
goddess. Her hair had never been more smoothly bound,
and natural color touched her large cheeks. Before the wedding, the wicked Giuseppe had seen her and run into her
arms. Smiling perpetually at no one, it was as though she
had created them all.

Signor Naccarelli had escorted Margaret Johnson to her
place and sat beside her. He kept his arms tightly folded
across his chest, and his face wore an odd, unreadable
expression, mouth somewhat pursed, his high, cold Florentine nose drawn toughly across the bridge. Perhaps his collar
was too tight.

Yes, Margaret Johnson saw everything, even the only
person to cry, Giuseppe's wife, who had chosen to put her
sophisticated self into a girlish, English-type summer frock
of pale blue with a broad white collar.

I will not be needed anymore, thought Margaret Johnson
with something like a sigh, for before her eyes the strongest
maternal forces in the world were taking her daughter to
themselves. I have stepped out of the picture forever, she
thought, and as if to bear her out, as the ceremony ended
and everyone started moving toward the church door, no
one noticed Margaret Johnson at all. They were waiting to
form the wedding cortege, which would wind over the river
and up the hill to the restaurant and the long luncheon.

She did not mind not being noticed. She had done her job,
and she knew it. She had played, single-handed and unad-
vised, a tricky game in a foreign country, and she had
managed to realize from it the dearest wish of her heart.
Signora Naccarelli was passing — one had to pause until the
suction of that lady in motion had faded. Then Mrs Johnson
moved through the atrium and out to the colonnaded porch,
where, standing aside from the others, she could observe
Clara stepping into a car, her white skirts dazzling in the
sun. Clara saw her mother: they waved to each other.

Fabrizio was made to wave, as well. Over everybody's head a bronze fountain in the piazza jetted water into the sunlight, and nearby a group of tourists had stopped to look.

Clara and Fabrizio were driving off. So it had really happened! It was done. Mrs Johnson found her vision blotted out. The reason was simply that Signor Naccarelli, that old devil, had come between her and whatever she was looking at; now he was smiling at her. The money again. There it was, forever returning, the dull moment of exchange.

Who was fooling whom, she longed to say, but did not. Or rather, since we both had our little game to play, which of us came off better? Let's tell the truth at last, you and I.

It was a great pity, Signor Naccarelli was saying, that Signor Johnson could not have been here to see so beautiful a wedding. Mrs Johnson agreed.

Though no one knew it but her, Signor Johnson at that very moment was winging his way to Rome. She had cut things rather fine; it made her shudder to realize how close a schedule she had had to work with. Tomorrow she would rise early to catch the train to Rome, to wait at the airport for Noel to land, but wait alone this time, and, no matter what he might think or say, triumphant.

He was going to think and say a lot, Noel Johnson was, and she knew she had to brace herself. He was going to go on believing for the rest of his life, for instance, that she had bought this marriage, the way American heiresses used to engage obliging titled gentlemen as husbands. No use telling him that sort of thing was out of date. Was money ever out of date? he would want to know.

But Margaret Johnson was going to weather the storm with Noel, or so at any rate she had the audacity to believe. Hadn't he in some mysterious way already, at what point she did not know, separated his own life from that of his daughter's? A defective thing must go. She had seen him act upon this principle too many times not to feel that in some fundamental, unconscious way he would, long ago, have broken this link. Why had he done so? Why, indeed? Why are we all and what are we really doing? Who was to say when *he*, in turn, had irritated the selfish, greedy nature of things and been kicked on the head in all the joyousness of his playful ways? No, it would be pride alone that was going to make him angry: she had gone behind his back. At least so she believed.

Though weary of complexities and more than ready to take a long rest from them all, Mrs Johnson was prepared on the strength of her belief to make one more gamble yet, namely, that however Noel might rage, no honeymoon was going to be interrupted, that Signor Naccarelli was not going to be searched out and told the truth, and that the officials of the great Roman church could sleep peacefully in rich apartments or poor damp cells, undisturbed by Noel Johnson. He would grow quiet at last, and in the quiet, even Margaret Johnson had not yet dared to imagine what sort of life, what degree of delight in it, they might not be able to discover (rediscover?) together. This was uncertain. What was certain was that in that same quiet she would begin to miss her daughter. She would go on missing her forever.

She was swept by a strange weakness. Signor Naccarelli was offering her his arm, but she could not move to take it. Her head was spinning and she leaned, instead, against the cool stone column. She did not feel able to move. Beyond them, the group of tourists were trying to take a picture, but were unable to shield their cameras from the light's terrible strength. A scarf was tried, a coat; would some person cast a shadow?

"Do you remember," it came to Mrs Johnson to ask Signor Naccarelli, "the man who fell down when the cannon fired that day? What happened to him?"

"He died," said Signor Naccarelli.

She saw again, as if straight into her vision, painfully contracting it, the flash that the sun had all but blurred away to nothing. She heard again the momentary hush under heaven, followed by the usual noise's careless resumption. In desperate motion through the flickering rhythms of the "event," he went on and on in glimpses, trying to get up, while near him, silent in bronze, Cellini's *Perseus*, in the calm repose of triumph, held aloft the Medusa's head.

"I did the right thing," she said. "I know I did."

Signor Naccarelli made no reply. "The right thing": what was it?

Whatever it was, it was a comfort to Mrs Johnson, who presently felt strong enough to take his arm and go with him, out to the waiting car.

Knights and Dragons

Knights and Dragons

PART ONE

1

Martha Ingram had come to Rome to escape something:
George Hartwell had been certain of it from the first. He
was not at all surprised to learn that the something was her
divorced husband. Martha seldom spoke of him, or of the
ten years she had spent with him. It was as though she feared
if she touched any part of it, he would rise up out of the
ground and snap at her. As it was he could sometimes be
heard clear across the ocean, rumbling and growling,
breathing out complaining letters and worried messengers,
though what had stirred him up was not clear. Perhaps he
was bored, thought Hartwell, who never wanted to meet the
bastard, having grown fond of Martha in his fussy, fatherly
way. He was her superior at the U.S. cultural office and saw
her almost every day, to his pleasure.

The bastard himself Hartwell had also seen in a photograph that Martha had shown him, drawing it from her

purse while lunching with him in a restaurant. But why carry his picture around? Hartwell wondered. Well, they had been talking of dogs the other day, she explained with a little apologetic shrug and smile, and there was the dashshund she had been so fond of, there on the floor. But Hartwell, staring, was arrested by the man — that huge figure, sitting in the heavy chair with some sort of tapestry behind, the gross hands placed on the armrests, the shaggy head and big, awkwardly tilted feet. Martha's husband! It made no sense to think about, for Martha was bright and cordial, neither slow nor light-headed, and she had a sheer look that Hartwell almost couldn't stand; he guessed it was what went with being vulnerable. "He looks German," protested Hartwell. She thought he meant the dog. "Dear old Jonesie," she said. Hartwell chuckled uneasily. "No, I meant him," he said. "Oh. Oh, yes. Well, no, Gordon is American, but it's funny your saying that. He studied in Germany and his first wife was German." "What happened to her?" Martha tucked the photograph away. "She died. . . . I was Gordon's student," she added, as though this explained something.

Why did the man keep worrying her? Why did she let him do it? Hartwell did not know, but the fact was, it did go on.

But sometimes the large figure with the shaggy head left her alone and she would be fine, and then she would get a letter from a lawyer she'd never heard of, speaking of some small lacerating matter, or an envelope addressed in a black scrawl with nothing but a clipping inside on a political issue, every word like a needle stab, considering that he knew (and never agreed with) how she felt about things. And if one thought of all the papers he had gone shuffling through to find just the right degree of what he wanted! And sometimes some admirer of his would come to Rome and say he wasn't eating at all well and would she please reconsider. "He never ate well," she would answer. "Only large quantities of poor food." She thought of all the hours spent carefully stirring canned cream of mushroom soup. And yet —

thinker, teacher, scholar, writer, financial expert and
heaven knew what else — he had been considered great and
good, and these people were, she understood, his friends.
She tried to be equable and kind, and give them the right
things to drink — tea or Cinzano or Scotch — and show
them around the city. "But *he* never says he would be better
off if I were there," she would make them admit. "He never
says it to you or me or anyone." Then she would be
unsteady for a week or two.

Nobody can change this, she decided; it will always be this
way. But she grasped George Hartwell's sympathy, and
knew that when he gave her some commission outside
Rome, it was really done as a favor and made her, at least,
unreachable for a time.

"Do you want to go to Genoa?" he asked her. It was
June.

He was sitting at his large friendly disorderly desk in the
corner office of the consulate, and he was round and cherub-
like, except for a tough scraggle of thin red hair. There was
always a cigar stuck in the corner of his mouth. He
scrambled around among manila folders. "Arriving in
Genoa," he explained, "cultural-exchange people, heading
eventually for Rome. But in the meantime they've excuses
for wanting to see Milano, Padova, Lago di Como, perhaps
going on to Venice. Italian very weak, but learning. Guide
with car would be great help."

"But who are they?" She always had a feeling of hope
about moving toward total strangers, as if they would tell her
something good and new, and she would go away with them
forever. She took the files as he found them for her. "Coggins . . . what an odd name. Richard Coggins and wife,
Dorothy, and daughter, Jean."

"That's the ones. Some friend of the family's wrote Grace
about them. We've got to do something a little extra for
them, but it just so happens I have to go to Florence."

Martha smiled. George's wife, Grace, out of an excess of
niceness, was always getting them into things. She wanted

everyone to be happy; she wanted things to "work out." And so it followed, since she herself was away in Sicily, that one wound up having to be helpful for a week or two to a family named Coggins. "Mr Coggins is an expert on opera, George, no kidding. Did you know that? Look, it says so here."

"That we should be floating somebody here to lecture the Italians on opera," George Hartwell complained. "Any six waiters in any one of a hundred trattorias in Rome can go right into the sextet from *Lucia* for fifty lire each. Italian women scream arias during childbirth. What can we tell any Italian about opera?"

"I wonder," said Martha, "if they listen to us about anything."

"Martha! That's the remark we don't ever make!" But he laughed, anyway, shuffling papers. "Here we are. The others make a little more sense. . . . James E. Wilbourne and wife, Rita. No children. Economist . . . thesis brought out as book — *New Economic Patterns in* . . . et cetera. He won't stick with the group much, as is more interested in factories than art galleries."

"Maybe the worst of the Cogginses is their name."

"You'll go, then?"

"Yes, I'll go."

"Atta girl."

But, certainly, she thought, moving through the sharp June shadows under the trees around the consulate, something will happen to change these plans — there will be a cable in the hall or someone will have come here. She entered her summer-still apartment through all the devious stairways, corridors and *cortili* that led to it. "Sequestered," George Hartwell called her, as though knowing it was not the big terrace and the view alone she had considered in taking a place one needed maps and even a compass to reach. The sun and the traffic noises were all outside, beyond the windows. There was no cable, no telephone message, but — she almost laughed — a letter. She recognized the heavy black slant of the writing and slowly, the laugh fading, slit it open. To her surprise the envelope was empty. There was nothing in it at all. He had probably meant to put a clipping in; it was a natural mistake, she thought, but some sort of menace was what she felt, being permanently lodged in the mind of a person whose love had turned to rejection. "Forget it," Hartwell had advised her. "Everybody has something to forget." But, alas, she was intellectually as well as emotionally tenacious and she had, furthermore, her question to address to the sky: how can love, in the first place, turn into hate, and how can I, so trapped in hatred, not suffer for it?

In his apartment, the expensive, oak-paneled, high-ceilinged place in New York's upper Seventies, crusted with books and littered with ashtrays, she had lived out a life of corners, and tiny chores had lengthened before her like shadows drawn out into a sun slant; she had worn sweaters that shrank in the back and colored blouses that faded or white ones that turned gray, had entertained noble feelings toward all his friends and tried to get in step with the ponderous designs he put life to, like training a hippopotamus to jump through hoops. There had been the long rainy afternoons, the kindness of the porter, the illness of the dog, the thin slashing of the brass elevator doors, the walks in the park. She still felt small in doorways. Not wanting to spend a lot, he had had her watched by a cut-rate detective agency, whose agent she had not only discovered at it, but made friends with.

She crumpled the empty envelope and dropped it in the wastebasket, bringing herself up with a determined shake rather like a shudder.

2

Martha Ingram would always remember the first sight she had of her new Americans at the dock in Genoa. She got a

chance to look them over before they saw her. She had to
smile — it was so obviously "them." They stood together in
clothes that had seen too much of the insides of suitcases and
small metal closets in ship cabins; they were pale from getting up early after an almost sleepless night at sea, and the
early breakfast after the boat had gone still, the worry over
the luggage, would have made them almost sick. The voyage
was already a memory; they waved halfheartedly, in a
puzzled way, to a couple who, for ten days, must have seemed their most intimate friends. They formed their little hud-
dle, their baggage piling slowly up around them, while the
elder of the two men — Mr Coggins, beyond a doubt —
dealt out hundred-lire notes to the porters, all of whom said
that wasn't enough. The Coggins girl's slip was too long;
she was holding a tennis racket in a wooden press. She looked as if she had just got off the train for summer camp. Her
mother had put on one white glove. The young man,
Wilbourne, gloomy in a tropical-weight tan suit, seemed
hung over. Was this Mrs Wilbourne sprinting up from
behind, her hand to her brow as if she had forgotten something? But it was somebody else, a dark girl who ran off crying, "Oh, Eleanor!" Mr Coggins had graying hair that
stood up in a two-week-old bristle. His lips were struggling
with a language he believed he knew well. He understood
opera, didn't he? *"Scusatemi, per favore. . . . "*

Martha hated to break this moment, for once they saw
her, they would never be quite like this again. "Are you, by
any chance, the Cogginses?" They were. How thrilled they
were, how instantly relieved. They had been expecting her,
but had not known where to look. It was all open and friendly beyond measure. Martha became exhilarated, and felt
how really nice Americans were. So the group formed instantly and began to move forward together. "Taxi! Taxi!"
It was a word everyone knew. . . .

Two weeks later George Hartwell rang them up. They
had crossed Italy by then and had reached — he had guessed
it — Venice. How was it going?

"Well, fine," Martha said. "It's mainly the Cogginses. Mrs Wilbourne couldn't afford to come and stayed behind. She's flying out to Rome in a week or so. George, did you ever know an economist who didn't have money problems?"

He chuckled.

"Mr Wilbourne doesn't stay with us much. He goes off to visit industries, though God knows what he can learn with sign language. It's churches and museums for the Cogginses — they're taking culture straight."

"Should I come up and join you with the other car?" His conference was over in Florence; he was feeling responsible and wondering what to do.

"We managed okay with the baggage rack. They've shipped nearly everything ahead." She felt obscurely annoyed at being found. "How did you know where we were?"

"I remembered that pensione, that little palace you like. . . ."

It was indeed, the pensione in Venice, a building like a private palace. It had once been some foreign embassy, and still kept its own walled campo, paved in smooth flagstones, ornamented with pots of flowers, boxed shrubs and bougainvillea. The tall formal windows opened on a small outdoor restaurant. "You mean we get all this and two meals a day?" Mr Coggins was incredulous. "And all for six thousand lire each," chanted Mrs Coggins, who was by now a sort of chorus. That was the first day. Jim Wilbourne, angrily complaining about some overcharge on the launch from the station, joined them from Padova just in time for a drink before dinner, and they felt reunited, eating out in the open with the sound of water, by candlelight. They decided to stay on for a day or two.

One afternoon they went out to the Lido — all, that is, except Martha, who had decided she would spend the time by herself, revisiting one or two of the galleries. When she came out of Tintoretto's Scuola into the quiet campo where the broad shadow of a church fell coolly (had everyone in Venice gone to the Lido?), there in a sunlit angle, a man, with a

leather briefcase but no apparent business, stood watching.
The campo, the entire area, all of Venice, indeed, seemed
entirely deserted. There had been no one else in the gallery
but the ticket seller — no guide or guard — and even he
seemed to have disappeared. The man with the briefcase
held a lighted cigarette in his free hand, a loosely packed
nazionale, no doubt, for the smoke came gushing out into the
still air. When he saw Martha pause and look at him, he
suddenly flung both arms wide and shouted, *"Signora,
signora! Che vuol fa', che vuol fa'?"* "I don't know," Martha
answered. *"Non so."* "Something has gone wrong!" he
shouted across the campo, waving the briefcase and the
cigarette. "Somewhere in this world there has been a terrible mistake! *In questo mondo c'è stato un terribile errore!"*

Martha walked away to the nearest canal and took a gondola. Mad people show up all over Italy in the summer; they
walk the streets saying exactly what they think, but this was
not like that: it was only *scirocco*. The air was heavy. She
remembered Tintoretto's contorted figures with some desire
to relax and straighten them out, and the cry from the man
with the briefcase, comic and rather awful at once, swept
through and shook her.

Already the sky was beginning to haze over. On a clothes-
line hung behind an apartment building, a faded red cloth,
like a curtain or a small sail, stirred languorously, as though
breathing in the heat itself. The boat's upcurving metal
prow speared free, swinging into the Grand Canal. Even
there the traffic was light; the swell from a passing *vaporetto*
broke darkly, rocking the gondola in a leaden way.

At dinner everyone was silent. Jim Wilbourne ate very little, and that with his elbow propped beside his plate. Martha
judged that the Cogginses bored him; they seemed another
order of creature from him. Some days before he had wanted
to know what Italian kitchen appliances were like. The kind
of apartment he wanted in Rome absorbed him.

Jean Coggins, who had sunburned the arches of both feet
at the Lido, looked about to cry when her mother said sharp-

ly, "If you insist on having wine, you could at least try not to spill it." Mr Coggins, whose brow was blistered, sent back his soup, which was cold, and got a second bowl, also cold

To Martha the silence was welcome, for always before when gathered together, they had done nothing but ask her about the country — politics, religion, economics, no end of things. She was glad they had at last run down, like clocks, and that they could find themselves after dinner and coffee out in the back courtyard because some fiddlers had happened to pass. The guests began to dance, first with one another, then with strangers, then back to known faces again. When the music turned to a frantic little waltz, Jim Wilbourne stumbled twice, laughed and apologized, and led Martha to a bench near the wall, where they were flanked on either side by stone jars of verbena.

"I'm so in love with that girl," he said.

Martha was startled. What girl? The waitress, one of the guests, who? There wasn't any girl but the Coggins girl, and this she couldn't believe. Yet she felt as the guide on a tour must feel on first noticing that no one is any longer paying attention to cathedrals, châteaux, battlefields, stained glass, or the monuments in the square.

Jim Wilbourne offered her a cigarette, which she took. He lighted it, and one for himself.

"Out at the Lido this afternoon," he went pleasantly on, "she got up to go in the surf. Her mother said, 'You're getting too fat, dear. Your suit is getting too small.' For once I could agree wholeheartedly with Mrs Coggins."

So then it was Jean Coggins. "But she's only a kid," Martha protested.

"That's what I thought. I was ten days on that damn boat and that's what I thought, too. Then I caught on that she only looks like a kid because her parents are along. She's nineteen, actually. And rather advanced," he dryly added.

"But when —" Martha exclaimed. "I've never seen you near each other."

"That's strange," said Jim Wilbourne.

She almost laughed aloud to think how they had so quickly learned to walk through walls; she felt herself to be reasonably observant, quite alert, in fact. But she was also put out — she and George Hartwell were not really delighted to have Americans who leaped into *la dolce vita* the moment the boat docked — if not, in fact, the moment they embarked. She got up and walked to the wall, where she stood looking over the edge into the narrow canal beneath. From under the white bridge a boat went slowly past, a couple curled inside; its motor was cut down to the last notch, and it barely purred through the water. Before Jim Wilbourne came to stand beside her, the boat had slipped into the shadows.

"Italy always has this romantic impact," Martha began. "You have to take into account that the scene, the atmosphere — "

" 'Generalizations,' " Jim Wilbourne teased her, quoting something she was fond of saying, " 'are to be avoided.' "

"No, it's true," she protested. "After a year or so here, one starts dreaming of hamburgers and milk shakes."

"Indeed?" He flicked his cigarette into the water and turned, his vision drawn back to where Jean Coggins was dancing with the proprietor's son, Alfredo, the boy who kept the desk. Her skirts were shorter, her heels higher; her hair, a shambles on her return from the beach, had been brushed and drawn back. She had put on weight, as her mother said, and she did, to Martha's surprise, look lovely.

Martha, who disliked feeling responsible for people, toyed with the idea of seeking the elder Cogginses and hinting at what she knew, but there in the faraway shadows, around and around a big oleander pot, the Cogginses were dancing cheek to cheek. Richard Coggins accomplished a daring twirl; Mrs Coggins smiled. The two grubby musicians, with accordion and fiddle, who had brought an empty *fiasco* and offered to play for wine and tips, had not even paused for breath for an hour. They could go on like this all evening.

Scirocco, Martha thought, deciding to blame everything on the weather.

She slipped away, walking inside the broad, dimly lighted hall of the pensione. It looked shadowy and lovely there, its wide doors at either end thrown open to the heavy night. On the beamed ceiling reflections from water were always flickering, breathing, changing. Behind the desk a low light burned, and the proprietor, a tubby, shrewd-faced man, was bending over one of his folio-sized account books. He had told Martha that the pensione was owned by a Viennese lady who came there unannounced twice a year. She might descend on him, like the angel Gabriel, he had said, at any moment. So he kept his nose to his figures, but now, as Martha went by on her thoughtful way upstairs, he looked up.

"Ah, signora," he said, "there's nothing to do about it. *Non c'è niente da fare.*" But what he meant, if anything, was not clear.

She heard the lapping of tiny waves from everywhere, and through a window saw the flowers against the wall, hanging half-closed and dark as wine.

3

In Piazza San Marco, where she went the morning after with some idea of keeping her skirts clear of any complications, Jim Wilbourne nevertheless appeared and spotted her. Through hundreds of tables and chairs, he wove as straight a line toward her as possible, sat down and ordered, of all things, *gelato*. He was wearing dark glasses as large as a pair of windshields, and he dropped off at once into a well of conversation — he must have enjoyed college, Martha thought. The scarcely concealed fascism of Italy troubled him; how were they ever to bring themselves out into democracy?

"Quite a number have jumped completely over democracy," Martha said.

"I simply cannot believe," he pursued, trying to light a

cigarette with any number of little wax matches, until Martha gave him her lighter, "that these people are abstract enough to be good communists. Or democrats, either, for that matter. I think when the Marshall Plan came along they just wanted to eat, and here they are on our side."

"Oh, I really doubt they're so unaware as you think," Martha said. "The idea of the simple-hearted Italian — not even English tourists think that any more."

"I don't so much mean simple, as practical, shrewd, mainly a surface life. What would happen, say, if this city turned communist right now? Would one Venetian think of hauling the bones of St Mark out of the cathedral and dumping them in the lagoon? I just can't see it."

"The Cogginses seem to like everything just the way it is," Martha laughed.

"Do you see that character as I do? As long as Richard Coggins can hear some *ragazzo* go by whistling *'O soave fanciulla,'* he's gone to paradise for the afternoon. The more ragged the *ragazzo* is, the better he likes it. I have two blind spots; want to know them? Opera and religious art. A million churches in this country and quite likely I'm not going to like a single one of them."

"So no wonder you keep escaping us."

"Oh, it's been pleasant enough. You've done your best to keep us happy. And then there's daughter Jean —" He paused, adding, "Don't get me wrong," though she had no idea what that meant. By now he was eating through a mountain of ice cream, striped with caramel and chocolate, piled with whipped cream and speared with wafers.

"The Cogginses are going down to Rome tomorrow," he went on. "As you know they've got this meeting with Coggins's opposite number, somebody who's going to the States to tell us all about jazz."

"I ought to know about it," Martha said. "I went to enough trouble to set it up. Anyway, it's chamber music, not jazz."

"Okay, Mrs Ingram. So you'll get me straightened out

some day. Keep at it. Anyway, I wondered if maybe you wouldn't stay on a day or so, with Jean and me. She thought it would be a good idea. We could all go to the Lido.''

"That might be fun," said Martha.

"If you're worried about the Cogginses — well, don't. Him and his bloody opera plots. Catsup all over the stage, women's heads bellowing out of sacks. Is he serious? Those people were born to be deceived.''

"The real hitch for me is that I have a schedule back in Rome. I only made this trip to please my boss.''

"It can't be all that important," he pursued, though it was obvious to her that by actually mentioning deception he had spoiled it all.

"Anyway," she pointed out gently, "in this weather the water will be no good at all for swimming. There's sure to be a lot of rain.''

"How nice to know so much."

She maneuvered easily, but the fact was, he puzzled her. Are they all turning out like this, she wondered, all of them back there? Yet he consistently gained her attention, if that was what he wanted; she had found him attractive from the start, though she had assumed he was accustomed to creating this sort of reaction and would not have thought it remarkable, if he noticed at all. As for herself, she wanted only to place a face value on him. Tanned, solid, tall, dressed even to his watchband with a sort of classical American sense of selection, he was like something hand-picked for export; if you looked behind his ear you might find something to that effect stamped there. He was very much the sort who returned in ten years leading a group of congressmen by the nose and telling them what to look for and where, though when on home leave she might encounter him even before that, being interviewed on some TV show. It would be like him to leap out at me, right in a friend's living room, she thought. And when he had appeared in Venice a few evenings back, she had been looking toward the bridge he crossed to reach them and had seen him mount

up angrily, suddenly, against the horizonless air. He gave
her then, and fleetingly at other times, as well, the impression of being seen in double, as people always do who carry
their own image in their heads.

"How can you smoke and eat ice cream at once?" she
asked him.

He stopped, both hands, with spoon and cigarette, in air.
He looked from one to the other. "Funny. I didn't know I
was." He dropped the cigarette at once, smashing it out
carefully.

"I've been wondering how to tell you this," he said, still
looking down, but straightening as he finished. "It just happens that I seem to know your former husband rather well."

The bright level surface between them on which she had,
in her own way, been enjoying the odd sort of quarrel they
had been having, tilted, and she slid definitely, her heart
plunging downward. So another one had arrived.

"Why didn't you say so before?" she asked him.

"It isn't so easy to say, especially if —"

"If you have a message," she filled in.

She sat looking out at the square. It had filled with
tourists, mainly Germans, moving in a slow, solemn,
counterclockwise procession, ponderous, disorderly, unattractive, as though under tribal orders to see everything.
There were the pigeons, more mechanical still, with their
wound-up motions, purple feet and jewel-set eyes. And then
there was a person, all but visible, right at home in Venice,
moving diagonally across the great colonnaded ellipse of the
piazza, head down, noticing no one, big shoulders hunched
forward under his old tasteless tweed jacket, gray-black hair
grizzled at the nape. He was going to the corner drugstore,
somewhere near East Seventy-first and Madison. The smell
of a late New York summer — just a morning hint of fall —
was moving with him, strong enough to dispel the scent of
European cigarettes, the summer-creeping reek of the back
canals. He would spread books on the counter, stir coffee

without looking at it, clumsily allow the bit of lettuce to drop
from his sandwich.

"Not so much a message," Jim Wilbourne said.

"You see, people are always turning up when I least ex-
pect them!" She longed now simply not to sound helpless.

"Oh, then," he said, in a relieved voice, "you must
already know about the accident."

" 'Accident!' " She started like a quiet, lovely insect into
which someone has suddenly stabbed a pin; her wings
quivered; her eyes were fixed.

"Oh, my God, now I've done it!" She tried twice to speak
but failed, and the voice below the green mask soon continued, "I think he's all right now."

"Oh. . . . Then nothing serious happened —" She drew
a shaky breath.

Jim Wilbourne glanced out across the square. "There was
some doubt about his being able to walk, but I think —" He
broke off again, tentative, mysteriously cold.

Martha stirred compulsively, as though to shake herself
free of whatever net had fallen over her. In doing so, her
knee struck the little table, rattling the cups and spoons. She
remembered the letter on the table in Rome, and the empti-
ness of the envelope was now her own. "He was always a
completely awful driver," she was presently able to continue. 'Go on, now you've started. Tell me the rest."

Were they reading lines to each other? Nothing, even
turning the table completely over, bringing three waiters
rushing down upon them with long arguments about paying
for the glassware, would have quite restored her bearings, or
loosed her from this cold current into which he seemed
deliberately to have plunged them both. "Tell me," she
insisted.

His vision seemed, behind the glasses, to pass her own.
"Oh, it wasn't a driving accident. But who should tell you
this — it's not my business to. He was out hunting with one
of his patients, up in the Berkshires. I never thought that

aspect of it made too much sense — well — to take a mental patient hunting, that is. Almost like an experiment, just to see if he'd do it on purpose. I never meant to get into all this. But since he is okay now, you naturally will be relieved to know —"

The entire piazza, thickening steadily in the closing weather, had become a total wet-gray illusion. "This isn't Gordon Ingram," Martha said. "It can't be."

"Gordon? No, Donald Ingram. The psychologist, you know. My wife studied with him at Barnard. Well, he does have an ex-wife in Italy. It was just that we were sure —"

Martha was really angry now. "I think you invented the whole thing!" She had not quite lost control. Sparing herself nothing, she had hoped, as though striking off a mask, to find something unequivocal and human facing her, to lose the sensation of conversing with a paper advertisement for shirts and whiskey.

"No, honestly. Quite sincerely, I promise you. It was just a natural mistake."

If there was a person back of the glasses, she had missed him completely. She was not going to succeed in confronting him with anything, for his voice, with as much sameness as a record, went on, "a natural mistake."

Well, she supposed it was true. She sat looking down into treacly dregs of espresso in her cup, into which a drop or two of the oppressive mist occasionally distilled and twinkled. She gathered up her bag, lighter, a couple of packages including a glass trinket and a book she had bought for a friend, and got up to leave.

Jim Wilbourne leaped to his feet. He was halted by the waiter, who had arisen from nowhere to demand payment. Now he was running after her. "Wait!" She turned. "If I don't see you . . . I may take the train down, to stop off in . . ."

Just as he reached her, a whole family of German tourists walked straight into him, knocking off his green glasses. Martha had the startling impression that an entirely new face had leaped into place before her, in quick substitution for the one she had been across from at the table. It was even saying different things: his tone now openly challenged her: "So you won't?" "No." "Not for even a day?" "Exactly."

Their faces, contesting, seemed for an instant larger than life. Yet she could remember, recalling the exchange, no further words than that, and the moment must have faded quickly, for in retrospect it seemed telescoped and distant in the vast sweep of San Marco. Jim Wilbourne was backing away as though in retreat, and Martha stood holding her packages while two pigeons at her feet plucked at the smashed bits of his glasses. There was no weakest blot of sun and she wandered out of the square into the narrow labyrinth of Venice, where the lions had mildew on their whiskers and St George slew the dragon on every passing well.

She had looked back once, in leaving the arcades, thinking she had left a camera on a chair, and had seen Jim Wilbourne with Jean Coggins, who must have been nearby all along. They were standing near the corner of the arcade, talking. The girl had a white scarf wrapped around her hair. The vision flickered, and was gone.

He would have been angry with me, anyway, she told herself. The story was only an excuse, a pretext. But why should I have angered him?

She walked, moving sometimes with clumps and clots of people, at other times quite alone, beginning to settle and stabilize, to grow gentle once more after the turmoil, the anguish, that his outlandish mental leap at her had, like a depth charge, brought boiling up inside her. She took a certain view of herself: someone, not unusual, who had, with the total and deep sincerity of youth, made a mistake. Now, the mistake paid for, agonizingly paid for, the only question was of finding a workable compromise with life. But now at this point did she have to learn that there was something in life that did not want her to have even that? The threat seemed distinctly to be hanging in the air, as thick as the threat of heavy weather.

I should have talked more with the man with the brief-case, she thought, for, far from being mad, he had got things exactly right. *Perchè in questo mondo c'è stato veramente un terribile errore.* Don't I really believe that Jim Wilbourne's *terribile errore* was deliberate? She had accused him of it, certainly, and she did believe it.

She had believed more than that, looking back. She had thought that he was simply stirring up the Jean Coggins romance to question her authority — but that was before she had actually seen the girl standing there.

Martha stopped and almost laughed aloud. She had been about to walk straight into a wall, an architectonic device painted upon it to suggest continuing depth where none ex-isted. The laugh would have bounced back at her, perhaps from the false corridors, the steps and porticos and statuary of that very wall. Laughter was a healthy thought, nonethe-less, that said that not so many things pertained to herself as she sometimes seemed determined to believe. And as she stood there a woman much older than herself, gray, but active, and erect, walking with the easy long stride of Vene-tians, who are good at walking because they are always doing it, went past and entered a doorway, bearing a net of groceries — *la spesa* — in one hand. Just before she entered, she glanced up, and a cat uncurled itself from the column base near the entrance where it had been waiting, bounded past the woman's feet and entered the door in one soft flow-ing motion. The door closed.

Martha recalled her apartment in Rome; how easily and comfortably it closed about her once she had got past the place where the messages waited and, beyond, found the *salotto* empty and free. How quietly then she took out her work and spread it on the table, opened the shutters out to the terrace in summer, or bent in winter to light the fresh fire the maid always left.

A new season lay ahead. Perhaps the messages would

begin to dwindle now and not so many couriers would show up; time perhaps had no other result but the dissolution of things that existed, and after this something new came on. Martha, if she never had anything worth calling a new life, would have settled simply for a new silence. It would happen, she believed, when Gordon Ingram finally went back totally to his friends, who would convince him that if his young failure of a second wife ever existed, she had had no right to. (And let it even be true, she thought; if it makes him content, why, I'll believe it, too.) She thought then of Jim Wilbourne and Jean Coggins, off somewhere together in the city's rich labyrinth.

Asking the direction of the Grand Canal from a young woman who was eating chocolate, she went off in the way she was told.

4

Sometime after four it began to rain — the city, more than ever like a gray ghost ship, a hypnotic evocation, nodded into the thicker element. The rush and whisper of rain came from every distance. Inside, the air clung like cloth. The maids at the pensione hastened about closing the shutters; they set the restaurant up indoors and brought candles out to decorate the tables — Martha felt she was viewing a new stage set, a change of scene. Like an opera almost, she thought, and at that moment, sure enough, here came the Cogginses skimming in together hand in hand through the rain. Now they were laughing together at the door and soon, from the desk, were appealing to her. "Have you seen Jean?"

She said she hadn't, but Jean herself came along not much later, walking alone through the rain. She had been sight-seeing in a palace, she said, and had got lost when she left it. "You go right upstairs and take a hot bath," Mrs Coggins said.

Jean went by, making wet tracks and looking curiously at Martha, of whom she was somewhat in awe. Her foreign clothes, her long fair smoothly put-up hair, her intelligence and near absence of makeup made her seem to Jean like a medieval lady in a painting. "I can't tell what she's thinking," she had complained to Jim Wilbourne. And he had said nothing at all.

The Cogginses called Martha aside and confided to her with shining eyes that they had experienced a most curious phenomenon since coming to Venice. They had been able to relive in great detail, vividly, their entire past lives. Martha, who could not think of anything worse, nodded, smiling. "How wonderful," she said. "Marvelous," they assured her.

In the heavy air Martha had all but dissolved, and went upstairs to take a nap. She left the two Cogginses murmuring below. Tomorrow they would all be in Rome; there would be the sun.

She slept and dreamed.

In the dream Gordon Ingram was standing along some country road in New England, among heavy summer trees, and saying, "You see, I have been severely injured in a hunting accident. I cannot come there. Please understand that otherwise I would." He looked very young, like the young man in photographs she had seen of him, taken long before they met, standing in the sort of hiking clothes he must have worn in walking over Europe in days, vacations, the like of which would never come again. She was reaching out her hand and saying, as in a formal note to someone, "I sincerely regret . . . I deeply regret. . . ." It seemed the first thing they had had to talk about in many years; the first time in many years that he had spoken to her in his natural voice. The rain-colored shadows collected and washed over the image and she half woke, then slept again, but could not summon up the dream. She remembered saying to herself, perhaps aloud, "What a strange city this is." For it lay like a great sleeping ear upon the water, resonant and intricate.

All the while the rain poured vastly down and could be heard even while sleeping and dreaming, speaking one continuous voice.

In a half daze she awoke and dressed and went downstairs, and at the desk found a note for herself. Jim Wilbourne had just left; he had probably let in the ragged splash of water near the door. He had written a scribble to say that he would see them all in Rome. She crumpled the paper and dropped it in a wastebasket back of the desk. She tried to ring George Hartwell, but could not reach him; the line seemed muffled and gave her only a vague wavering sound. The operator, after a time, must have shut her off for the day. But she remembered that George had said once, one evening when he had drunk too much, that Americans never lose their experience abroad, they simply magnify it. "It's the old trick of grandfathers," he had said. "Before the fire they make little motions and big shadows dance on the wall. Europe is the wall the shadows dance on." His voice went with her for a step or two.

There was nothing to do till dinner, and she went upstairs again. The smell of cigarettes hung stagnant in the upper hall and from somewhere a shutter banged in the shifting wind. She pursued stairways and long halls, passed alcoves and sudden windows. Everything was as dark as her dream had been when it faded. A lance had whistled past her ear, and the impression persisted that she moved in a house of death.

PART TWO

5

In Rome that fall she stopped herself just before telling a friend that her husband had been wounded in an accident. This was very odd, for the fall was bright and sane, and she was at the time nearly eclipsed in cleaning up a lot of George

Hartwell's extra chores. The cultural effort had taken on new life that year; the lectures were well received, the social events congenial; pools, lakes, marshes of American good-will were filling up everywhere, and all Italians, you would think at times, were eventually going to splash and mingle in them, and the world would never be the same again.

A letter from a lawyer came to Martha, suggesting a price for some property she had owned jointly with Gordon Ingram. It should have been settled long before; it was only since they had gone so happily into it — this small wooded crook of land beside a stream in New York State — that she could never bear to discuss it. But why wouldn't he write me about it? she wondered. Why get somebody else? She sat with the letter and realized something: that if he had had an accident it would have been about here that it happened, right on this bit of land. There were some rocks and a stream below a slope, screened by maple trees.

At last she wrote: "Dear Gordon: Do take the property outright. I do not want any money for it. Will sign whatever transfer is necessary. Martha."

But he could not stand brief notes, simple transactions, direct generosities. Her motives now would suspend him for days. When people dealt with him too quickly, he always suspected either that he had made them too good an offer, or that they were trying to shake away from him; and so, suspicious, obscurely grieved, he would begin to do what he called considering their own good; he would feel it his duty to make a massive reevaluation; he would call all his friends. He would certainly call them all about Martha.

They had all discussed her to death, anyway; for years she had interested them more, it seemed, than they interested themselves. They had split her up and eaten her, some an arm and some a leg and some the joints of her fingers.

Sitting at her desk on a Sunday morning, in sunlight, Martha pressed her palm to her brow. Should she mail the letter at all, or write to the lawyer instead, agreeing to everything, or write to her own lawyer to take it over? And must all life, finally defeated, turn itself over with a long expiring grateful sigh into the hands of lawyers? No, she thought with sudden force. I will keep it a personal matter if both of us have to be accidentally wounded. It is, after all, my life.

So in the end she wrote two letters, one to the lawyer and one to Gordon Ingram. Once, before she had left the States for Italy, a year after her divorce, she had run squarely into him in New York, getting out of a taxi she had hailed, and before she could stop herself she had almost screamed, and that must have been terrible for him — poor Gordon. But she well knew that if she deceived herself by thinking she knew how he felt, she might act upon it, with sympathy, and trap herself, falling a victim of his pride.

It seemed to her in retrospect that while she debated her letter that Sunday morning, the sun went away; sensually, in recollection, she could almost feel it slipping from her hair, her cheek, her shoulder, and now Rome was deep in winter, with early dusks, blurred neon on the rush of shining streets. *Tramontana*, the wind from the mountains, struck bitterly, or heavy weather moved in from the sea; the great *campagna* around Rome became a dreary battlefield of contentious air, and one had to be sorry for the eager Americans, there for one year only, who now had to learn that a sunny, amiable, amusing, golden land had passed in one night into a dreary, damp, cold dungeon of a world where everybody was out to cheat them and none of them could get warm. Martha was used to it. She had been there several years and she liked it. Far stranger to her had been that sudden shift of weather in Venice, back in the summer. It had plunged her, like a trapdoor opening under her feet, into a well of thought she could not yet get out of. She must have been deeply in it the very day when, going home in an early dark after tea with friends, she had run into Jim Wilbourne.

She had seen the Wilbournes fairly often during the fall. Rita Wilbourne, though somewhat more flamboyant than

Martha cared to think about — she wore chunky jewelry, bright green and corals, colored shoes — was energetic in getting to know people. She studied Italian, learned it quickly, and took up a hobby — she would make ceramics. It had been a Grand Idea and now it was beginning to be a Great Success. All one room of the Wilbourne apartment had become a studio. It exuded the smell of solvents and plasters.

There had been intermittent invitations. George and Grace Hartwell, the Wilbournes and Martha Ingram often found that they had gravitated into the same corner at a party, or were ringing one another up to come over for supper on rainy Sundays. What did they talk about so much as the Cogginses?

Jean Coggins had a job in a glove shop on the Piazza di Spagna. About once a week, every young Italian in Rome made a point of coming in and buying gloves. Some did nothing but walk back and forth before the window for hours. The owner was having to expand.

Richard Coggins was the success of the entire cultural program. His Italian, once it quit rhyming like opera, was twice as fluent as anyone else's; he learned, he learned! He was invited — a great coup for the American image — to address the opera company in Milan. His lectures were packed and ended with cheers and cries. (*Bravo! Bis, bis!*) Oh, no one had ever furnished more party talk than the Cogginses. Yet there was something enviable about their success.

One night at the Wilbournes' apartment after dinner, Jim Wilbourne remarked, "Jean Coggins's effect on Italian men began to happen the minute the boat docked. It was spontaneous combustion. Do you remember Venice, Martha?"

Martha looked puzzled. She shook her head. The trouble was she remembered nothing but Venice; it was a puzzle that had never worked out for her; what exactly did he mean?

"There was some boy who kept the desk — Alfredo, his name was."

"Oh, yes, the proprietor's son."

"What happened?" someone — Hartwell's wife — wanted to know.

"Well, they were hitting it off so well that she wanted me to persuade Martha — you must remember this, Martha — to stay on a day or so, so that her parents would let her stay, too. The only catch was she didn't want me to mention Alfredo: it seems the Cogginses believe that Italian men are incorrigibly passionate or something. She nagged me until I promised to do it, but the only excuse I could think of was to say I was interested in her myself."

Everyone laughed. "So what happened?" they wanted to know.

"Well, I got nowhere with Martha. She got out of it very well."

"What did you say?" Hartwell asked her.

"I forget" — she let Jim Wilbourne finish his story.

"She said she'd like to stay on, but she had some appointments or other — very grand she was."

Hartwell, after a hard week, had had a drink or two more than usual. He gave Martha a hug. "I love this girl."

"But I was in the dark myself," Martha protested. She soon followed Rita into the next room to look at her workshop.

"So she tried to be philosophic, which for a Coggins is something of a strain, to put it mildly. She went off in the rain with Alfredo, off in Venice somewhere, and called it a day."

"I wouldn't have thought these two colors would go at all," Martha said to Rita, who had joined her. "But you've made them work."

"Yes, but Italians are so bold with their colors. I think it must be something in the sunlight here — when there's any sun, of course." She picked up two sections, handle and basin, from an unfinished hors d'oeuvres dish. "You see, you wouldn't think that would do well, but I find the more I experiment —" Her bracelets jingled together as her hands

moved. They were thin, quick, nervous hands with tinted
nails. Grace Hartwell had told Martha that the Wilbournes
were expecting a child. Why is George such a puritan?
Martha wondered. You'd think I'd struck a blow for
freedom by keeping lovers apart.

"Did you, by any chance," Martha asked Rita, "know a
Professor Ingram at Barnard?"

"Oh, yes, but not at Barnard. I went to Columbia. He
teaches there occasionally, one semester every so often. Yes,
I not only knew him, but we were sure for a time that you
must be the former Mrs Ingram. She's somewhere in Italy.
It's odd your asking that."

"I'd just recalled when we were talking of Venice that Jim
mentioned him to me there. And several other times," she
lied, "people have assumed that he — I never met this person, of course."

"But beginning to feel you know him rather too well?"

"I also heard he had been in some sort of accident last
summer. Did you know anything about that?"

"Oh, that must be another Ingram still. No, unless
something happened just recently —"

The ceramics were laid out in a bare, chilly servant's
room on a large makeshift table, strips of wallboard held up
by a smaller table underneath and supported on either end
by chairs. The effect was of a transferred American look,
makeshift and practical, at no pains not to negate the parquet floor, a scrolled mirror now layered with cement dust.
A small French escritoire had been pushed into a corner,
and beside it, a gilded baroque angel holding a torch stood
face to the wall. The room had probably been intended as a
smoking or drawing room off the *salotto*. They had dined on
frozen shrimp from the PX, and only in here with the
ceramics was the odor escapable. Why would anyone buy
frozen American shrimp in Italy? Martha had wanted to
ask, but had not. It had been answered, anyway, at dinner;
Rita was afraid of the filth in the markets. But the markets

were not filthy, Martha thought, murmuring how delicious
it was.

"Hey, Martha!" Hartwell again.

"We're busy," Rita called.

"Information required," Grace Hartwell said.

"They always want you to tell them things, don't they?"
said Rita with a moment of woman's sympathy. "If I were
you, I wouldn't."

Martha came to the doorway, her shawl tugged around
her. Her hands felt cold. Hartwell was lighting his third
cigar. Would he not, singlehanded, eventually drive out
both shrimp and ceramics smell? "Martha, I thought *scirocco*
was a wind. Jim here says it's not. He says in Venice it's
nothing but heavy weather. Now you settle it."

"I believe it's an African wind," she said, "and causes
storms all along the coasts, but sometimes the wind doesn't
get as far as Venice, especially in the summer, so then you
have heavy weather and rain."

Jim Wilbourne laughed. "You mean it is and it isn't."

"I guess that makes you both right," she agreed, and
smiled.

All their faces were momentarily turned to her. There was
some way, she realized, in which, in that moment, she drew
them, the two men primarily, and because of the men, in-
evitably, the women, as well. She would have as soon dropped from her the complex self that was for them, in separate
ways, her force, dropped it off like a shawl on the threshold
and walked away. But where? Toward other eyes, of course,
who could look, be looked at, in a new and simpler way.
Why not? The coil of her own being held her, and she could
not; that was all.

Yet the possibility continued to tease her mind until the
night she ran into Jim Wilbourne, down in the low
Renaissance quarter of the city, in the windy, misty,
December cold. In brushing past they recognized each

other, and for some reason, startled, she slipped on an uneven paving stone, so that he caught her back from falling. Then he asked her into a café and they had a drink together. She felt she was seeing him after a long absence.

He had changed somewhat; she noticed it at once. He was paler than in Venice, no longer seemed so well turned out, needed a better haircut, had a cold. He was complaining about Italian medicine; it was his wife's having a miscarriage only a week or so after their dinner party that had got them so sensitive to these matters. Martha thought how soon the bright young Americans began to look tarnished here. The Wilbournes had had some squabble with the landlord about their apartment. He had believed that Rita, who had begun to sell her ceramics, was obviously using the place for business purposes, so he drew up papers demanding either eviction or a larger rent. Martha had heard this through the grapevine, in the same way she had learned that there had been some disagreement with American friends about a car. All these were the familiar complications of Roman life, which only the Cogginses seemed to escape. *Their* landlord had dreamed of an opera career when young, and as a result brought them fresh cheeses from the country, goat's milk, ropes of sausages. The Wilbournes, stubbornly American, were running against the Italian grain, so of course everything was going wrong. Yet Jim Wilbourne did work hard; it was this that Hartwell always said, as though making up for something.

Jim Wilbourne asked her the name of the pensione where they had all stayed in Venice. A friend of his was going up. "But do you think they'd enjoy it this time of year?" she asked. "What's the matter, the weather?" The weather, obviously; she hardly needed, she thought, to nod. "I must be thinking of Verona." He frowned. "There was a big fireplace — " She shook her head. "I don't think so."

The door of the café stuck on the way out; getting it to work, he gave her an odd smile. He walked along with her for about a block, then, saying something about somewhere he had to be, he turned abruptly and went back the other way.

She turned around in the cold misty street, looking after him. The street was long and narrow and completely deserted, the shop windows covered over with iron facings that had been bolted to the pavement. Almost involuntarily, she lifted her hand. "Wait!" She did not speak very loudly and it was a wonder he heard her at all. He did stop, however, and looked back.

She began to walk toward him, and presently he even came a step or two to meet her. She stood huddled in her dark coat. The damp got in everywhere. She shifted her feet on the cold wet stones. "It's a silly thing to ask — I keep meaning to mention it whenever I see you, then I always forget. Do you remember a conversation we had in Venice when you said that someone you knew named Ingram — you mistook him for my husband — had been shot in a hunting accident?"

"I had hoped you'd forgotten that. It was a hell of a conversation. The whole place was depressing. Some start for a year in Europe." He did not exactly look at her, but past her in a manner so basically unsatisfactory to her she would have liked to complain about it. Then when he did look at her, her face, she realized, slanting up to him, must have become unconsciously strained. She laughed.

"I'm shivering in this cold. This is ridiculous, of course. I wouldn't have remembered it at all, but Rita mentioned it to me, not long ago — this same man, I mean. But what she said was that he never had any accident at all. Neither he nor anyone else she knew."

"Well?"

"Well, I simply wondered what the connection was. Why did you say it at all?"

"I must have got him confused with someone else."

"Oh, I see. Someone you know and she doesn't?"

He did not reply.

"Was that it?" she insisted.

"Lots of questions," he remarked, amusing himself, though he was not what she could call light about it. "I guess I just don't remember it so well as you."

"It was in San Marco, in Venice. You ran after me and broke your dark glasses and just after that Jean Coggins came there — to meet you."

Watching him was like looking up into a dark mirror, or trying to catch some definite figure embedded in glass. Yet his features were singularly without any motion at all. She had, as she had had before, the impression of a photographed face.

"Oh, yes, Jean Coggins. . . ." She thought for a moment he would not continue. "She wanted you to stay on. She got me to ask you. I told you that," he added impatiently. "In fact, I went to some trouble to tell you. As for her coming there, I don't remember that — I don't think it happened."

A Lambretta sputtered behind her, turning with a cough into the narrow, resounding street. The echoes clapped, climbing up to the high tile eaves above them. Pools of rain, surfaced in the uneven paving, seamed and splashed. Jim Wilbourne and Martha Ingram stepped back into a shallow alcove against an iron door, where large white letters were painted, advertising the name of the shop. The roar mounted with an innocent force and turmoil that seemed close to drowning them. Then it passed, faded, turned a corner. They both stepped back into the street.

"All this seems to have got on your mind in some sort of way," Jim Wilbourne said. "Here, come on, I'll walk you home."

The damp chill had crept up to her ankles, but she did not stir, though he caught her elbow to urge her forward. Her private idea of him was beginning to form; namely, that he was a sort of habitual liar. He might, if this was correct, be incapable of telling the truth even when it would do him no shred of harm to do so, even when it might be better that way. Any exact nature of things he was called upon to reconstruct might seem always to escape him. Hartwell had called her in once about a mix-up that had involved Jim Wilbourne and she had said then that she thought he was absentminded, but Hartwell protested, "That simply won't hold a thing like this." Then she said, "I don't think he would do anything to damage his work." They were, between them, she and Hartwell, aware of new Americans, newer than themselves, perhaps different, perhaps more nearly right, than they who had been "out here," "away from things" for longer. The feeling was that people, like models of humanity, might quickly become obsolete in some overruling set of American terms even now, beyond their knowledge or power, being drawn up; so their confidence grew weak before the solid advantage of the Wilbourne image. He was so definitely American-looking, while Hartwell had recently given in to shoes with pointed Italian toes that looked extremely odd on him, and Martha went habitually to Roman dressmakers and looked extremely well, though hardly Fifth Avenue. So with this thinking interchanged between them, Hartwell agreed not to make an issue of the Wilbourne default, and let the matter slide.

Martha said to Jim Wilbourne, "Naturally it got on my mind. It concerned me, didn't it?"

"Not at all. It concerned me, Jean Coggins, and a man you used to be married to."

She gave a laugh that did not sound altogether pleasant, even to herself. "A rather close relationship," she said. Rambling about in those half dreams that Gordon Ingram's giant mahogany bed, like being lost on a limitless plateau with the same day's journey always in prospect, seemed both to encourage and deny, she had often thought the relationship could be a lot closer. Yet now she regretted most the times that it had been. She would have liked to extinguish those times not only out of memory but out of time itself.

They began to walk off together in her direction. She protested against being any trouble to him, but he did not seem to hear her, and soon he was walking ahead at a rapid, nervous pace she found hard to keep up with in her thin shoes.

His long legs and narrow heels were striking accurately down before her. The streets were narrow and dark and his raincoat went steadily on, as though its light color cut a path for them.

"Jean Coggins," he told her with his short hoarse laugh, "has a lot of boyfriends but never gets to bed with any of them. We found this out from the maid whose sister works for the family of one of the boys. She's a great girl in *topolinos*, picnics, out among the tombs. She could probably make love in a sarcophagus. Her morals are well defined, but what if she never gets over it?"

"How do her parents get along with all this?" Martha asked.

"Her parents," said Jim Wilbourne, "are still in Venice, dancing around a flower pot."

This was not only funny, but true; Martha often saw them there herself.

He slowed his step, letting her catch up even with him, and for a moment caught her hand. "Why do I always talk to you about Jean Coggins?"

"It does get monotonous," she admitted.

"I can't think why I do it. She's comical. All the Cogginses are comical."

"You told me you loved her. You're probably still trying to get out of that."

"I don't know. It was the Italian boy —"

"Yes, I know. Alfredo."

"I remember now I told her to ask you herself, about staying on in Venice, but she didn't have the nerve. She found you awe-inspiring, your intelligence, authority, something — I don't know. As for me, I had some sort of strong feeling for you, right from the first. I imagined you felt the same, but then — " He broke off, but added, rather dryly, "Your attention was elsewhere. You seemed — enclosed."

She said nothing, walking, hearing their footfalls on the stones, and how sometimes the sound of them interlocked and sometimes not.

"I try not to think of myself at all," she ventured. And this was true; she would have put herself quite outside her own harsh, insistent desire for him, if this had been possible. As it was not, she meant simply to hold it aside.

"Well, you don't succeed," he said pleasantly. "Nobody does."

"You took that way of getting my attention by telling me that Gordon — that my husband —" Only to get that question out of the way! She felt she could get herself intellectually right, at least, and as for the rest — But striving with him to get it answered only drew her deeper in, and her feeling mounted that it was no more possible to make him speak openly to her than to make an intelligent animal consent to converse.

"I kept trying to get out of it, once I started it," he reminded her. "But nothing seemed to work. I had some notion you were slipping away from me. You did it repeatedly — it was a question of whether anything on earth could reach you at all. On that peculiar day, the question seemed what you might call urgent."

"But even on a peculiar day," she argued, "to make up death like a parlor game —"

He stopped walking. "I didn't invent any death. You did — or seem to have."

It was true. Her heart filled up with dread. Not even her dream had mentioned death. The wildest leap of all had been her own.

"Oh, God!" she murmured. "Oh, my God!" She stood before him, her head turned severely aside. They had reached the top of her street, and from the far end there came, in the narrow silence, the trickle of a commonplace little fountain. The mist, shifting, prickled sharply against her cheek. Some minutes back, from high up among the roofs and terraces, a cat had mewed, trapped on a high ledge.

He drew her in, quickly, easily, against him. The motion for them both was accurate beyond measure, and the high tension between them broke up almost at once. At its sudden departure, she gasped sharply. His arm still tightly around her, he brought her to her doorway and leaned against it with her. A small boy went past without a glance, and then a girl in a swinging coat, who looked twice and then away. The street came back to them, constricted, gray-black, high and dim.

"You've made too much of a mystery of this," he said. "I wanted to see you before, but — well, obviously, it was difficult. And, then, how could I be certain what went on with you?"

"I don't know," she said, but rousing somewhat out of the muffled clamor of her senses, she thought to ask, "How did you know that anything went on?" To which he did not reply.

She thought of his various hesitances and evasions in terms of his life being elsewhere: how could he manage to get into hers without disturbing his own? The problem could have any degree of intensity for him. She fully intended to say this, when he said,

"There's nothing very unusual about all this that I can see. You've wanted him out of the way all along. You wanted me to get rid of him. You see that, don't you?"

And he had cast her, with one casual blow, straight into madness.

She was back in her terrible private wood where the wind howled among the thorn trees; she was hearing the roar of the gun down by the stream, the crash of the autumn-garish leaves. She was racing to get there in time and the thorns tore her gown and her flesh. "Out of the way," "get rid of him" — these phrases were plainly and diabolically murderous, and she could not hear either one or echo it without a shudder. How could Jim Wilbourne speak with such an absence of horror? An accomplice speaks this way, she thought, brought too late into the action to have any but the most general notion of it, but once there, what way can be taken back to the time before him? With a staggering mental effort, nothing short of heroic, she closed down the lid on her chestful of bedlam, and said to him calmly,

"You must understand. Hatred is too much for me. I can't face it. You have to believe that." He stirred, shifting her weight entirely against his arm and shoulder, but as he said nothing, she presently hurried on. "We would be here, anyway, whether you had told me that miserable story in Venice or not. We'd still be here — I know that's true!"

This declaration was so swift and plain, it caught them in like all of truth, in one warm grasp, so that she felt it might never have ended, until he drew back to point out, "My darling, of all places in the world to make love! Do I break the door down? Haven't you got a key?"

She drew herself back, collecting the shreds and rags of what she had been thinking. Something was being ignored; she found it about the same time as she located the key. "But you do see what I mean to say." Her hand lay urgently on his arm. "It's important to me to know you understand."

"I understand it isn't true. You'd never have called me back tonight if it hadn't been for what you call my miserable story in Venice. And you know that, Martha, don't you?" He gave her a demanding shake. "Denying it — that's no good."

"I know, I know, but I —" The words rushed out at last like a confession. She felt a deep pang of relief, and was unable to finish what she had begun by way of protest. She felt shaken and outdone. All her life she had longed for some world of clear and open truth, reasonable and calm, a warm, untroubled radiance (the sort of thing that Gordon Ingram wrote about so well). But though she thirsted like the dying for it, it never appeared to her, and she wondered if every human being was not surrounded by some dark and passionate presence, opaque and confusing, its face not ever to be discerned without enormous cost. The rush of her emotion had thrown her fully against him, and she disengaged herself slowly. He let her go.

"I never meant to injure you," he said at last. "It's only

that — well, I suppose in this case it matters, keeping straight on things.''

Straight! She almost burst out laughing. Well, she thought somewhat wearily, all her rush toward him brought to a complete stop, she supposed he *had* gone to some high degree of concentrated effort to keep her straight. As for the straight of *him*, it was such another question, it made her dizzy to think about it. The truth about even so slight an episode as the Coggins girl alone would have quite likely baffled a detective force. And where, for that matter, had he been going tonight? In a return to her native aristocratic detachment, she could not bring herself to ask him things like this; perhaps it was because she did not really want to know.

She turned, finding her key in her bag, and tucking her hair up with one hand, unlatched the door. It was a small winter- and night-time door cut within the larger *portone*, and sprang easily back so that she stepped inside the dimly lighted interior at once. She looked back reluctantly to observe him. He had not pressed in behind her but stood as she had left him. It was only that one arm was thrown out against the door. The crumpled sleeve of his coat, the white inch of cuff, the set of his hand, pressed into her senses like the bite of a relief. His gaze, meeting hers, did not implore her for anything. His face was simply present, and would be, she recognized, as it had been for a long time now, present and closely with her whether she shut it out or not. From somewhere she had gained the strength to take it now, deliberately, whenever the moment came, between her two hands.

She nodded, and bending sideways to avoid the low frame, he stepped inside. The closing door made a soft definitive thud, echoing strongly within, but only once, dully, in the narrow street outside. She mounted the long stairs, proceeded through corridors and turnings, archways and landings. She did not look back or speak, but moved quietly on ahead of him.

She had lived a year at least, she thought, since running into him in the Via de' Portoghesi.

PART THREE

6

George Hartwell got the news in Milan. By then it was summer, summer even in Rome, which he had left only two days ago to help maneuver the Milan office through a shake-up; and the weather finally pleased everyone. The old damp, closed medieval shrunken city, which had all but destroyed them, had evaporated in one hour of this glorious new season. And what could have happened in it that was not gone with it? he wondered, and read the letter once more.

On Sunday morning he was driving there. It's the least I can do for her, he thought, just in case. In case of what? The road flickered up, the sea appeared and melted away and crashed in again. In case, in case, he thought, and soon might even make a song of it, and go bellowing as operatically as Richard Coggins all along the sea road south, past Santa Margherita, Portofino, with Tarquinia ahead and Santa Marinella . . . the plains, the mountains and the sea.

In some ways he wondered if it was a serious matter at all. Is any personal matter, he asked himself, a serious matter any longer? Isn't a personal matter simply a bug in the machine? Get rid of it as quickly as possible, or one of the rockets in your space capsule might jam. Push button C with all due reverence, for any other one will be your doom. The sea grew pink, then crimson, then a blue so deep and devastating he thought he would give up all considerations and sit out several days on a rock. Then life would change, if we would do that. If every other person, every other week . . .

A Lambretta roared up out of a curve, all but shaving the paint from his left front fender. He did not slacken speed, but drove on. He was not going to go and sit on any rock, ever, not even if they dropped the bomb next week.

Martha Ingram, all this time, was serenely alone upon her terrace, drying her long hair in the sun. Observant as a cat in the morning still, she had just seen far down in the little square below, where the fountain twinkled, the last courier come and go, a rich little white-haired lady from Connecticut, some cousin or friend (was it?) of Gordon Ingram's — Martha could not remember her name. The sun stood at ten and a large daytime moon floated in the sky; pale, full-blown as a flower, it seemed a contrivance of the imaginary sort, fragilely mounted for effect. Was it because she could not remember the name that she had not gone to the door? The name, actually, had been called to her attention no earlier than yesterday, when a note had come, written from the lady's hotel — the Grand, of course, nothing less. (Martha had often thought that Gordon Ingram was in Rome and staying at the Grand, which would have suited him so; they had large fronded palms in the lobby, and the steps that broke the interior floor between the reception area and the lounge were so long you could never find the end of them.) Martha wondered what she had done with that note — she didn't know.

Just now, through the beautiful weather, an hour earlier in the summer morning, the Italian messenger from the embassy had come with a dispatch case for her: she was to add a stack of reports for Hartwell and take them in the next morning. Well aware of the season, the Italian, whose name was Roberto, was amiable and conversant and invited her for an afternoon at the beach. He had his sister's car, he said, by way of recommendation, and had recently visited the States. Martha agreed the beach would be nice; she had got together with him on several minor problems recently and had found him astute. He was, in a pleasant way, a sort of social spy; he could tell an *arrivato* a mile off, and he knew ways of isolating, or deflecting, people. If Hartwell had found some way of listening to someone like Roberto during the winter past, the Cogginses would not have leaped to such prominence in the cultural program that people now had the Americans all taped as opera lovers. So what Roberto was in turn going to want . . . questions like that flowed along easily with Roman life; they were what it was about. She thought of that gently sparkling sea and what a slow progress she had made toward it through heavy weather a year ago, back when it all began.

Going out, Roberto passed by the porter and the little lady in blue. Martha could hear by leaning over the terrace that the porter (whom she had bribed) was saying over and over, "*La Signora Ingram non c'è . . . la Signora Ingram è fuori Roma.*" Roberto stopped by the fountain; turning swiftly, he seemed to stamp himself with a kind of ease on his native air. "*Sì, sì, c'è . . . la signora c'è . . . l'ho appena vista.*" Then, catching some glance from the porter, he retreated. "*O, scusi . . . uno sbaglio. . . .*" He turned, a little gray Fiat, the sister's car, no doubt, his goal, but the little lady shot after him, quick as a rabbit. She caught his sleeve. "I am looking for Mrs Ingram. She lives here. Now would you be so kind." "*Non parlo inglese, signora. Mi dispiace. . . .*" How quickly, Martha thought, they did solidify. She had always, from the first, had some knack of getting them on her side. But was it fair that poor little lady friends of the family should get the runaround? *Le prendono in giro*, Martha thought. They are leading her in a circle. A little more and she would go down and open the door, come what might.

She never saw any friends, messengers, from the States anymore. She never read her mail. And when the little lady looked up, she ducked cleverly behind the parapet of the terrace, bringing her hair, which she had just shaken damp from the wet scarf to dry, down with her. She loved the warmth on the back of her neck, the sun's heat reaching to the roots of her hair, through the fabric of her dress. Who would leave it for a minute to descend three stone flights that still smelled like winter?

So the rich lady cousin went away in her fitted blue summer coat with the funny squat legs V-ing down from the broad behind into the tiny feet in their specially ordered shoes. What a world of shopping, the kind these ladies did, came back to Martha as she watched her go. And there was her loud English to the porter (the louder we speak the more chance we have), and then for the sweeter part, her brave attempt at Italian: *"Voglio parlare con la Signora Ingram, per cortesia."* It was as if someone had said that if the lady's duty lay in climbing a mountain at once, she would not even have stopped to change clothes.

The porter was not touched in the least. *"No, signora. La Signora Ingram non c'è. L'appartamento è vuoto."* They went on and on, their voices in counterpoint, echoing in the wide-open hallways below, now touching the fountain, now climbing to the terrace. If I could think of her name, Martha thought, I might weaken and let her in. Surely she has nothing to do with, knows nothing about, the property in New York State that they must have got me to sign something in regard to or they would not now be so determined to get me to sign something releasing it. You would think they had found a deposit of gold and diamonds six inches beneath the soil, though it is quite possible that I am holding up a real-estate development. Who can tell what goes on back in that green dream across the Atlantic?

The porter kindly called a cab. Now he would earn two ways — the tip from the lady and Martha's bribe. All he had to do was be as adamant as a barred door, which was his true nature, anyway. The lady rode off in her hat of blue-dyed feathers with the tight veil, fitting sleekly as it had been carefully planned to do, over her white hair, her two million wrinkles. She held her neck up straight, giving orders to the driver, an indomitable little white duck.

If I could have thought of her name, I would have let her in, thought Martha as the cab disappeared from the square. She wasn't as bad as the rest of them, I do remember that.

Martha knew, too, by the slight degree of feeling by which even mad people recognize character, as though fingers upon a fine string in the dark had discovered a knot in it, that the lady in blue was not indulging in ugly suspicions as to if and why lies had been told her. She was saying that she simply did not know. That was all.

Oh, mythical bird, vanishing American lady! She had been, Martha felt certain, the last courier.

Martha picked up her hairbrush and, drawing her chair close to the edge of the terrace, she began to brush her hair. The bells had begun to ring, and she had put her hair up, when George Hartwell drew up in the square below, hot and rumpled and jaded, hitching up the hand brake sharply. So I was right to have the papers ready for him, Martha thought, but it wasn't especially the papers he had come there for. He tossed his hat aside and sat down in the sun.

He held out a letter to her, though it had come to him. "Your sister says you don't answer your mail," he told her, stirring the coffee she brought him. "She also wants you to know that Gordon Ingram is very sick. He is in New York Hospital."

"I haven't answered much mail recently," Martha admitted. "I've scarcely read my mail at all."

A long silence grew up between them. Hartwell's wife was in the States attending their son's graduation from prep school in Massachusetts. Everyone had begun to be displaced. The Wilbournes were gone, Jim to take a job on some new economic council for advising private industry, and Rita to open a ceramics shop, having shipped loads of material, not quite legally, through embassy channels. They had left their flat in a mess, having sneaked out unexpectedly three days early. Hartwell still had calls from the landlord. The parquet was ruined, the mirrors . . .

How was it that the sun seemed literally to warm one's heart? Hartwell now thought kindly of Martha Ingram's husband for the first time in his life. The poor old bastard, was what he thought. A man that age. Quite likely he's dying.

"So will you consider going there?" he asked her. "It can be arranged."

In the sun her hair shimmered like a fine web. Hartwell had once said about Martha Ingram when he was drunk, "Being from Springfield, Missouri, I am moved by women with grave gray eyes," which, as everyone told him, made no sense at all. It was a flight that failed. He had had some reference to his mother, aunt, some old magazine picture, or advertisement, maybe, showing a lady who wore her long hair up, face partly turned aside, serious and quiet. It was his way of worrying out loud. For his wife had speculated that there was undoubtedly a man in her life, but who? Hartwell used to think it over in the office alone and then wad paper up and hurl it at the wastebasket.

A slight movement just now of a curtain through one of the terrace windows made him think of Jim Wilbourne's even, somewhat longish, smoothly observant face, his nervous gesture of banging the heel of a resoled American shoe against a desk or chair leg when he talked, his cough and cigarettes and short hoarse laugh. Anybody, thought Hartwell, but Jim Wilbourne. Yet there she was, shining and fair, surfaced out of a long hard winter.

"Going there?" she repeated, as if he had mentioned a space ride. "It's nothing he's suggested. Don't tell me she said that."

"No," Hartwell admitted, "but look at it, anyway. . . . You haven't even read it." She had taken it, but it was lying on her lap. When she moved, it slid to the terrace and she did not pick it up.

"But I know, anyway," she said. "The last time I saw him was in Venice. He did not even look my way."

"Venice! Your husband was not in Venice," Hartwell corrected her with a slightly chilly feeling.

She tucked one foot meditatively beneath her. "You see how crazy I am," she pointed out.

After some time, Hartwell said, "Intentionally crazy, I take it?"

"It's necessary," she finally replied.

At this Hartwell stopped drinking coffee, perhaps forever.

"What are you thinking?" she asked him.

"I think the weather is better," he said.

"That isn't what you think," she said gently, and gently, too, she went so far as to pick up the letter and place it — most untrustworthily — upon the table.

A small bell in a small church rang close by. It had a lovely clear sound and one actually looked about, expecting to see it, as though for a bird that had burst out singing.

"If only you could have got by without Wilbourne!" Hartwell cried, astonishing himself.

Martha built a pyramid out of burned matches beside the milk pitcher. "He's gone. And anyway, what was it to you?"

"I didn't like him," said Hartwell arbitrarily. "This has happened before. It's nothing new. Those tall young men . . ." It had happened all his life, in fact; he never having been one of them. At Harvard he had seen them, in the clothes of that day, older, of course, than himself, their strong easy step moving down corridors. And at Oxford, English tall with heavier bone structure, their big knees ruddy and tough in the blear cold. Now they were younger and would be younger still, but the story was still the same. "One expects such brilliance, and what happens? A moderately adequate work program, someone dear to me damaged —" she gave him a glance but did not stop him "— and now this headache of an apartment going on and on into the summer."

They had wrecked their apartment when they left, Jim and Rita Wilbourne. The parquet, the mirrors, the plumbing, the furniture. It was a vengeance on the landlord,

whose nature was infernal and who had made their life a
grating misery for the whole year. Now Hartwell had to
listen to the landlord; he came once or twice a week to Hartwell's office; he would come tomorrow. "*Signor console, devi
capire che sono un uomo giusto e gentile. . . .* You must understand I am a just and honorable man." The world was
smeared and damaged, and Martha's craziness obsessed
him, the more because she having completed herself he was
in some ways crazier than she, else why would he let the
landlord in for these interminable visits complaining of
something that he could be said to be responsible for only in
the vague sense of directing an American program in which
Jim Wilbourne had, for a short time, taken part?

"You are linking me, George," she half teased him, "to
what the Wilbournes did to the landlord. Is that reasonable?"

"No, it isn't. It isn't reasonable at all. It just happens to
be the truth, that's all. And anyway, you didn't see it — you
didn't get the guided tour after they carried out the crime
and ran away to Naples in the night. Carelessness is one
thing, disorder left by people who aren't so tidy, something
not at all nice about it, smelly maybe, but still human. But
Rita and Jim Wilbourne had taken hammers, crowbars,
scissors . . . !" He had begun, somewhat ludicrously, to
shout.

Martha thought it was time somebody repaid a Roman
landlord in kind, though anything short of crucifixion
seemed genteel, but even to think of a Roman landlord
seemed out of place in the timeless non-bitterness of a Sunday morning full of sun.

"If he found that was the only way to get even," she said,
"there may even have been some logic in it. I'm sure he got
no more than even, and maybe no less. You forget he was an
economist, so that might have something to do with the way
he felt. I really don't pretend to know."

"I'm sure you would know more than I would," Hartwell
said, somewhat recovering himself.

"I know he was the only one who could deal with Gordon Ingram — I do know that. But I never thought of him as smashing apartments up, though now that you mention it —"

The little church bell stopped ringing about then, and she wondered at Hartwell, this stupor of moral horror in his face, and predicted, the instant before he did it, that he would ask for a drink. She went and got it, drifting free and anchorless through her apartment, then going off to rearrange some flower pots, having no more ties than a mobile, invisibly suspended in the sun. Yet she was kind enough to reassure him. "If my judgment of him is worth anything, he seemed more quiet than not."

"Quietly murderous?" Hartwell murmured, and fell into the Scotch with a sigh.

She had to recognize, for by turning her head she could even see what made a space for itself rather constantly in her mind — how the room just beyond the tall windows onto the terrace looked now. They would have both known a long chain of rooms like that from childhood on, known their quiet, with shadowy corners and silent chairs and pictures that look only at one another, ornaments of no earthly connection to anything one knows about or can remember, and known, too, the reason for their precise quality, even down to the slow wind of dust motes in the thin slant of winter sun, the cool rest the marble has in summer and the small light of the lamps: the reason being that somebody has been got rid of in them. In spite of her, their thoughts like profiles in a modern painting, merged and coalesced. She appeared as one of a long line of women who have rooms like this; invariably handsome, well dressed, detached, goalless, they have struck at life where it lived, unnaturally, because it grew unbearable.

He recalled from his long-lost Missouri days, various women, their features indistinct but their spirits clear to transparency, who lived in shady white houses with green latticework under the porch where the land sloped away. In

varying degrees of poverty and wealth, they gave up their
lives day by day, like sand running through a visible hour-
glass, to some trembling cross old father or invalid brother
or failure of a husband or marvelously distorted and deeply
loved child. But out and away from this monotony, they
ranged far and wide among friends of the town, accepted,
beloved, understood, praised. He saw them shift through
that lost world with the sureness of angels, and though he
said to himself it was lost, the thought occurred to him that it
was perhaps only he who was lost to it; for certainly it was
there still: what made him think it wasn't? It was still there
and going on, and repeating moreover its one relentlessly
beautiful message: that you had to stand what you couldn't
stand, or else you couldn't live at all. And for the first time it
came to him that Martha Ingram did not, any longer, exist.
He felt a pang of missing her, as though sometime back
somebody had come in the office and told him the bad news
and he had done all the decent things.

Whereupon she looked at him, reflectively, through the
sun, and all the fabric of his fantasy crumbled. At least in the
warm intelligent effigy of the flesh she was still there and still
able to get through to him. She was all but pointing out to
him that he didn't really know, how could he know just how
it was? It was inhuman; it was monstrous — that was the
first thing to know. Therefore, who was to say what she had
or hadn't had the right to do about it?

7

As to whether or not she was really there anymore, she could
have said that she had simply become the winter past. Its
positive motion against her, which seemed at times as blindly relentless as a natural force breaking up her own life,
would always be with her. But it could not, unlike a natural
force, ever be forgotten, for human faces had appeared in it
and voices had cried to her, human motion had struck her

down, and by these things, grasped at, sometimes only half understood, she had been changed for good and could never escape them. It had been a definitive season.

But why George Hartwell now had to rush back into its devastating glooms and vapors, the flicker of its firelights and quick gasps of its passions, so grotesquely lighted up in shadow play against the walls of his good and gentle heart — that she could not say. She did not really want to say. He seemed distant to her. She was fond of him. She could not have been any more or less than that if he had wanted her to, and he would never say so if he did, even, she supposed, to himself. She could, however, indulge him. He had his curiosity, so much a part of his affection — she could honor both by letting him in on things. She doubted if she would ever go so far as to say very much about the evening she had run into Jim Wilbourne on the Via de' Portoghesi, but in a way by just recalling it, it could be in some way shared by George Hartwell's openness in her direction, which she might have been leaning over to pat on the head, like a house pet. But then of course, he would want to get past all that as hastily as possible and on to the next thing, the next stone in her private torrent, and she guessed, looking back, that that would have been the Boston lawyer. In January, wasn't it?

Yes, she could share that with George. She could even tell him about it, for she would not forget a single detail of it, even down to the gray suit the lawyer was wearing. He was all gray, in fact, all over, even to his cuff links, hair and tie, and his name was gray, as well — Bartram Herbert. He was a close friend of Gordon Ingram's. She had known him for years.

He flew in in the afternoon, to Ciampino, just as his telegram had said he would. She did not meet the plane, and had even decided that she would leave the city for Naples, but unable to make herself do so, showed up exactly where he had asked her to, the Flora lobby near the Porta Pinciana. She even arrived on the exact hour, clasped his hand with a

pale smile and turned her chilly cheek for a token kiss. He
took her down to have a drink with him in the bar. Next he
ordered a cab to Ranieri's (had he reserved by cable, she
wondered?), which is an old-fashioned Roman restaurant
where the carpets sink deeply in and the soft chandeliers
swing low and the waiters murmur in French, bending at
monsieur's elbow, and he said (this being the kind of place
his voice was best adapted to), "Gordon feels some income
should be set up from the land for you. It is on his conscience
because you may remember that some of your parents'
legacy went into the original purchase. It was not noted in
the deed of sale, and indeed could not be. This is only a matter of personal conscience, as I'm sure you must appreciate
correctly."

She was wearing a stern black suit and noticed, in a discreet but enormous mirror in a heavy frame, how pale she
looked, though perhaps it was only the lighting, how subdued she sat, almost clipped out with scissors. She watched
the neat insertion of his pointed spoon in the melon he had
discovered on the menu and was now enjoying, and longed
to say, "But you and Gordon were directors in that trust
company that failed in the crash — I heard all about it —
and somehow you never got precisely ruined, though of
course 'ruined' was the word you used for yourself, but it
was never visible." But she did not. She wondered if it was
not too easy to suspect dishonesty where people are really
only loyally seconding one another's ideas, echoing one
another's politics and views of humanity that sound despic-
able, only to prove their common ground of affection. Then
she said, "I think the trouble with all these messages, these
visitors and plans and letters and schemes, is that everyone
is looking at things only as Gordon sees them." His glance
was sheer genius. "Oh, not at all, my dear. If it's what you
feel, why that's unfortunate, but certainly in Mrs Herbert's
— Ruth's — view and my own, you and Gordon were
simply too dissimilar to manage a happy arrangement."
Dissimilar! She tried desperately to keep the word from

clanging in her head. Had Gordon really poisoned the dog, as she suspected? she wanted to ask, for certainly the vet had told her so, clear and round, and he had said, "If you think I will stoop to so much as answer this degrading nonsense. The dog was not poisoned. They are either confused or are deliberately telling you something to cover some mistake on their own part." There was, of course, another word like dissimilar: incompatible. "I have often wondered, however, granting the fact that no one can really say what causes such desperate conditions in a marriage that divorce is the only way out — I have often wondered what I did to turn all Gordon's friends against me. Why did you hate me so much?"

"It looked that way to you, did it?" He took a small sip of French wine. "I can see how it might. We all felt, you see — protective of Gordon. He has meant, through the years, so much." "So you wanted him back to yourselves?" "There was some sort of reaction." "There certainly was," Martha agreed. "I wanted to love you," she added. "I'm sure we made it difficult for you," he admitted. "I, for one, was somewhat conscious of it at the time. I tried, in some way, do you remember, to make amends." "I remember," she said, "that you took me down to see the fish pond." "So I did." He smiled. "And wasn't that pleasant for you?" "Yes," she said, "but it was scarcely more than decent. You never said anything to let me know you saw the difficulties I was half drowning in, with everyone else." "Well, but wouldn't that have been disloyal to Gordon?"

There was the thin sound of his spoon touching down on the plate, and she said, "I suppose now that this bit of land is turning out to have some value I have not heard about."

"There is no attempt afoot to give you less than every cent that could possibly be due you."

"I did not mean there was," she said. Good God! she thought, how old he makes me feel. "I only meant that I have a reasonable interest in business."

"Well, then, you may as well know that the area is being opened up as suburban property — quite in the junior executive line. Maybe you aren't familiar with the term."

"Oh, yes."

"Has someone else got to you, then?"

"Oh, no, it's only that I guessed that I was being treated rather well for there not to be better than average sums involved." I shouldn't have said that, she thought. Of course, I make them angry. They don't like it, of course, they don't like it, and why do I do it? "Listen," she said intensely, "I'm sorry. I never meant to —"

"You must remember, my dear, that Gordon only got interested in finance through having to manage property you were left with. He saw what a sorry mess things were in where you and your sister were concerned and he so interested himself that he could now earn fifty thousand a year as a market analyst, that is, if he cared to. Your sister Annette says she never goes to bed without thanking God for Gordon Ingram."

In Martha's view her sister Annette was a near illiterate who would have gone on comparing prices of soap powders if she had a million dollars. She felt a blind white tumult stir inside, the intellectual frustration, of always being — she could only think deliberately, but how was one to know that — misunderstood.

"I think it's wonderful how well he manages money, but that wasn't the point of what I was saying."

"Why don't we take our coffee elsewhere, if you're agreeable." In the *carrozza* he hailed for them in the narrow empty street, he conversed intelligently about the city, telling her in the course of some chance recollection several things she didn't know. And in the *carrozza* she experienced the tug of motion as one doesn't in a car, and the easy sway of the wheels, the creak of leather. He handed her down in a comfortable way. "Well, and what a pleasant thing to do!" Moving her toward a quiet café, "Shall we just have some coffee here?"

How charming they would all be, she thought, if only one could utterly surrender the right ever to disagree with them.

She wished she could have sat in the handsome bar, all white rococo and gilt, and bring him out on some old story or other: reminiscence, that was what they loved, but she had desperately to try once more, for the bar was teeming with Italians: he was all she had of America here.

"I only wish that someone would admit that a man can be as wonderful as a saint to everyone in the world, but behave like a tyrant to one person."

He gave her a quiet gray look. "I cannot see anything tyrannical about Gordon wishing you to have your share of this property settlement."

"I only want to be forgotten," she said.

"Surely a rather singular wish."

It was right there on the table that she signed it. She remembered the crash of the gun down by the stream's edge. The ink flowed easily from the pen. It was only, she thought, a question of money. His hands in receiving documents were extremely adept.

"There will of course be other papers," he said. "They will reach you through the mail."

8

And all this time in the thick or cutting weather of that winter she had been blown adrift about the city, usually going to put in a social appearance somewhere that the Hartwells didn't have time for, and when George saw her as he did see her once, driving by in his little car — she was on the Veneto — it gave him the odd sensation that all was not well. As if to confirm it she stopped still and laughed. The sight was pleasant, but the idea worrying; she had told him something even back that far about the Boston lawyer, whom he had actually seen her having cocktails with at the Flora, but, in the days that followed the laugh, he fell to wondering what his responsibility was. He recalled the sudden break in her walking there by the high wall just past the embassy, and the giant twin baroque cupids playing with a basin into which a fountain gently spilled, and thought that if Martha was in New York she would be swelling some psychiatrist's income by now, a thing he withdrew himself from even considering. He sat meditating evenings before a Florentine fireplace covered with Della Robbia cherubs, a full-length angel or two that he called his "dancing girls," and with sighs of joy sank his stone-chilled feet deeply into hot water poured into a copper pot that his wife had bought from a peasant in the Abruzzo and that was someday going to be filled to abundance with bronze chrysanthemums in some white American home among the flaming autumn hills, but right now . . . she poured another boiling kettle in. "I wish to heaven you would find out definitely once and for all that of course she does have a lover. Or even two or three. Or decide that you want her yourself. Just tell me please, so I don't have to overhear it at the opera." "It's too hot," he protested for the third time. "You don't have to scald me. And anyway, I hope she does have somebody if he's the right sort. I just don't want her jumping out of a top window of the Colosseum, or off St Peter's balcony, or even her own terrace, for Christ's sake. You know about the suicide we had in Germany." "But why should she —" "I don't know, I can't tell. It's just a feeling I have."

An old bathrobe he had bought in Missouri to take with him to Oxford, where it had been his heart's comfort and one sure joy, was hugged round his shoulders, and cupids, winged but bodiless, alternating with rich purple clusters of grapes and gently prancing unicorns, looked down upon him from the low, beamed Rinascimento ceiling, justly famed. Their palazzo was listed in guidebooks and it seemed a shame that they could never remember once having been warm in it. His wife was bundled up in sweaters and an old ski jacket; she even sometimes wore gloves indoors in the damper weather, and George himself was turning into an alcoholic just from trying to get enough whiskey in himself to

keep out the vicious mists. A glass of Bourbon sat beside him
on the marble floor.

9

What George Hartwell now recognized that in those days he
must have been fighting off was no more than what Martha
herself had spent so long fighting off — that around one corner he was going to run headlong into Jim Wilbourne. He
told himself he was afraid she had got mixed up with an
Italian, though it might not in the long run perhaps mean
very much — Italians generally left the American women
they made love to, or so ran the prevailing superstition. The
question of her divorce would have been in it from the first,
thus practically guaranteeing she would get hurt. But then
he worried, too, that it might be the English or the
Americans, whom one counted on really to mean it, or so
the legends went, and hence might get lulled into trusting
too implicitly for anything. That might be more damaging in
the long run.

"Who is it?" he came right out at lunch once and asked
her. "Who is it, Martha?" But as he had not led up to this
demand in any way, she assumed, quite naturally, that he
was referring to somebody who had just passed their table
and told him a name they both knew of a girl from Siena
who used to work at the consulate but had had to return
home to live with her aunt, but what was she now doing
back in Rome. He said he didn't know.

The day was misty and the light blurred, lavender and
close all day, dim as the smoke from the chestnut braziers,
on the branched trees of the Villa Borghese, where the gravel
smashed damply under the thin soles of Roman shoes. The
crowds flowed out, engulfing and persistent; a passing tram
blocked out whatever one might have thought one saw.
Hartwell gave up worrying; suicide seemed out — she

looked invariably blooming. He had enough to bother him, what with new government directives that occasioned the reorganization of the entire staff (by a miracle he stabilized himself, Martha and one or two others he wanted to keep upon the shaky scaffolding until it quieted down — these earth tremors left everybody panting). Then there was the thing of the ambassador's getting poison off the ceiling paint — *Ceiling paint?* No Roman ever believed this, just as no American ever doubted it. Solemn assurances eventually were rendered by a U.S. medical staff that the thing had actually taken place. The Romans howled. You could judge how close you came to being permanent here by how much you doubted it.

Martha forgot to come one evening and help Grace Hartwell out with the Cogginses, who had to be invited somewhere occasionally; they had to be acknowledged or clamors went up from their admirers. George made a monstrous effort and kept them out of the festival plans now being talked in reference to Spoleto where no one who remotely resembled them would be included, a thing they would never have understood. Martha rang up late, excusing herself on the grounds of some trouble with her maid. Maid trouble was always a standard excuse among Americans, and though it seemed almost Italian to lie to close friends, Grace Hartwell accepted it not to risk upsetting George.

"You abandoned me, just the same," she told Martha. "And that girl now is into some trouble over her work permit."

"She never had one at all," said Martha, who knew the straight of the story. "She agreed to help at the shop or be allowed to hang around just to learn Italian. She wanted experience instead of money."

"I don't know how much experience she got," said Grace, "or for that matter had already, but the proprietor had a fight with his relatives, who are all out of work, and say she's taking food out of their mouths and now she's been reported somewhere. The Cogginses seem to have got her out of it just by having so many friends at the Istituto Musicale di Roma, but now she's out of work.''

"Unemployment is on the rise," said Martha flippantly, making Grace cross.

"There is so little for young people in Rome," said Grace, "they don't know what to do with her. It seems all the young Italians —"

"They can always send her back," said Martha.

But seeing that she had made Grace Hartwell angry, an almost impossible feat, she invited Grace and Dorothy Coggins to tea at Babbington's on the Piazza di Spagna. They were joined by Rita Wilbourne, who had been at Grace's. Dorothy Coggins said she used to come here often before Jean left the glove shop, which was right across the street. Grace Hartwell gave full attention to Rita, who always looked tentative in Italy, rather like an ailing bird, but who, at least today, was subdued in what she wore, a navy dress and dark beret. Grace seemed to feel that given enough scones to eat she might actually be fixed in place in some way so far lacking. But Rita protested that she felt much better since some friends took her up to Switzerland, a civilized country.

Martha, who liked Grace and often used to confide in her, now felt herself so utterly bored she wondered if she could make it through to a second cup of tea, when suddenly, as if a signal had been given, they all found themselves deeply involved in talking about a new couple who had just come out from the States. They were soon examining these people in about every verbal way that exists, briskly, amiably, with enormous, almost profound curiosity, not at all unkindly, hoping for the best and not missing anything, from the two children's immediate cleverness with the language (they reminded Grace of *English* children. "Oh, yes, you're right," Martha enthusiastically agreed. "It's their *socks!*") to the woman's new U.S. clothes and probable family background, somewhat superior, they thought, to the husband's, who had worn a huge Western hat (he taught in Texas) down the Via Nazionale and was trailed around by knots of people, some of whom believed him to be a famous movie director. This was really rather funny, when one considered that he was actually an authority on Virgil, though Grace said she did not know which was funnier, to consider an authority on Virgil in a cowboy hat on the Via Nazionale, or in Texas in any sort of headgear, and Dorothy Coggins said that Texas was getting way way up, culturally speaking; that remark only proved what an ancient Roman Grace was getting to be. And Rita said that Jim loathed Italian hats and would not have one. Martha did not recall he ever had a hat at all.

"Richard doesn't mind anything Italian," said Dorothy. "He's simply gone on the place. Jean has a modeling job now," she told Martha. "I thought at first I'd have to arrange for her to go home. She was running around too much, meeting too many of these boys who just hang around places. I don't know what they do. I can never understand. Their families are well off, I suppose, but still I — You got it for her, didn't you, Martha?" "Why, no," said Martha, "I don't think so." "She mentioned you to that designer — what's her name — Rossi. The little elegant one on the Via Boncompagni, and you were just the right one for her to know. She had to lose fifteen pounds — she ate nothing but salami for ten days. They were to call you up and she was sure —" "They didn't, but it's all right." "She thinks you got it for her." "Well, I —" Martha suddenly knew nothing to say. It looked clever of Jean to go to that one shop and mention her; but it had been perhaps merely luck. It was the sort of haphazard luck the girl had. "She admires you so," said Dorothy Coggins with housewifely openness. "She always did. It really is amazing," she added. "I can't see anything amazing about it," said Grace with her generous laugh. They had all paused and were looking, with more admiration than not, at Martha, and Rita said, "What a lovely pin — I must borrow it sometime to copy it." It was something she had had forever. She felt silent and alone in a certain shared secrecy with the pin — its quiet upcurving taste enclosing amethysts — and though she said she would lend it to Rita sometime she had no intention of doing so.

The women sat together, in their best suits and hats, shoes damp from the streets, handbags beside them at a corner table, while the early dusk came on and the soupy traffic thickened outside. The ceiling was low, dark, and beamed in the English manner, the place a favorite haunt of the quieter English colony. The Brownings might have just gone out. Yet under the distant assurance of even that name lurked some grisly Renaissance tale. Martha found her gloves and asked for the check.

Afterward she drove with Grace to carry Dorothy Coggins up the Gianicolo to the American Academy to meet her husband. They left Rita to catch a cab home. "It will be a blessing," said Dorothy as Grace fended through traffic, "if she has another baby as soon as she can. She's not going to be happy until she does. I know that from my own experience."

"Well, if she could just —" Grace Hartwell broke off, fighting traffic for dear life. She and Martha were quite solidified in not wanting to hear just what Dorothy's experience had been.

When she dropped Dorothy off, she drove around for a time among the quiet streets above the city, also above the weather, for up here it seemed clear and cold, and glimpses of the city showed below them framed in a long reach of purple cloud.

"You didn't mind my bringing Rita?" she asked Martha.

"No," said Martha, and then she said, "I see a lot of Jim, you know."

"I thought something like that, this afternoon, I don't know why. I really cannot think why. I think it was when she asked you for that pin. Isn't that amazing? Well, I won't tell George."

"I know you won't," said Martha.

"I just hate seeing nice people get hurt," said Grace somewhat shyly. She and George had fallen in love at a college dance. They had never, they did not need to tell you, loved anybody else but each other.

"I don't know who is supposed to be 'nice people,' " said Martha with a little laugh.

Grace did not answer and Martha added, "I don't want, I honestly do not want, to embarrass George in any way."

"Why, it's possible he won't ever hear about it at all. Unless everybody does. Or unless the marriage breaks up or something. Is that what you want to happen?"

Martha fell completely silent. This was the trouble with the run of women, considered as a tribe, with their husbands — George, Jim and Richard — to talk about and other families to analyze. How they assembled all those alert, kind-tongued comparisons! How instantly they got through an enormous pot of tea and a platter of pastries! How they went right straight to the point, or what they considered to be the only point possible. To Martha it was not the point at all. The fact of her trusting Grace was the more remarkable in that she understood, even in advance, that they would from now on in some way be foreign to each other.

"I don't know that I want anything to happen," said Martha.

"Rita came over," said Grace, "to talk about —"

"Oh, do stop it," said Martha, laughing, but somewhat put out as well. "You're trying to say it wasn't about me."

"You know, I honestly feel tired of it already," Grace said. She paused. "I'll think of it all as we were, as you and George and I always have been, all these years. I'm going to do that," she reiterated, and began to accelerate. Pulling her chin up sharply, a habit for preserving her chin line, and gripping the wheel with her hands in worn pigskin gloves, she went swinging and swirling down the Gianicolo, past the high balustraded walls of those tall terra-cotta villas. She remained firm and skillful — a safe driver — her reddish-brown hair, streaked with gray, drawn up rather too tall from her wide freckled brow so forthrightly furrowed (like many people with warm, expressive faces, the thin-skin texture of nice women, she was prematurely lined). But now, Martha noticed, her face looked strained, as well.

"Confidences are a burden, I know," said Martha. "I'm sorry, Grace."

"It isn't keeping secrets I mind. You know that. No, it isn't that at all."

Martha did not ask her to define things further, for to encounter love of the innocent, protective sort that George and Grace Hartwell offered her and that she had in the past found so necessary and comforting seemed to her now somewhat like a risk, certainly an embarrassment, almost a sort of doom. Grace did not press any further observations upon her, did not kiss her when she was ready to get out of the car. She waved and smiled — there was something touching about it, a sort of gallantry, and Martha was sensitive to the exaggeration, the hint of selfishness, which this reaction contained. She did not blame Grace, but she read her accurately. She was protective of her husband, the sensitive area was here, and here, also, was written plainly that Martha was more of a help to George Hartwell than she herself had known. Somehow she thinks now I'm in bad faith and she in good, Martha saw. Does she think I can live for George Hartwell?

She took off her damp topcoat and the hat with which she had honored the tea and saw on the telephone pad a note saying that Signor Wilbourne had called.

10

"Martha?"

Whether at home or in the office, at whatever time of day, the name, her own, coming at her with the curious, semi-hoarse catch in it, seemed to fall through her hearing and onward, entering deep spaces within her. She listened as though she had never heard it before, and almost at times forgot to answer. Hurried, he was generally going on, anyway, to what he meant to tell her; the clatter of some bar in the background, he would be shifting whatever clutch of books or briefcase he had with him to unfold a scrap of paper and read an address. Then she would write it down. There were streets she'd never heard of, areas she did not know existed, bare-swept rooms at the tops of narrow stairs, the murmur of apartment life from some other floor or some distance back of this one, the sounds of the street. The wires of small electric stoves glowed across the dim twilights of these rooms, and if she reached them first, she would sit quietly waiting for him to come, drawing the heater close to warm her damp feet, wearing one of the plain tweed suits she wore to work, her scarf and coat hung up, her face bent seriously forward. She thought of nothing, nothing at all.

She would hear his footsteps on the stair striking, as his voice on the phone did, directly against her hearing, but when the door opened she would scarcely look up, if at all, and he on his part gave her scarcely more than a passing glance, turning almost at once to put his coat up. Yet the confrontation, as brief as that, was absolute and profound. It was far more ancient than Rome.

"Is it okay here? Is it all right?" To a listener, he might have been a landlord speaking. She sat with her hands quietly placed beside her. "It's like the others. There's nothing to say about it, is there?" "Well, it's never warm enough. Someday we'll . . ." "Do what?" "I don't know. Go right into the Excelsior, I guess. Say to hell with it." "But I like it here." "You're a *romana*."

His cheek, the high bone that crossed in a straight, horizontal line, pressed coldly against her own; it was damp from the outside air. His hands warmed momentarily beneath her jacket. His quick remarks, murmured at her, blurred off into her hearing — stones thrown in the sea. In the long upswing of her breath she forgot to answer, and tumbled back easily with him against the bed's length.

"God, there's never enough time!" "Forget it." "Yes . . .I will . . . yes. . . ."

In these beginnings, she often marveled to know if she was being made love to or softly mauled by a panther, and that marveling itself could dwindle, vanishing into the twin bars of the electric fire or the flicker of a white shirt upon a chair. She could reach the point of wondering at nothing.

Yet something — some word from without them both did come to her — either then or in recollection of those widely spaced-out little rooms hidden among the crooked roofs of Rome, where the mists curled by and thought stood still and useless, desiccated, crumbling, and perishing; it was only a phrase: "Run slowly, slowly, horses of the night." It fell through her consciousness as her own name had done, catching fire, mounting to incandescence, vanishing in a slow vast cloudy image silently among the gray skies.

Sometimes he gave her coarse Italian brandy to drink out of a bottle he might have found time to stop in a bar and buy, and she sometimes had thought of stuffing bread and cheese in her bag, but they were mainly almost without civility — there was never any glass for the brandy or any knife for the cheese, and if anyone had hung a picture or brought in a flower or two their consciousness of each other might have received, if not a killing blow, at least a heavy abrasion.

She asked him once why he did not simply come to her, but there was something about Rome he instinctively knew from the start and chose to sidestep. Ravenous for gossip, the Romans looked for it in certain chosen hunting fields — nothing would induce them to rummage around in the poorer quarters of Trastevere or wonder what went on out near San Lorenzo. And anyway —

And anyway, she understood. It was merely a question, perhaps, of furniture. The time or two he did stop by her place, ringing her up from a tobacco shop or restaurant nearby, they almost always disagreed about something. Disagreed was not quite the word; it was a surprise to her that she still found him, after everything that went on, somewhat difficult to talk to. She remembered the times in Venice and later in Rome that she had sparred with him, fighting at something intractable in his nature, and the thought of getting into that sort of thing anymore made her draw back. She just didn't want to. Perhaps it was a suprise to him that she never asked him anything anymore; she never tried to track him down. Did he miss that, or didn't he? Did he ask himself? And if he had would he have known what to answer? He was busy — that was one thing, of course. Committees had been set up — there was a modest stir about economic planning on certain American lines proceeding at a level far below the top governmental rank, only in educational circles, but still — He thought of plunging off into fieldwork, studying possibilities of industry in the south of Italy. "Then you might never come back," said Martha. "You mean to Rome?" "Oh, no, I meant — it's a separate world." She did not think he would ever do it. "You don't think I'll ever do it, do you?" She seemed even to herself to have drifted away for a time, and finally murmured or thought she had said, "I don't know." She was tired herself, with mimeograph ink on her hands and a whole new library list to set up, and her brain gone numb at so much bandying about of phrases like "the American image abroad." "What did you say?" he asked her. "I said I don't know." She rallied. "It's a worthwhile project, certainly." "Thank you, Mrs Ingram." His tone stung her; she glanced up and tears came to her eyes. "I'm sorry," he said with a certain stubborn slant on the words.

He had been leaning against her mantelpiece talking down to where she sat in the depths of a wing chair, sometimes toying with objects — small statuary, glass clusters, and paperweights — distributed on the marble surface. When he pulled her up against him by way of breaking off a conversation that had come to nothing, his elbow struck a china image to the floor. The apartment was rented furnished, only half such things were hers and this was not. He helped her clean the fragments and must have said a dozen times how much he regretted it, asking, too, "What was it?" "A little saint, or maybe goddess . . . I don't know." "If you don't know, then maybe it wasn't so good, after all." She smiled at the compliment. "I wish we were back in some starved little room," she said, "where nothing can get broken." "So do I," he agreed, and left soon after.

Reflecting, she was not long in coming upon the truth the little rooms made plain: that they had struck a bargain that lay deeply below the level of ordinary speech; in fact, that in rising toward realization in the world where things were said, it only ran terrible risks of crippling and loss.

And yet one afternoon, when the rain stopped and there was even a red streak of late sun in the clear simple street below, she felt gentle and happy and asked him to walk down in the street for just a little way. And then when he consented a dog trotted up and put its nose in her palm; it would have laid all of life at her feet like a bone. A cat purred near the open furnace of a pizzeria, which burned like a deep-set eye of fire in the stony non-color of a winter day, and a child ran out with bare arms in the cold, its mother following after, shouting *"Pino! Pino!"* and holding up a little coat. When they left the pizzeria, he lighted a cigarette leaning against a damp wall and said all right, all right, if she wanted to they would go away for the weekend somewhere. She looked up, startled and gratified, as though at an unexpected gift. It had been somewhat offhandedly thrust at her and yet its true substance was with it.

11

They drove to the sea in what started out to be fine weather but thickened over damply. Nevertheless, he had been full of a run of recklessly funny talk and stories ever since he got off the tram and crossed the sunlit street to meet her, way out near the Laterano, and the mood persisted. The feeling be-

tween them was, though nobody had mentioned it, that they
would never be back at all. They took turns driving.

Martha admired the artichoke fields warm in the new sun
and recalled a peasant who had plowed up a whole
Aphrodite in his field and didn't know what to do with her,
for if he told anybody his little farm would be made an
archaeological area; he wouldn't get to raise any more artichokes for a decade or two. So he and his family kept hiding
the statue and every now and then someone would be smug-
gled in to have a go at wondering how much could be got for
her in devious ways and the whole thing went on for a year
or so, but in the end the farmer buried her again and let her
rest in peace; he could never decide whom he could trust, for
everybody had a different theory, told a different story and
offered him a different sum. He then went back to raising
artichokes. "So every field I see I think of Aphrodite under
it," said Martha. This was not true, but she did think of it
now — the small compact mindless lovely head, the blank
blind exalted eyes, deep in the dark earth. "Imagine finding
Aphrodite and not knowing what to do with her," he said.
He began to cough.

The racking of this particular cough had gone on for
weeks now. He said he would never understand Martha for
never being sick. The Wilbournes were always in the thick of
illnesses; there had not only been Rita's miscarriage, which
had afflicted him with a tenacious sort of despair, a sense of
waste and reasonlessness, the worse for being almost totally
abstract. What kind of home could be had in this city, in this
entire country? (Here the sun, distinctly weakening, had
about faded out; he seemed to be grasping for it.) The
Italians didn't even have a word for home. *Casa.* It was
where you hung your hat, and slept, and froze, and tried to
keep from dying. Oh, Lord, thought Martha, getting weary
of him. To her, Rome was a magnificent city in any weather
and she moved in it easily with friends in four languages at
least — she had not been Gordon Ingram's student for
nothing. The city's elegant, bitter surfaces were hers natural-

ly, as a result of his taste and judgment, and there were
people about who knew this, in their own way of knowing,
from the instant she stepped across the threshold of a *salotto*.
She had luck, as well. She rented from a contessa in Padova,
who counted her a friend; if she told all this to Jim Wilbourne he would class her with the Cogginses who had got
invited to a *vendemmia* in Frascati a short time after they
arrived.

At the sea they sat before a rough fire in the *albergo* (there
were no other guests) and her mind wheeled slowly around
him like a gull. It was going to dawn on him someday, she
thought, how well she got along, how easily she got things,
not the sort of things the Cogginses got, which nobody
wanted, but the sort of things one coveted. She started out of
this, startling herself; this was wrong, all wrong — he was
better than that. He was self-amused, even in his furies, and
never lost the thread of reason (this being one reason Italians
preyed on him; the reason in a reasonless quarrel delighted
them; they would probably have gone on fighting with him
for a generation or so, if he had remained, for when the maid
stole the case of economics texts on loan from the States and
was forced to admit it, she returned to him books in the same
case, weighed within an *etto* of the original weight, the books
even being in English and some, she pointed out, having
been printed in the States: they were mainly mystery novels,
but included a leather-bound history of World War I dedicated to the Veterans of Foreign Wars — he found this
appropriate). And even he would admit that what he needed
most for his nerves in a country so uncivilized was an evening at the bowling alley, a stroll through a drugstore, a ride
down the turnpike, an evening at the neighbourhood movie
house. These things were not as much a myth to Martha as
might be thought to look at her, in her classic Roman grays
and black, for Woolworth's and Radio City had once
stabilized her more than human voices. He believed this,
and the rain sprang up off the sea, lashing in ropes against
the tall windows. Her heart sank. "It's so nice here in sum-

mer,'' she said faintly. His face had turned silent; in Italy he had acquired a touch of despair that she felt sorry for. He could make her feel responsible for the weather.

She never knew if he heard her at all. A shift of wind off the sea had blown one of the glass doors wide, and a maid rushed through to close it, but they scarcely noticed, if at all. They had reached the shore, an extremity of sorts, and had already discovered themselves on the other side of a wall, shut, enclosed, in the garden that everyone knows is there, where even the flowers are carnivorous and stir to avid life at the first footfall. He had caught her hand, near the cup, among the silver. She sat with her face half-turned aside, until her hand and arm reddened from the fire. She did not remember leaving the table and going upstairs.

The room where they stood for a time, clinging together a step from the closed door, was unlighted, dark, though on this troubled coast it seemed a darkness prepared and waiting with something like self-knowledge, to be discovered, mapped, explored, claimed, possessed and changed for good, no inch of it left innocent of them, nothing she had ever felt to be alive not met and dealt with. They were radical and unhurried, as if under imperial orders, and it seemed no one night could contain them; yet it managed to. As she fell asleep she heard the rain stop; it had outdistanced them by a little, as though some sort of race had been going quietly on.

The next morning there was a thin light on the sea, which hung leaden and waveless below their windows, its breast burnishing slightly, convexly meeting the fall of the light, like a shield. She saw a bird on the windowsill outside. Its feathers blew, ruffling in the wind, and once it shifted and looked in for a moment; she saw the tiny darting gleam of its regard.

The silver light held through the whole day. They drove far up the coast toward Pisa and she feared for a moment toward midday, voicelessly without decision as they seemed to be, they would come full circle at Genoa, where she had first seen him, in which case the sky would fall in broken masses of gray light. But the way is longer than it might be thought to be, and the slowly unwinding journey seemed perpetual, the fields and villages strict and sharply drawn with winter, the coast precipitous and wild, vanishing only to reappear, and their own speed on nearly deserted roads was deceptive — no matter what the speedometer said, they seemed adrift. They came on a fishing village and stayed there; she could never remember the name of it, but perhaps she never knew.

Where they were drifting, however, was not toward Genoa and the sky falling, or to any mythical kingdom, but like thousands of others before and after them, it was only toward Sunday afternoon. He was sitting putting on his shoe in the pension, when the shoelace suddenly snapped in his narrow fingers, jarring him into a tension that had seemed to be gone forever; if there was anything he immediately returned himself to, after the ravishment of strange compelling voyages, it was order; he was wrenched by broken shoelaces, and it was to that slight thing she traced what he said when they were leaving: "It disturbs me to think I'm the one you aren't going to forget — yet it's true, I know it is."

His arms were around her; he was human and gentle; but she filled up instantly with panic — it was time he had let in on them, in one phrase. Had he meant to be so drastic as that? But it had always been there, she reasoned desperately, and though watching the abyss open without alarm is always something of a strain, she tried to manage it. Yet going down the stair she felt numb and scraped her wrist against a rough wall surface. Reaching the car ahead of him, she sat, looking at the surface of the harshly rubbed skin, which had shaved up in places like thinly rolled trimming of chalk, and the flecking of red beneath, the wonder of having blood at all at a moment when her ample, somewhat slow, slightly baroque body had just come to rest as finally as stone.

Miles later on the way back to Rome she asked him, "What about you? Are you going to forget it?" He glanced at her at once. "No." And repeated it, "No."

On that she would be able to stay permanently, she
believed; it was her raft on the long, always outflowing tide
of things, and once back in Rome could linger, not being
obliged to be anywhere, in the bare strict narrow rented
room, and ride the wake of his footsteps hurrying down
toward the empty street, but one day she discovered on
walking home alone that the rain had stopped for once, and
traveling a broad street — Via Cola di Rienzo — that rose
toward a high bridge above the Tiber, the sky grew gray and
broad and flashed with light into which the *tramontana* came
bitterly streaming, drawing even the wettest and deadest
leaves up into it, and the whole yawning city beneath was
resonant with air like wind entering an enormous bell. This
is the center of the world, she thought, this city, with a certain pride, almost like a native might, or should have.

And passing through the post office, far across the gigantic
enclosed hall of a thousand rendezvous and small disburse-
ments for postal money orders and electric bills and letters
sent *posta aerea* to catch the urgent plane and the smell of ink
and blotted bureaucratic forms and contraband cigarettes,
she saw Gordon Ingram leaning on a heavy mahogany cane,
the sort of thing he would either bring to Europe with him or
find for himself the instant he arrived. His back was toward
her, that heavy-shouldered bulk, and he was leaning down
to write on a sheet of paper, but even while she watched,
something must have gone wrong with the pen, for he shook
it twice, then threw it aside and walked away. The letter flut-
tered to the ground and she soon went there and picked it
up, but by that time a heel or two had marked it in walking
past.

Yet she made out clearly, in handsome script, the best
Italian: *"Sebbene* (whereas) . . . *tu m'abbia accusato di ció che ti
piace chiamare inumanitá . . ."* (you have accused me of what
it gives you satisfaction to call inhumanity, you must realize
if you have any mentality at all, that this man in spite of his
youth and attractiveness is far less human than anyone of
my generation could possibly be, without the least doubt.
He takes an interest in you because he must live in this way

to know that he is alive at all, and his behavior is certain to disappoint a woman like yourself, such as I have taught you to be, in such a manner as to make you wish that it could never be said by anyone including yourself that you were ever in any contact with him. You know that whatever else you may say or think I have never lied to you — this you cannot deny — I have never once lied to you, whereas you have done nothing but pride yourself on your continual lying as though it were some sort of accomplishment, an art you had mastered so well you could use it carelessly —.)

She went home holding the letter in one hand, and reached the apartment with the heel of one shoe in the other, limping, because she had twisted the heel off in the irregular paving of the *piazzetta* below. She had spent the morning helping George Hartwell draw up a new lecture program, and there had been the interview with the priest who wanted to start a liberal newspaper in a small town near Bari. At last, anyway, she had a letter, a direct word. She hung up her umbrella, coat and scarf, but dripped still a limping trail into the big *salotto*, which, awaiting her in the quiet, looked utterly vacant, as disinhabited as if it were rented out afresh every three months, and she thought, He can't have written this; he is dead. Nobody is ever coming here again.

She fell face downward on the couch and slept, half recalling and half dreaming — which, she did not know, and why, she did not know, though the whole held no horror for her whatsoever any more than some familiar common object might — the story of a man who shot and wounded a she-wolf on his way home through the woods at twilight, and coming home, found his wife dead on the couch, a trail of blood leading inward from the door. She was awakened by a banging shutter.

She went out to the terrace and saw that the clouds had cleared before the wind and were racing in long streamers like swift ships, and that a moon, so deeply cold it would always do to think of whenever cold was mentioned, raced without motion. The city beneath it lay like a waste, mysterious, empty discovery, cold and vaulted beneath it, channeling the wind. It came to her for the first time to wonder, standing out on her empty, winter-disarrayed terrace, if a cold like that might not be life's truest definition, since there was so much of it.

And certain cold images of herself were breaking in upon her now, as though she had waked up in a thunder-ridden night and had seen an image of herself in the mirror, an image that in the jagged and sudden flash seemed to leap unnaturally close. What am I doing? Am I asleep sitting straight up? A thousand times she had said to life in the person of a bird, brilliant and wise in the cage of a friend, or a passing dog (just as she had said to Gordon Ingram), I forgive you everything, please forgive me, too, but getting no answer from either, her mind went on discriminating. She had not been Gordon Ingram's student for nothing and she longed to discuss with him:

If life unreels from an original intuition, what if that intuition were only accident, what if it were impulse, a blind leap in the dark? An accident must be capable of being either a mistake or a stroke of luck, depending on what it is in relation to whom it happens to. So what do you think of this one, since you were the victim of it? Before you are quite gone, forever and ever, answer that for me at least.

But he was silent; Gordon Ingram was always silent.

Jim Wilbourne, however, told her many things about himself and (she had not been Gordon Ingram's student for nothing) none of them were supremely interesting things; she listened but was not utterly arrested, sometimes she half listened. So he said, "Listen, Martha — listen," and she did stop the car (it being her turn to drive) coming back from the sea in the wet sea-heavy night, and she did try to listen, but traffic sprang up from everywhere — there was a confluence of roads and they all led to Rome, a glare and snarl and recklessness in the rain and dark, and someone shouted, *"Stupida! Ma guarda! Guarda!"* They poured past her like the hastening streams of the damned. She turned her face to him and he was talking, haltingly; he fell almost at once into platitudes and she wondered that the person whose face she encountered in the depths of her dreams had nothing more remarkable to say than this.

It did not escape him. He wanted to return everything to its original clear potential, to say that love, like life, is not remarkable, it is as common as bread. But every contact between the two of them was not common; it was remarkable. He was stopped before he started. "I'm listening. I'm listening," she said.

"It's the way you're listening."

"Don't let that matter to you," she said gently, kindly, for the shadow of some nature far beyond anything that had happened to her occasionally came to her. "I live in a mirror, at the bottom of a mirror somewhere."

"I think we both do. It's why we make love so well."

"There must be some way to stop it . . . to go back to where we might have been, to change. I always wanted to think of it differently. You remember I told you —"

"Yes, I remember." He urged her to drive on, the stop was dangerous, and presently said out a long sequence of thought not told to her, "I simply can't ever believe there's any way back from anything." The force of the statement reached her, and she sensed it as distantly related to fury. He had made another jump, she realized, and now there was no turning back from that, either. She had finally, like any other woman, to hold on the best way she could.

PART FOUR

12

Coming up from the winter's recollections was what she and George Hartwell had to do every so often to keep from drowning.

They were still on the terrace, and it was still Sunday morning, a healing timelessness of sun, though Hartwell went on gnawing at things he drew up out of fathomless reservoirs.

"And did you know," he was saying, "and did you fully realize, that Wilbourne got me to recommend him for an Italian-government grant? He was going to study the economic picture south of Naples — the self-sacrificing servant of his times, he was harkening to duty's voice, he was going to leave the world a better place. Then what did he do but turn around and use that very grant as a lever to land his fat job back in the States."

"I'm not surprised," said Martha.

"But think what a hell of a position it put me in," Hartwell complained.

"Well, why did you let him talk you into it?"

"I thought you wanted him here. I thought you —"

"You thought *I* did it?"

"Something like that."

"It wasn't my idea," she said. "It was only that he did talk about it. I suppose, for a time, he considered staying on. He may even have believed that he meant to."

"But you said you weren't surprised."

"I wasn't . . . no . . . when he changed his mind, you mean? No, I wasn't too surprised. He only existed in relation to Gordon." There had always been the three of them, she thought; they had got stuck in the same frame forever.

"You mean destructively, of course," George Hartwell grumbled. He wondered what portion of the service they had reached in mass, for though not a Catholic, he could hope that it was some deep and serious portion that could bite him up whole and take elaborate care to lift him back out of this pit he had blundered into on a fine Sunday morning.

"Did you see a little white-haired American lady on your way in?" Martha asked. "She was wearing a blue feather hat with a close veil over her hair and face and a matching blue coat. She was bowlegged."

"Martha," said Hartwell, "aren't you going to spare me anything?"

He had begun to laugh. The whole thing was crazy, and probably had been all along. There wasn't any little old lady in blue. That was one certain fact. It was something to tie to. It enabled him to keep on laughing.

But there had been no laughter for him at all from any source on that February day back in the winter when the phone rang in his office and the voice said,

"This is Gordon Ingram, Mr Hartwell. May I see you for a short time?"

"Where are you? Where are you?" was all he could think of to say; that and, "Yes, Albergo Nazionale . . . of course, right away."

To his amazement a chill like a streak of ice had run down his spine; he went out in no time, breaking three appointments, grabbing a cab rather than taking the car. Had the man already called his wife? Did she know? If so, she was likely driving blindly somewhere, fodder for the next highway crash; or more deliberately, walking straight off into the Tiber would do just as well. He felt himself in the grip of fates and furies. In the dank, gusty February day, every step seemed bringing him nearer to the moment when statues speak and old loves appear.

Albergo Nazionale ran inward from a discreet doorway. The rugs were heavy and the decor firm. He searched among the sofas, the coffee tables, the escritoires, the alcoves and bronze gods taming horses, for a shape ponderous and vast, a heavy thigh and a foot like an elephant's, and toward the last he was spinning like a top and had whirled upon the desk clerk, saying, "I'm looking for a Signor Ingram, *un professore americano.*" But before he could get that out altogether, a hand touched his sleeve, and it was only Robert Inman, English and slight with sandy hair severely thinned, a classmate at Balliol. "I say, George, I've tried this makes three times to stop you, can't have changed so much as all that, you know.'' It could not have been Robert Inman who had telephoned. Yet it had been. There was no Ingram on the register.

George Hartwell lived through a weak Scotch in an armchair that threatened to swallow him whole, so small was he already in addition to feeling unreal, extended a dinner invitation, reviewed old histories, and afterward, still in bleary weather, he walked up to the Campidoglio and stood looking through a heavy iron grill at something he had remembered wondering at before, back in his early days in Rome, the enormous hand from the statue of an emperor, standing among other shards in the barred recess. It was the dumbness of the detached gesture, there forever, suggesting not so much the body it was broken from as the sky it was lifted toward — one could be certain all through the centuries of similar skies. And with very little trouble he could find which step Gibbon was probably sitting on when he thought of *Decline and Fall*, but why do it unless perhaps he wanted to plant himself down on the cold stone and catch pneumonia? And what indeed did he have to think of that was a match for Gibbon? He had to realize that in missing three appointments at least — two of which had to do with Italian cultural organizations interested in cooperating with American exchange programs — he had not done a good thing and that now he would have to dictate letters explaining that his son was in an accident and that he had thought for a time of flying home. Anyway, it was too late now.

He walked a bit and in passing near the post office saw the Wilbourne car, which was now fairly well-known in Rome because so much had got stolen off it at one time or another and certain quarrels had centered about it as it had once been jointly owned with another couple who complained that the Wilbournes (though the car was in their possession each time it was rifled) insisted that the expense of each misfortune be shared and shared alike. The body was a sort of dirty cream, which Hartwell did not like, possibly because he did not like the Wilbournes, so why be called upon to stop and wait and why, when Jim Wilbourne appeared alone, ask him into the German beer hall nearby to share a stein and bend his ear about this odd thing — this misunderstood telephone call — as if by talking about it, it would be just odd and nothing more. And it seemed, too, that only by talking could he say that from the first he had felt a concern for Martha, that she had stirred his sympathies from the first and he had learned her story a little at a time. This, too, he judged, was only a way of talking about people for once, instead of programs, programs — one built up a kind of ravenous appetite for individuals, for the old-time town life he, back in Missouri, had had once and called the past. He was winding up by saying, ''Of course, don't repeat any of this to Martha,'' and there was a certain kind of pause hanging in the air, and Jim Wilbourne carefully lighted a cigarette behind his hands, worrying the match five or six times before it went out, and Hartwell thought, Oh, God, oh, my God, having caught it on one side now I'm catching it on the other. I didn't know and yet I must have known.

He also thought, She is not this important to me, for all this about her to happen in one afternoon.

Neurotic to the last notch, she had dragged him into her exile's paranoia as into a whirlpool. He foresaw the time when the only individuals would be neurotics. They were the only people who still had the nerve to demand an answer. He doubted if Jim Wilbourne was neurotic or that he would qualify as an individual, but he without a doubt had a sort of nerve balance that so obviously related him to women it seemed in the most general sense to be a specific of blessing, like rain or sun, and why shouldn't she, in common with everybody else, have sun and rain? Who was to rule her out of golden shores? But with her there would always be more to it than that. Hartwell had blundered into this picture and now he wanted out.

''Did you ever know this guy?'' Jim Wilbourne asked.

''Who, her husband? Well, only by reputation. He was at

one time a leading American philosopher, or that was the direction he took early on. There were a couple of books . . . some theories of goodness, relating action to idealism . . . something like that. I remember one of them excited me. I read half of it standing in the college library one afternoon. . . .'' One long-ago fall afternoon at Harvard. What reaches out of nowhere to touch and claim us? At a certain age, on a certain sort of afternoon, it may be any book we pick out from a shelf. "But perhaps you've read it, too.''

"Oh, Lord, no. I read practically nothing out of my field. I know that's not a good thing. It makes me laugh to think — I'd laid all sort of plans for doing some catching up on reading in Italy, after I learned the language, of course.'' He ended by coughing badly.

"You have learned it,'' Hartwell said, complimenting effort.

"Damned near killed me. It was a hell of a lot of work.''

"You're telling me.'' Hartwell gulped his way into a second beer.

At the end of the encounter, catching a cab back to the office, refusing a ride, Hartwell felt outdone and silly. He envied Jim Wilbourne his cool intelligence, his quick judgments, his refusal to drink too much. I am the world's most useless citizen, he thought, an impractical cultural product, a detached hand reaching out, certainly changing nothing, not even touching anything. I am the emperor of Rome — I shall be stabbed in a corridor.

He longed for his own warm table and his wife's brown eyes, under whose regard he had so often reassembled his soul.

13

"There was always something rather depressing to me,'' said Hartwell with a laugh, "about all those damn ceramics. She kept on turning them out as if her life depended on it, and every one of them was in the worst possible taste.''

''She knew the market back in the States,'' Martha said kindly. ''I think that's what she had in mind.''

''It's no wonder the Italians preyed on them. There was something about some chickens.''

''The landlord's cousins kept some chickens out on the terrace next door, which was disturbing,'' Martha related, ''and then when the Wilbournes got an order through the *condominio* to remove the chickens, they put some ducks there, instead. The Wilbournes killed and ate the ducks. That was not as bad, however, as the fight over the electric bill.''

''Oh, Lord,'' said Hartwell. ''Even we had one of those. Martha, you never had a fight with Italians in your life.''

''Never,'' said Martha, ''but then I never tried setting up a business.''

''I'm frankly glad as hell they're gone,'' said Hartwell. ''If she started a business,'' he went on unwisely, ''it was probably out of desperation. She never seemed very well. If a vote of sympathy was taken, she'd get mine.''

They had taken Rita Wilbourne for a drive one day to Tivoli — he and his wife — and had discovered near there in the low mountains a meadow full of flowers. It was as close to a miracle as they could have hoped for, for it was misty when they left Rome and raining when they returned, but here she grew excited and jumped out of the car and walked out into the sun. Hartwell and his wife Grace sat in the car and spoke of her; she was unhappy, displaced in life and alone far too much.

She had walked on away from them, here and there, in a brightly striped raincoat, always with her back to them, so that it was easy to imagine she might be crying. She talked about too many different things. Grace Hartwell worried about her. ''Men like Jim Wilbourne are difficult,'' she said. ''They're bitter, for one thing. I dislike bitter men — they are nothing but a drain.'' Yet when Rita came back to the car she had not been crying at all that Hartwell could see. She had found some bits of mosaic to copy in the bramble-covered remains of something — a villa, a bath, a tower — a whole acanthus leaf done in marble; her eyes were flat, bright, almost black; she was like a wound-up doll. She said it was marvelous to see the sun; she said it was wonderful to find a meadow full of flowers; she said it was quite unusual to find a whole acanthus leaf in marble. Who was she to demand George Hartwell's fealty? She was an American girl who happened to be walking across a meadow near Tivoli; she thought automatically of what she could do with what she found there. Martha Ingram hardly heard him when he spoke of sympathizing with her; she correctly judged that he was attacking Jim Wilbourne.

"What have you got against Jim? I doubt his being so bad as you think. There was nothing whatever bad about him, in an extraordinary sense."

"Yes," said Hartwell, "but who do you think is? Always expecting Gordon Ingram, of course?"

She fell silent; he wondered if he had got to her. Self-appointed and meddlesome, she could certainly call him, but he would stop her if it killed him, he thought, and it probably would. It was then she flashed at him with sudden definition, like an explosion of tinder.

"But I love them both. Haven't you understood that was the reason for it all?"

And the one to be stopped was himself.

He sat and mopped his brow as though in a period of truce, by himself, at least, much needed.

So they finally turned to business, having worn each other out.

The papers came out of her desk and he was leaning close to the shadow of the terrace wall to glance at some notes she could and did explain from memory — one thing clearly emerging from all this, like a negative from a slow developer, was how excellent she was; she seemed to have got up one morning and put her work on like a new dress.

People were always calling George Hartwell up to tell him in assorted languages how lucky he was to have her, how lucky the United States of America was to have her, and in truth he himself had to marvel at how intelligently she could appear at varied distances in the conversation of *salotti, terrazzi, giardini.* He thought she would grow the torch of liberty out of her hand any day now, or at least show up photographed in some sleek expensive magazine, a model of the career woman abroad. She might even eclipse him: had he thought of that? He thought of it now, and decided that it did not supremely matter. In view of his long ambitious years, what a surprising thing, right now, to learn this about himself. Grace in leaving had been brimful of talk about their son, graduating at home, the solemn black mortarboard procession stretching and contracting, winding beneath green elms, every sun splotch another sort of hope and promise; the twin tears in Grace's eyes meant grandchildren beyond a doubt. Even when packing to leave, her son's future was infinitely exploding within her. She at some unknown hour had acquiesced to something: the shift in women's ambitions — true augur of the world. It was known to all, George realized, how much he drank, and Martha now was fetching him another, moving in and out among the azaleas. The truth at last emerges (he took the glass), but it had been there, relentlessly forming all this while.

"But what if the poor old bastard wants you, needs you? What if he dies?"

"I've been there already," she said, remembering how they had got the land away from her where it had all happened, she had signed the papers at Colonna's on the Piazza del Popolo and heard how the gun's roar faded along with the crash of the leaves.

"That isn't good enough!" said Hartwell, but her gray regard upon him was simply accidental, like meeting the eyes in a painting.

So there was no way around her.

I'll go myself, thought Hartwell, halfway down the Scotch. In the name of humanity somebody had to, and it seemed, for one sustained, sustaining moment, that he actually would. He would go out of the apartment, reach his car, drive to the nearest telephone, call the airport for space on the first plane to New York. He could smell the seared asphalt of a New York summer, could see soot lingering on windowsills in the coarse sunlight, feel the lean of the cab turning into the hospital drive, every building in an island aspect, turning freely. An afternoon of dying. . . . A strange face in the door's dwindling square, rising above the muted murmur of a hospital at twilight. "I have come from your wife. You must understand she would come if she could, but she cannot. You must understand that she loves you, she said so. I heard her say so. She has been unavoidably detained . . . restrained? . . . stained? . . .maimed?"

Then he knew it was time to go. He picked up all the documents, and put the last swallow down. The stairs were below. "Lunch with me this week." "Poor George, I think I upset you."

Poor George (he kept hearing it). Poor George, poor George, poor George. . . .

PART FIVE
14

But she had never said Poor Jim, though he, too, had gone down that very stairway as shaken as he had ever been in his life or would ever be. Their parting had torn him desperately — she saw it; it was visible. And all this on the first day of sun.

"Love . . . love . . .love . . ." The word kept striking over and again like some gigantic showpiece of a clock promptly, voraciously, at work to mark midnight, though actually it was noon. Returning to her was what he kept talking about. "Yes, yes, I'll always be here," she replied.

But this total motion once begun carried him rapidly down and away, *cortile* and fountain, stairway and hidden turning — the illusion was dropping off like a play he had been in, when, at the last flight's turning, he came to an abrupt halt and stood confronting someone who had just come through the open *portone* and was now looking about for mailboxes or buzzers, a fresh-faced young man whose clear candid eyes had not yet known what stamped a line between the brows.

He was wearing a tropical-weight suit that would have been too optimistic yesterday, but was exactly right today. Second-year university, just arrived this morning, Jim Wilbourne thought, holding to the banister. The young man seemed to have brought the sun. Jim Wilbourne, fresh air from the *portone* fanning his winter-pale cheek, thought for the first time in months of shirts that never got really white and suits that got stained at the cleaners, of maids that stole not only books but rifled drawers for socks and handkerchiefs, of rooms that never got warm enough and martinis that never got cold enough and bills unfairly rendered, of the landlord's endless complaints and self-delighting rages, the doctor's prescriptions that never worked, the waste of life itself to say nothing of fine economic theory. He coughed — by now a habit — and saw, as if it belonged to someone else, his hand at rest on the stone banister, the fingers stained from smoking, the cuff faintly gray, distinctly frayed. He felt battered, and shabby and old, and here was someone to block not only the flow of his grief, but the motion of his salvaging operation, that was to say, the direction of his return; for every step now was bringing him physically closer to the land he had had to come abroad to discover, the land where things rest on solid ground and reasons may be had upon request and business is conducted in the expected manner. It all meant more than he had ever suspected it did.

"Could you possibly tell me — you are an American, aren't you — I don't speak much Italian, none at all, in fact

— maybe you even know who I'm looking for — does a Mrs Ingram live here?''

''She isn't here just now, at least I don't think so. Come to think of it, she's out of the city, at least for the time being.''

He grasped at remembering how she felt about it — about these people who kept coming. She did not like it; he knew that much. But a boy like this one, anybody on earth would want to see a boy like that. He retreated from her particular complexities, the subtly ramified turnings were a sharp renewal of pain, the whats and whys he could of course if necessary deal in had always been basically outside his character, foreign to him, in the way a clear effective answer was not foreign whether it was true or not.

''Very odd. I got her address just before leaving from the States.''

''When was that?''

''Oh — ten days ago.''

''Well, then, that explains it. She's only left a couple of weeks back, or so I understand.''

He ran on down the stairs. The boy fell in step with him and they went out together. The fountain at the corner played with the simple delight of a child. ''You see, I have this package, rather valuable, I think. I would have telephoned, but didn't know the language well enough — the idea scared me off. Now I've gone and rented this car to go to Naples in, that scares me, too, but I guess I'll make it. I just wonder what to do with the package.''

''Mail it — why not? Care of the consulate. She works there. Your hotel would do it, insured, everything.''

''Did you know her well, then? You see, I'm her nephew, by marriage, that is. When I was a boy, younger than now at least, she used to —''

''Listen, it's too bad you and I can't have a coffee or something, but I happen to be going to catch a plane.''

They shook hands and parted. He had begun to feel that another moment's delay would have mired him there

forever, that he had snatched back to himself in a desperate
motion his very life. Walking rapidly, he turned a corner.
He went into a bar for coffee and was standing, leaning his
elbow on the smooth surface and stirring when somebody
said, "Hi, Jim!" and he looked up and there was Jean Coggins. She was eating a croissant and gave him a big grin,
whiskery with crumbs. He laughed in some way he had not
laughed for a year. "What d'you know?" he asked. As
usual, she didn't know anything back of yesterday. "I was
going down to Capri yesterday, but it rained. It even hailed!
And the storm last night! Now look at it. Wouldn't it kill
you?" "It shouldn't be allowed." He paid for her bill and
his and while doing so wondered if at any time during the
entire year in Italy she had ever actually paid for anything.
She skimmed along beside him for a short way, going on like
a little talking dog; he soon lost track of what she was saying;
she always bored him — everything named Coggins bored
him, but she was at least fresh and pretty. Walking, he flung
an arm around her. "I heard from Alfredo," she said, "you
remember in Venice?" "I remember something about some
stamps," he said. She giggled.

(Because that day they got back from the Lido, with
Martha out somewhere, or so the proprietor said, and the
weather getting dim, the air covered with a closing sort of
brightness, she had tried to buy stamps at the desk, feeling
herself all salty in the turns of her head and creases of her
arms, but the proprietor said he was out of stamps and Jim
Wilbourne, going up the stairway, heard her, though he was
already a flight up and half across the lobby, and he said,
"I've got some stamps, so just stop by number something
and I'll let you have them," but when she went and
scratched at the door and thought he said come in, he was
asleep — she must have known they weren't talking entirely
about stamps, yet when he woke up, scarcely knowing in the
air's heaviness, the languor the surf had brought on and the
boat ride back, the lingering salt smell, exactly where he
was, and saw her, he could not remember who she was, but

said at once, "My God, you've got the whitest teeth I ever saw," and pulled her down under his arm. But she didn't want to. She liked fighting, scuffling, maybe it was what she felt like, maybe it was because he was what she told him right out, an Older Man, which made him laugh, though on the street that day coming out of the bar, almost exactly a year later, it wouldn't have been funny one bit, not one little bit, and then she had bitten him, too, which was what he got for mentioning her teeth. Otherwise, she might not have thought about it. He had cuffed her. "Let's stay on," she said, "I love this place. All across Italy and couldn't even swim. That old lake was slimy. Anyway, I'm in love with the boy at the desk. Get them to let us stay." "You mean get rid of your parents," he said, "that's what you're driving at. Or is it her, too?" "You mean Martha? Well, she makes me feel dumb, but she's okay." She came up on one elbow in sudden inspiration. "She likes you." "Oh, stop it." "I know." "How do you know?" "I just know. I always know. I can tell." "But maybe it's you that I —" "But it's Alfredo that I —" "Alfredo? Who's that?" "You don't ever listen. The boy at the desk." She had squirmed out from under and run off, snatching up a whole block of stamps off the table — he actually had had some stamps, though this surprised him, and later in the pensione, walking around restless as a big animal in the lowering weather, he had heard her talking, chattering away to the boy who kept the desk, sure enough, right halfway down on the service stairs, and the little maids stepped over and around them with a smile. *"Ti voglio bene, non ti amo. Dimmi, dimmi — Ti voglio bene."* One way to learn the language. He thumbed an ancient German magazine, restless in an alcove, and saw Martha Ingram go by; she had come in and quietly bathed and dressed, he supposed; her hair was gleaming, damp and freshly up; her scent floated in the darkening corridor; she did not see him, rounding the stairs unconsciously in the cloud of her own particular silence. Some guy had given her one hell of a time. He thought of following her, to talk, to what? He flipped the

magazine aside; his thoughts roved, constricted in dark
hallways. . . .)

"I've got his picture, want to see?" "I don't have time,
honey." Next she would be getting his advice. She loved
getting advice about herself. He told her goodbye, taking a
sharp turn away. Would he ever see her again? The thought
hardly brushed him.

(Would she ever see him again? The thought did not
brush her at all. What did pass through her mind — er-
roneously, anyone but Jean Coggins would have thought —
she did not know a word like that — was a memory of one
day she was in Rossi's, the fashion shop where she worked
on the Via Boncompagni, and had just taken ten thousand
lire from the till — and not for the first time — to lend to a
ragazzo who took pictures on the Via Veneto and was always
a little bit behind, though he kept a nice *seicento*. She would
have put it back before the lunch hour was over at four, but
the signora found it gone and was about to fire her, though
she denied having done it except as a loan to her mother's
donna di servizio, who had forgotten money for the shopping
and had passed by on the way to the market. She would
bring it right back from home. She faded off toward the back
of the shop, for the signora was waggling her head darkly
and working away in an undertone. *Figurati!* And while she
was in the back, way back where the brocade curtains and
satin wallpaper faded out completely and there were only the
brown-wrapped packages of stuffs, *tessuti*, stacked up in corners of a bare room with a gas jet and a little espresso
machine and snips and threads strewn about the floor, she
heard a voice outside and it was Martha Ingram and the
signora was saying with great *gentilezza*, "O, signora, the
American girl you sent me, the Signorina Co-gins . . ." and
then she heard, in the level quiet poised educated voice,
almost like a murmur, "Oh, no, there was some mistake
about that. I never sent her to you, signora, there was some
mistake. . . . However, *nondimeno* . . . . I am sure she is
very good . . . *è una brava ragazza, sono sicura.* . . ." And

then there was something about some gloves. *Addio*, she thought in Italian. *Adesso comincia la musica* . . . now the music will really begin. She thought of running out the back door. She liked working up near the Veneto, where it was fun. And then the Signora Rossi herself appeared in her trim black dress with her nails all beautifully *madreperla* and her gold Florentine snake bracelet with the garnet eyes and her sleek jet hair scrolled to the side and her eyes that were always asking how many *mila* lire, and she twitched at the curtain and said, "Signora Co-gins, you are a liar — it is always *la stessa cosa*. . . . You have given the money to that *paparazzo*, and the money was not even yours, but mine. It would have been *gentile* indeed if you had first asked me if *I* — *io, io* — had had some debt or other to pay. *Davvero*. But, then, I do not drive you out to Frascati in a *seicento* — not often, do I? No, not at all. But as for using the name of Signora Ingram, *mia cliente*, to come into *mia casa di moda* . . ."

It went on and on like this, a ruffling stream of Italian, unending; as though she had stuck her head in a fountain, it went pouring past her ears. And then she remembered, out of her scolded-child exterior, that pensione in Venice, and Jim Wilbourne this time, rather than Alfredo — the dim concept of the faceless three of them — him and her and Martha Ingram — afloat within those rain-darkening corridors and stairways. She remembered tumbling on the damp bed and how he was taller than she and that made her restless in some indefinable way, so she said what was true: "She likes you." "Oh, stop it." "I know." "How do you know?" "I just know. I always know. I can tell." For the truth was she was not at all a liar: she was far more honest than anybody she knew. It was the signora who had said all along, just because she said she knew Martha Ingram, that she had been sent there by Martha Ingram, who was close to the ambassador, and the signora could tell more lies while selling a new gown than Jean Coggins had ever told in her life, and another truth she knew was that Martha Ingram was bound to come in and "tell on her" someday to the signora. It had been a certainty, a hateful certainty, because women like Martha would always fasten to one man at a time. She remembered her awe of Martha Ingram, her even wishing in some minor way to be like her. And then she saw it all, in a flash; perhaps, like that, she turned all the way into her own grown-up self, and would never want to be like anybody else again, for she suddenly pushed out of the corner where a tatter of frayed curtain concealed a dreary little delivery entrance from even being glimpsed by accident by anyone in the elegant *negozio*, started up and flung herself full height, baring her teeth like a fox, and spit out at the signora, "*Che vuole? Non sono una donna di servizio.* I am not a servant. *Faccio come voglio* . . . I will do as I like. *Faccio come mi pare* . . . I will do as I please. *Che vuole?*"

There was a sudden silence, rather like somebody had died, and the street door to the *negozio* could be heard to open. Signora Rossi broke into a laugh, at first an honest laugh — possibly the only one she had ever given — shading immediately into a ripple of pleasant amusement of the elegant *padrona* at her pretty little *assistente*; she turned on her narrow black stiletto heels and, having touched her hair, folded her hands in that certain pleasing way and moved toward the door.)

When Jim Wilbourne reached his own apartment, there at the head of the first flight of steps that ran down into the open courtyard, the landlord was lurking, paunchy and greasy haired with a long straight nose and tiny whistle-sized mouth, a walking theater of everything that had been done to him by the Wilbournes and all he could do in return because of it; here was the demon, the one soul who proved that inferno did exist, at least in Italy. Jim Wilbourne felt the back of his neck actually stiffen at the sight of Signor Micozzi in his white linen suit. The demon's energy, like the devastating continuous inexhaustible energy of Italy, was always fresh and ready for the fray; the time was always

now. Jesus, another round, Jim Wilbourne thought; will I
die before I leave this place? Smoking, saying nothing, he
climbed the stair to within two steps of the waiting figure
that had bought that new white suit, it would seem, especially to quarrel in. The two of them, on perfect eye level, stared
at each other. Jim Wilbourne dropped his cigarette, stepped
on it and walked deliberately past. His hand was on the bolt
when the first words fell in all the smear of their mock
courtesy.

"Scusi un momento, Signor Wilbourne, per cortesia."

For a moment, at the door, they ran through the paces of
their usual nasty exchange. It was all he could do to keep
from striking physically; in Italy that would have involved
him so deeply he would never be free; Italy was the original
tar baby; he knew that; getting out was the thing now; he
had a sense of salvage and rescue, of swimming the ocean.

"Scusi, scusi!"

"Prego!"

They were shouting by now, their mutual contempt ooz-
ing wretchedly out of every word. He stepped inside and
slammed the door.

His wife poked her head into the corridor. She was working; she was always working. Thin, in a pair of knee-length
slacks of the sort nobody at all in Italy wore, which hung
awkwardly, showing how much weight she'd lost in one nag-
ging illness after another, her dark hair lank and flat, lying
close to her head, framing like two heavy pencil lines her
sharp face and great flat eyes. "All that bastard had to do
was stand a few inches to the left when he passed the window, and I would have dropped this right on him," she said.
She pointed to a ceramic umbrella stand she had made herself. It must have weighed seventy pounds at least. Her
voice, slighly hoarse by nature with a ready tough fundamental coarseness in everything she observed when they
were alone (she was never much "like herself" with other
people), was a sort of life to him. He could not even
remember life without it. "They called from the university

about some survey on Neapolitan family management. It was due last week. I called your office, but nobody answered." "I was there all morning, but nobody rang." A world of old quarrels hung in shadowy phalanxes between every word of an exchange like this one, but both of them wearied to pour enough energy into any one of them to make it live. He stood in the doorway of her studio where she had even hung up a Van Gogh reproduction — the whole place looked American now. The Italian furniture had acquired the aspect of having been bought in a Third Avenue junk shop. "The dear old telephone system," she said, turning away, the corner of her mouth bitten in. He picked up the paper and stood reading it, leaning against a gilded chest of drawers, pushing at the dark hair above his ear with restless fingers. How would she have picked it up, he wondered, the umbrella stand? She would doubtless have managed. It was then the phone started ringing. "If that's the landlord —" he said. He knew it was. It was a favorite trick of Signor Micozzi's, when the door slammed in his face, to circle down to the bar on the corner and ring upstairs, continuing the argument without the loss of a syllable. Martha Ingram would never get into this sort of mess — The thought wrote itself off the page. He crashed the paper to the floor. His wife whirled around and saw the way he looked. "Now, Jim, please!"

"Look, you realize how much deposit he took on this place? Three hundred and fifty dollars. If he so much as hesitates about giving it back." "That's what he came for! Of course he hesitates. He's never had the slightest intention of giving it back." "All right. Okay. He's in for a surprise or two." "But not to him, not to him! Don't you touch him!" She suddenly began to sob without crying, a grating desperate sound, biting out between the jerks of her breath, "If you touch him we'll never get out of here, we'll be here forever in this country, this horrible place, I'll die, I'll die here!" She leaped at him, latching on to his arm with both hands, and she had grown so light and he had grown so angry that when he lifted his arm she came up with it, right off the floor, as handy as a monkey. They both began to laugh — it was ludicrous, and it must have been soon after that they started figuring things out.

Her cry was over; she had even combed her hair. Then she began to bully and mock and dare him slightly; as totally disenchanted as ever, she had begun to be herself again. In some ways he listened, in others he didn't have to; most of all he was drawn back to where he was a few streets after he departed from Jean Coggins for all eternity, when, abruptly halting in a little crooked alley all alone, at some equi-distance — mentally speaking, at least — between Martha and his wife, he gave over to wonder; for the first time, astringent and hard with himself, he allowed it to happen, he allowed the wonder to operate; fully, beautifully, he watched it curve and break in a clean magnificent wave.

What had he taken there, what had he conquered, so much as a city — a white, ample, ripe city, with towers, streets, parks, treasures? One bold leap of the imagination back there in Venice (the sort of thing he had always wanted to do but had never brought off quite so perfectly) had taken him soaring across the stale and turgid moat of her surrounding experience, had landed him at her very gates. It had been all blindly impulsive, perhaps cruel, but one thing had to be said for it — it had worked.

But there was something he knew and this was it: he could never have created her, and a thousand times, in turning her head, or putting on a glove, she had silently, unconsciously, praised whoever had put her together, ironically, the object of their merciless destruction — Jesus, what a trap! He rebelled at the whole godawful picture: it wasn't true. Love did not have to refer to anybody; that could all be changed in five minutes of wanting to. He had only to tell her, say so, absolutely — For an instant his mind crazed over like shat-tered glass, and it was some time before he hauled himself together, as though after another blind charge, this time at a wall, the first of many. Was it there or later, he allowed himself — briefly, but he did allow it — a moment's wonder at himself, recognizing a young man not even thirty and what he had challenged, taken, known. He knew in what sense he was the possessor still, and in what sense no matter when he left he would always be.

(About here he came to a corner, and frowning, leaned against a wall. Grace Hartwell saw him; she was coming down from the dressmaker, hurrying home to pack.)

He was clearly aware of the many ways in which his Italian year wore the aspect of failure, of an advance halted, his professional best like chariot wheels miring in the mud, nothing, in short, to be proud of.

He walked on, at last, with a dogged, almost classical stubbornness. This was what it had worn down to. He would live beyond himself again; he would, in future, be again gleaming and new, set right like a fine mechanism; he had to go to the States for that. But in this hour, blazed at by a sudden foreign sun, he presented to himself neither mystery nor brilliance, any more than he did to his wife or the landlord, in whose terms he did not even despise to live, if only his energy held out till the shores of Italy dropped behind him forever. But Martha, too, had been Italy — a city, his own, sinking forever. There was the wall again, blank and mocking. He could go crashing into it again, over and over and over, as many times as he wanted to.

15

It was George Hartwell who got the full force of the Wilbourne departure after they had left Rome earlier than they had said they were going to, in the night. Now every day or so, the landlord, Signor Micozzi, called Hartwell and "Yes," he said, *"Va bene,"* he said, and *"Grazie, signor console, molto gentile, sissignore,"* said Signor Micozzi.

Hartwell gave Signor Micozzi appointments when no one else could get one, while the important people went across the hall to see Martha; he swiveled back in his chair and

listened and listened . . . his mind wandered, sometimes he
dozed; he could pick up the refrain whenever he cared to.
*"Gente cattiva, quei Wilbourne. Cosa potevo fare . . .
cosa? Sono assolutamente senza . . ."*

"Ma Signor Micozzi, lei ha già ricevuto il deposito, non è vero?"

*"Si, ma questo, signor console, non deve pensare che il deposito è
abbastanza per questo . . . hanno rotto tutto! . . . Tutto è
rovinato!"*

One day soon now, he was going to haul himself together.
One has to wake oneself; one cannot go on forever, unravel-
ing the waste, the inconsequential portions of a dream that
was not even one's own. So one day soon now he was going
to stop it. He was going to say, like any tourist in the
market, *"Quanto allora?"* He might even write a check. It
was his American conscience, that was it. . . .

Poor George Hartwell, there was one success he had had.
Everyone assured him of it — the Cogginses, of course. He
could take pride in them; who would have thought that
Italians would let any American tell them about opera?

He left Martha's doorway. The sun struck him a glorious
blow and the little fountain pulsed from white to green in the
new season.

Ah, yes, the Cogginses. *Veni, vidi, vici.*

He looked for his car and found it. Dorothy, Richard and
Jean.

They had gone off triumphantly to take the boat at
Genoa, had been waved off at the station by contingents of
Roman friends, leaving time to go by Venice and revisit that
same pensione, having sent on ahead to the boat crate upon
crate of tourist junk, a whole case of country wines (a gift
from the landlord, by now a lifelong friend). There were also
a package of citations and awards from a dozen appreciative
music companies, autographed photos of half the singers in
Italy and ninety percent of all the chocolate in Perugia,
which had been showered upon Jean by admirers from
Trastavere to the Parioli, from Milan to Palermo. Perhaps
at this moment she was talking to Alfredo again in the pen-

sione, giggling at his soft Venetian accent, all in a palazzo
set on waters crackling in the brilliant light, or strolling
about the garden, hearing a motorboat churn past. Waiting
for Sunday dinner in the central hallways, with one or two of
the same old guests and the proprietor with his head in the
books . . . waiting for Sunday dinner. It was a Western
tradition, a binding point for the whole world. And why not?
In his vision of Venice, for a moment, Martha Ingram and
all her long mad vision stood redeemed. But not for long.
Jim Wilbourne was never far enough away; his head turned
slowly; his regard scorched slowly across the scene; as
though the Cogginses had been in an eighteenth-century
engraving deployed in each pleasant detail about their Venetian casa, the edges curled, the loosely woven paper bent
backward, the images distorted, changed — one turned
away.

Hartwell at last got home, and opened the windows in an
empty flat, fetched bread and cheese from the kitchen,
fought steadily against the need for whiskey and sat down to
unlock the dispatch case. His wife, so easily evoked, crossed
the ocean at his nod to stand at his elbow and remark with
her warm wit that along with all those dispatches, briefings,
summaries, minutes and memoranda from the embassy, he
might possibly draw out a poison toad, a severed hand, some
small memento of Martha Ingram.

But he did not.

The reports she had done for him were smooth and crisp,
brilliant, unblemished. Their cutting edge was razor-keen;
their substance unrolled like bolts of silk. There was nothing
to add, nothing to take away. It was sinister, and he did not
want to think about it alone. But he had to. Who has been
destroyed in this as much as me? he wondered. Gordon
Ingram is not alone. No, it was against George Hartwell's
present and fond breast that the hurled spear struck.

Knowing this, he could not stand it any longer.

Getting up, slamming out, he got into his car and went
nosing about the streets again. The Grand Hotel, a Sunday

vision, also, elegance and the Grand Tour, too little exercise, every wish granted, marmalade for tea, and if you're willing to pay extra, tours can be arranged through the —
He had charged halfway across the lobby before he stopped to think, to inquire.

"A little *signora americana* in blue, *sissignore*. She is there, *eccola là*."

And there she was. He saw her. She was real. Martha was not that crazy.

She was over in a far corner before some enormous windows reaching to the ceiling, canopied with drawn satin portières, and she was not alone. The Italian floor cleaner who had mopped and dusted the lobby there for at least ten years but had never once before this moment sat down in one of the sofas was now beside her. She had gone upstairs and, using her dictionary (as Hartwell was later to hear), had written down the message that she had to give to someone, and now she was reading it off. A piece of light blue letter paper trembled in her little crooked hand.

"*Ho un amico che sta morendo* . . . I have a friend who is dying. *Questa mattina ho ricevuto la notizia* . . . only this morning I received the news."

"*O signora!*" cried the floor cleaner. "*Mi dispiace* . . . I am so sorry!" He leaned toward her, his small-featured Latin face wrung instantly with pity. He, also, had lost friends.

"*Mio amico era sempre buono* . . . *è buono* . . . *buono*. . . ."

It was then that George Hartwell appeared. The floor cleaner sprang to his feet. "*S'accomodi* . . . sit down," said Hartwell. "*In nome di Dio*."

There was no one really around. The bright day was subdued to the decor of the great outdated windows, which made a humble group of them. And really, thought Hartwell, I've got no business here, what am I doing with these two people? Once I had a little kingdom here. It is stolen. It is gone. Should I tell them? Would they cry?

He sat and listened.

Now the sentiment, the inaccuracy, of the usual human

statement was among them; irresistibly as weeds in a great
ruin, it was springing up everywhere around what was being
said of Gordon Ingram. His books, his wisdom, his circle of
friends, his great heart, his sad life. . . . Hartwell was
translating everything to the floor cleaner, who had forgotten that he was a floor cleaner. He was, above all, a
human being, and he accordingly began to weep.

George Hartwell told the lady in blue that Martha Ingram
was out of town.

16

On a day that now seemed long, long ago, had seemed long
ago, in fact, almost the precipitate instant its final event occurred, she had gone out of her apartment, which Jim Wilbourne had been in for an hour or so, for the last time. It was
a matter of consideration to them both to give him time to
get well away before she went out behind him, leaving rooms
she could not for the moment bear to be alone in. She did not
know that he had been delayed on the stair. She saw him,
however, come out of the bar with Jean Coggins, laughing
with her over something; she stepped back, almost from the
curb into the street, which at that point was narrow, damp,
still in winter shadow, and then a car passed and she looked
up in time to see Gordon Ingram's nephew driving by. She
never doubted that was who it was. He had grown a lot, that
was all. He did not see her; the car nosed into a turning that
led away from her, away, she realized too late, icily, from
her apartment. He had been there already; he had gone.
From out of sight, in the chilly labyrinth where the sun
would slowly seep in now and warm and dry and mellow
through the long summer months, she heard Jean Coggins
laugh. The boy had grown so much; she used to give him
books and read to him: what college was he in, would no one
tell her? She had stopped still — after her first futile steps,
begun too late, of running after the car — in a small empty

square. The direction of the car pulled against the direction of the laugh, in an exact mathematical pivot, herself being the central point of strain, and in this counterweight, she felt her life tear almost audibly, like ripping silk. She leaned against a wall and looked out on the little empty space, an opening in the city. The sun brought out the smell of cigarettes, but no one was about; only dumb high doorways and shadows sliced at a clear, straight angle across a field of sun.

He was driven away from me, she thought: Jim Wilbourne did it; I know that it is true. I am no more than that meeting point of shadow and sun. It is everything there is I need to know, that I am that and that is me.

It was the complex of herself that her spirit in one motion abandoned; those intricate structures, having come to their own completion, were no longer habitable. She saw them crumble, sink and go under forever. And here was what was left: a line of dark across a field of sun.

When the small package arrived for Martha — a strand of pearls that had belonged to an aunt who had left them to her in memory of — she hardly read the letter, which was not from Gordon Ingram but from the nephew who was now in Greece. The lettering on the package had been done by Gordon Ingram. There was no message inside. She went carefully, in a gentle way, downstairs and laid the strand in the crevice of the palazzo wall, like an offering to life. She felt as a spirit might, rather clever, at being able to move an object or leave a footprint. Some Italian would be telling the story for many years, waving the pearls aloft. *"Dal cielo! Dal cielo! Son cadute dal cielo!"*

George Hartwell's saying to the lady in blue that Martha was out of town was no lie; perhaps he was incapable of telling one. She was driving to the sea to meet Roberto there, possibly the sister and the sister's husband, possibly not; the plans were generous, promising and vague. She more and more arranged to do things alone, a curious tendency, for loneliness once had been a torment, whereas now she regarded almost everything her eyes fell on with an equal sense of companionship; her compatibility was with the world. The equality of it all could of course be in some purely intellectual, non-nervous way disturbing. Things were not really equal, nor were people; one explanation might be that she simply did not care very deeply about anything; the emotional target she had once plainly furnished had disappeared. Was this another name for freedom? Freedom was certainly what it felt like. She bent with complete compassion, fleshless, invisible and absent, above the rapidly vanishing mortality of Gordon Ingram; at the same time she swung happily, even giddily (there went that streak again, the necessary madness), around the Colosseum, where the fresh glittering traffic, like a flight of gulls, joyous in the sunlight, seemed to float and lilt, fearless of collision. Children's bones and women's skulls had been dug up there and conjectures could be easily formed about what sort of undemocratic accidents had overtaken these fine people, but now the old ruin stood noble and ornamental to Rome, and views of it were precious to those apartments that overlooked it.

Faceless and nameless, the throng rushed on; they always had and would forever, as long as the city stood.

It was not Gordon Ingram who had died, nor was it Jim Wilbourne who was absent. It was herself, she thought. I am gone, she thought; they have taken me with them. I shall never return.

If only George Hartwell could understand that, he would know better about things; he could even bear them. But then, she saw, he might be compelled to trace a similar path in his own life; for knowing it arose merely, perhaps only, from being it. Let him be spared, she thought; let him be his poor human soul forever.

She was of those whom life had held a captive, and in freeing herself she had met dissolution, and was a friend now to any landscape, a companion to cloud and sky.

The Cousins

The Cousins

I could say that on the train from Milan to Florence, I recalled the events of thirty summers ago and the curious affair of my cousin Eric. But it wouldn't be true. I had Eric somewhere in my mind all the time, a constant. But he was never quite definable, and like a puzzle no one could ever solve, he bothered me. More recently, I had felt a restlessness I kept trying without success to lose, and I had begun to see Eric as its source.

The incident that had triggered my journey to find him had occurred while lunching with my cousin Ben in New York, his saying, "I always thought in some way I can't pin down — it was your fault we lost Eric." Surprising myself, I had felt stricken at the remark as though the point of a cold dagger had reached a vital spot. There was a story my cousins used to tell, out in the swing, under the shade trees, about a man found dead with no clues but a bloody shirt and a small pool of water on the floor beside him. Insoluble mystery. Answer: he was stabbed with a Dagger of Ice! I looked up from eating bay scallops. "*My* fault! Why?"

Ben gave some vague response, something about Eric's

need for staying indifferent, no matter what. "But he could do that in spite of me," I protested. "Couldn't he?"

"Oh, forget it." He filled my glass. "I sometimes speculate out loud, Ella Mason."

Just before that he had remarked how good I was looking — good for a widow just turned fifty, I think he meant. But once he got my restlessness so stirred up, I couldn't lose it. I wanted calming, absolving. I wanted freeing and only Eric — since it was he I was in some way to blame for, or he to blame for me — could do that. So I came alone to Italy, where I had not been for thirty years.

For a while in Milan, spending a day or so to get over jet lag, I wondered if the country existed anymore in the way I remembered it. Maybe, even back then, I had invented the feelings I had, the magic I had wanted to see. But on the train to Florence, riding through the June morning, I saw a little town from the window in the bright, slightly hazy distance. I don't know what town it was. It seemed built all of a whitish stone, with a church, part of a wall cupping round one side and a piazza with a few people moving across it. With that sight and its stillness in the distance and its sudden vanishing as the train whisked past, I caught my breath and knew it had all been real. So it still was, and would remain. I hadn't invented anything.

From the point of that glimpsed white village, spreading outward through my memory, all its veins and arteries, the whole summer woke up again, like a person coming out of a trance.

Sealed, fleet, the train was rocking on. I closed my eyes with the image of the village, lying fresh and gentle against my mind's eye. I didn't have to try, to know that everything from then would start living now.

Once at the hotel and unpacked, with my dim lamp and clean bathroom and view of a garden — Eric had reserved all this for me: we had written and talked — I placed my telephone call. "*Pronto*," said the strange voice. "Signor

Mason," I said. "Ella Mason, is that you?" So there was his own Alabama voice, not a bit changed. "It's me," I said, "tired from the train." "Take a nap. I'll call for you at seven."

Whatever Southerners are, there are ways they don't change, the same manners to count on, the same tone of voice, never lost. Eric was older than I by about five years. I remember he taught me to play tennis, not so much how to play because we all knew that, as what not to do. Tennis manners. I had wanted to keep running after balls for him when they rolled outside the court but he stopped me from doing that. He would take them up himself and stroke them underhand to his opponent across the net. "Once in a while's all right," he said. "Just go sit down, Ella Mason." It was his way of saying there was always a right way to do things. I was only about ten. The next year it was something else I was doing wrong, I guess, because I always had a lot to learn. My cousins had this constant fondness about them. They didn't mind telling what they knew.

Waking in Florence in the late afternoon, wondering where I was, then catching on. The air was still and warm. It had the slight haziness in the brightness that I had seen from the train, and that I had lost in the bother of the station, the hastening of the taxi through the annoyance of crowds and narrow streets, across the Arno. The little hotel, a pensione, really, was out near the Pitti Palace.

Even out so short a distance from the center, Florence could seem the town of thirty years ago, or even the way it must have been in the Brownings' time, narrow streets and the light that way and the same flowers and gravel walks in the gardens. Not that much changes if you build with stone. Not until I saw the stooped gray man hastening through the pensione door did I get slapped by change, in the face. How could Eric look like that? Not that I hadn't had photographs, letters. He at once circled me, embracing, my head right against him, sight of him temporarily lost in that. As was his of me, I realized, thinking of all those lines I must have added, along with twenty extra pounds and a high count of gray among the reddish-brown hair. So we both got bruised by the sight of each other, and hung together, to blot each other out and soothe the hurt.

The shock was only momentary. We were too glad to see each other. We went some streets away, parked his car and climbed about six flights of stone stairs. His place had a view over the river, first a great luxurious room opening past the entrance, then a terrace beyond. There were paintings, dark furniture, divans and chairs covered with good, rich fabric. A blond woman's picture in a silver frame — poised, lovely. Through an alcove, the glimpse of an impressive desk, spread with papers, a telephone. You'd be forced to say he'd done well.

"It's cooler outside on the terrace," Eric said, coming in with drinks. "You'll like it over the river." So we went out there and talked. I was getting used to him now. His profile hadn't changed. It was firm, regular, Cousin Lucy Skinner's all over. That was his mother. We were just third cousins. Kissing kin. I sat answering questions. How long would it take, I wondered, to get around to the heart of things? To whatever had carried him away, and what had brought me here?

We'd been brought up together back in Martinsville, Alabama, not far from Birmingham. There was our connection and not much else in that little town of seven thousand and something. Or so we thought. And so we would have everybody else think. We did, though, despite a certain snobbishness — or maybe because of it — have a lot of fun. There were three leading families, in some way "connected." Eric and I had had the same great-grandfather. His mother's side were distant cousins, too. Families who had gone on living around there, through the centuries. Many were the stories and wide-ranged the knowledge, though it was mainly of local interest. As a way of living, I always told myself, it might have gone on for us, too, right through the present and into an endless future, except for that trip we took that summer.

It started with ringing phones.

Eric calling one spring morning to say, "You know, the idea Jamie had last night down at Ben's about going to Europe? Well, why don't we do it?"

"This summer's impossible," I said. "I'm supposed to help Papa in the law office."

"He can get Sister to help him —" That was Eric's sister Chessie, one way of making sure she didn't decide to go with us. "You all will have to pay her a little, but she wants a job. Think it over, Ella Mason, but not for very long. Mayfred wants to, and Ben sounds serious, and there's Jamie and you makes five. Ben knows a travel agent in Birmingham. He thinks we might even get reduced rates, but we have to hurry. We should have thought this up sooner."

His light voice went racing on. He read a lot. I didn't even have to ask him where we'd go. He and Ben would plan it; both young men who studied things, knew things, read, talked, quoted. We'd go where they wanted to go, love what they planned, admire them. Jamie was younger, my uncle Gale's son, but he was forming that year — he was becoming grown-up. Would he be like them? There was nothing else to be but like them, if at all possible. No one in his right mind would question that.

Ringing phones. . . . "Oh, I'm thrilled to death! What did your folks say? It's not all that expensive what with the exchange, not as much as staying here and going somewhere like the Smokies. You can pay for the trip over with what you'd save."

We meant to go by ship. Mayfred, who read up on the latest things, wanted to fly, but nobody would hear to it. The boat was what people talked about when they mentioned their trip. It was a phrase: "On the boat going over. . . . On the boat coming back. . . ." The train was what we'd take to New York, or maybe we could fly. Mayfred, once redirected, began to plan everybody's clothes. She knew what things were drip-dry and crush-proof. On and on she forged through slick-paged magazines.

"It'll take the first two years of law practice to pay for it, but it might be worth it," said Eric. *"J'ai très hâte d'y aller,"* said Ben. The little French he knew was a lot more than ours.

Eric was about twenty-five that summer, just finishing law school, having been delayed a year or so by his army service. I wasn't but nineteen. The real reason I had hesitated about going was a boy from Tuscaloosa I'd been dating up at the university last fall, but things were running down with him, even though I didn't want to admit it. I didn't love him so much as I wanted him to love me, and that's no good, as Eric himself told me. Ben was riding high, having got part of his thesis accepted for publication in the *Sewanee Review*. He had written on "The Lost Ladies of Edgar Allan Poe" and this piece was the chapter on "Ulalume." I pointed out they weren't so much lost as dead, or sealed up half-dead in tombs, but Ben didn't see the humor in that.

The syringa were blooming that year, and the spirea and bridal wreath. The flags had come and gone, but not the wisteria, prettier than anybody could remember. All our mothers doted on their yards, while not a one of us ever raised so much as a petunia. No need to. We called one another from bower to bower. Our cars kept floating us through soft spring twilights. Travel folders were everywhere and Ben had scratched up enough French grammars to go around so we could practice some phrases. He thought we ought at least to know how to order in a restaurant and ask for stationery and soap in a hotel. Or buy stamps and find the bathroom. He was on to what to say to cab drivers when somebody mentioned that we were spending all this time on French without knowing a word of Italian. What did *they* say for hello, or how much does it cost, or which way to the post office? Ben said we didn't have time for Italian. He thought the people you had to measure up to were the French. What Italians thought of you didn't matter all that much. We were generally over at Eric's house because his mother was away visiting his married sister Edith and the grandchildren, and Eric's father couldn't have cared less if we had drinks of real whiskey in the evening. In fact, he was often out playing poker and doing the same thing himself.

The Masons had a grand house. (Mason was Mama's maiden name and so my middle one.) I loved the house especially when nobody was in it but all of us. It was white, two-story with big high-ceilinged rooms. The tree branches laced across it by moonlight, so that you could only see patches of it. Mama was always saying they ought to thin things out, take out half the shrubs and at least three trees (she would even say which trees), but Cousin Fred, Eric's father, liked all that shaggy growth. Once inside, the house took you over — it liked us all — and we were often back in the big kitchen after supper, fixing drinks, or sitting out on the side porch, making jokes and talking about Europe. One evening it would be peculiar things about the English, and the next, French food, how much we meant to spend on it, and so on. We had a long argument about Mont St Michel, which Ben had read about in a book by Henry Adams, but everybody else, though coaxed into reading at least part of the book, thought it was too far up there and we'd better stick around Paris. We hoped Ben would forget it: he was bossy when he got his head set. We wanted just to see Versigh and Fontaineblow.

"We could stop off in the southern part of France on our way to Italy," was Eric's idea. "It's where all the painting comes from."

"I'd rather see the paintings," said Mayfred. "They're mostly in Paris, aren't they?"

"That's not the point," said Ben.

Jamie was holding out for one night in Monte Carlo.

Jamie had shot up like a weed a few years back and had just never filled out. He used to regard us all as slightly opposed to him, as though none of us could possibly want to do what he most liked. He made, at times, common cause with

Mayfred, who was kin to us only by a thread so complicated I wouldn't dream of untangling it.

Mayfred was a grand-looking girl. Ben said it once, "She's got class." He said that when we were first debating whether to ask her along or not (if not her, then my room-mate from Texas would be invited), and had decided that we had to ask Mayfred or smother her, because we couldn't have stopped talking about our plans if our lives depended on it and she was always around. The afternoon Ben made that remark about her, we were just the three of us — Ben, Eric and me — out to help Mama about the annual lining of the tennis court, and had stopped to sit on a bench, being sweaty and needing some shade to catch our breath in. So he said that in his meditative way, hitting the edge of a tennis racket on the ground between his feet and occasionally sight-ing down it to see if it had warped during a winter in the press. And Eric, after a silence in which he looked off to one side until you thought he hadn't heard (this being his way), said, "You'd think the rest of us had no class at all." "Of course we have, we just never mention it," said Ben. So we'd clicked again. I always loved that to happen.

Mayfred had a boyfriend named Donald Bailey, who came over from Georgia and took her out every Saturday night. He was fairly nice-looking was about all we knew, and Eric thought he was dumb.

"I wonder how Mayfred is going to get along without Donald," Ben said.

"I can't tell if she really likes him or not," I said. "She never talks about him."

"She just likes to have somebody," Ben said tersely, a thread of disapproval in his voice, the way he could do.

Papa was crazy about Mayfred. "You can't tell what she thinks about anything and she never misses a trick," he said. His unspoken thought was that I was always misjudg-ing things. "Don't you *see*, Ella Mason," he would say. But are things all that easy to see?

"Do you remember," I said to Eric on the terrace, this long after, "much about Papa?"

"What about him?"

"He wanted me to be different someway."

"Different how?"

"More like Mayfred," I said, and laughed, making it clear that I was deliberately shooting past the mark, because really I didn't know where it was.

"Well," said Eric, looking past me out to where the lights were brightening along the Arno, the towers standing out clearly in the dusky air, "I liked you the way you were."

It was good, hearing him say that. The understanding that I wanted might not come. But I had a chance, I thought, and groped for what to say, when Eric rose to suggest dinner, a really good restaurant he knew, not far away; we could even walk.

. . . "Have you been to the Piazza? No, of course, you haven't had time. Well, don't go. It's covered with tourists and pigeon shit. They've moved all the real statues inside except the Cellini. Go look at that and leave quick. . . ."

"You must remember Jamie, though, how he put his head in his hands our first day in Italy and cried, 'I was just being nice to him and he took all the money!' Poor Jamie, I think something else was wrong with him, not just a couple of thousand lire."

"You think so, but what?"

"Well, Mayfred had made it plain that Donald was her choice of a man, though not present. And of course there was Ben. . . ." My voice stopped just before I stepped on a crack in the sidewalk.

"Ben had just got into Yale that spring before we left. He was hitching to a *fu*ture, man!" It was just as well Eric said it.

"So that left poor Jamie out of everything, didn't it? He was young, another year in college to go, and nothing really outstanding about him, so he thought, and nobody he could pair with.''

"There were you and me.''

"You and me,'' I repeated. It would take a book to describe how I said that. Half question, half echo, a total wondering what to say next. How, after all, did *he* mean it? It wasn't like me to say nothing. "He might just have wondered what *we* had?''

"He might have,'' said Eric. In the corner of the white-plastered restaurant, where he was known and welcomed, he was enjoying grilled chicken and artichokes. But suddenly he put down his fork, a pause like a solstice. He looked past my shoulder: Eric's way.

"Ben said it was my fault we 'lost' you. That's how he put it. He told me that in New York, the last time I saw him, six weeks ago. He wouldn't explain. Do you understand what he meant?''

'' 'Lost,' am I? It's news to me.''

"Well, you know, not at home. Not even in the States. Is that to do with me?''

"We'll go back and talk.'' He pointed to my plate. "Eat your supper, Ella Mason,'' he said.

My mind began wandering pleasantly. I fell to remembering the surprise Mayfred had handed us all when we got to New York. We had come up on the train, having gone up to Chattanooga to catch the Southern. Three days in New York and we would board the *Queen Mary* for Southampton. "Too romantic for anything,'' Mama had warbled on the phone. ("Elsa Stephens says, 'Too romantic for anything,' '' she said at the table. "No, Mama, you said that. I heard you.''. "Well, I don't care who said it, it's true.'') On the second afternoon in New York, Mayfred vanished with something vague she had to do. "Well, you know she's always tracking down dresses,'' Jamie told me. "I think she wants her hair restyled somewhere,'' I said. But not till we were having drinks in the hotel bar before dinner did Mayfred show up with Donald Bailey! She had, in addition to Donald, a new dress and a new hairstyle, and the three things looked to me about of equal value, I was thinking, when she suddenly announced with an earsplitting smile, "We're married!" There was a total silence, broken at last by Donald, who said with a shuffling around of feet and gestures, "It's just so I could come along with y'all, if y'all don't mind." Another silence followed, broken by Eric, who said he guessed it was one excuse for having champagne.

Mayfred and Donald had actually got married across the state line in Georgia two weeks before. Mayfred didn't want to discuss it because, she said, everybody was so taken up with talking about Europe, she wouldn't have been able to get a word in edgewise. "You better go straight and call yo' Mama," said Ben. "Either you do, or I will."

Mayfred's smile fell to ashes and she sloshed out champagne. "She can't do a thing about it till we get back home! She'll want me to explain everything. Don't y'all make me . . . please!"

I noticed that so far Mayfred never made common cause with any one of us, but always spoke to the group: y'all. It also occurred to me both then and now that that was what had actually saved her. If one of us had got involved in pleading for her with Ben, he would have overruled us. But Mayfred, a lesser cousin, was keeping a distance. She could have said — and I thought she was on the verge of it — that she'd gone to a lot of trouble to satisfy us; she might have just brought him along without benefit of ceremony.

So we added Donald Bailey. Unbeknownst to us, reservations had been found for him, and though he had to share a four-berth, tourist-class cabin with three strange men, after a day out certain swaps were effected, and he wound up in second class with Mayfred. Eric overheard a conversation between Jamie and Donald, which he passed on to me. Jamie: "Don't you really think this is a funny way to spend a honeymoon?'' Donald: ''It just was the best I could do.''

He was a polite squarish sort of boy with heavy, dark lashes. He and Mayfred used to stroll off together regularly after the noon meal on board. It was a serene crossing, for the weather cleared two days out of New York, and we could spend a lot of time on deck, playing shuffleboard and betting on races with wooden horses run by the purser. (I forgot to say everybody in our family but Ben's branch were inveterate gamblers and had played poker in the club car all the way up to New York on the train.) After lunch every day Mayfred got seasick, and Donald in true husbandly fashion would take her to whichever side the wind was not blowing against and let her throw up neatly over the rail, like a cat. Then she'd be all right. Later, when you'd see them together, they were always talking and laughing. But with us she was quiet and trim, with her fashion-blank look, and he was just quiet. He all but said ''Ma'am'' and ''Sir.'' As a result of Mayfred's marriage, I was thrown a lot with Eric, Ben and Jamie. ''I think one of you ought to get married,'' I told them. ''Just temporarily, so I wouldn't feel like the only girl.'' Ben promised to take a look around and Eric seemed not to have heard. It was Jamie who couldn't joke about it. He had set himself to make a pair, in some sort of way, with Mayfred, I felt. I don't know how seriously he took her. Things run deep in our family — that's what you have to know. Eric said out of the blue, ''I'm wondering when they had time to see each other. Mayfred spent all her time with us.'' (We were prowling through the Tate Gallery.) ''Those Saturday night dates,'' I said, studying Turner. At times she would show up with us, without Donald, not saying much, attentive and smooth, making company. Ben told her she looked Parisian.

Eric and Ben were both well into manhood that year, and were so future conscious they seemed to be talking about it even when they weren't saying anything. Ben had decided on literature, had finished a master's at Sewanee and was going on to Yale, while Eric had just stood law-school exams at Emory. He was in some considerable debate about whether he shouldn't go into literary studies, too, for unlike Ben, whose interest was scholarly, he wanted to be a writer, and he had some elaborate theory that actually studying literature reduced the possibility of your being able to write it. Ben saw his point and, though he did not entirely agree, felt that law might just be the right choice — it put you in touch with how things actually worked. "Depending, of course, on whether you tend to fiction or poetry. It would be more important in regard to fiction because the facts matter so much more." So they trod along ahead of us — through London sights, their heels coming down in tandem. They might have been two dons in an Oxford street, debating something. Next to come were Jamie and me, and behind, at times, Donald and Mayfred.

I was so fond of Jamie those days. I felt for him in a family way, almost motherly. When he said he wanted a night in Monte Carlo, I sided with him, just as I had about going at least once to the picture show in London. Why shouldn't he have his way? Jamie said one museum a day was enough. I felt the same. He was all different directions with himself: too tall, too thin, big feet, small head. Once I caught his hand. "Don't worry," I said, "everything good will happen to you." The way I remember it, we looked back just then, and there came Mayfred, alone. She caught up with us. We were standing on a street corner near Hyde Park and, for a change, it was sunny. "Donald's gone home," she said cheerfully. "He said tell you all goodbye."

We hadn't seen her all day. We were due to leave for France the next morning. She told us, for one thing, that Donald had persistent headaches and thought he ought to see about it. He seemed, as far as we could tell, to have limitless supplies of money, and had once taken us all for dinner at the Savoy, where only Mayfred could move into all that glitter with an air of belonging to it. He didn't like to bring up his illness and trouble us, Mayfred explained. "Maybe it was too much honeymoon for him," Eric specu-

lated to me in private. I had to say I didn't know. I did know
that Jamie had come out like the English sun — unexpected,
but marvelously bright.

I held out for Jamie and Monte Carlo. He wasn't an intellectual like Ben and Eric. He would listen while they finished
up a bottle of wine and then would start looking around the
restaurant. "That lady didn't have anything but snails and
bread," he would say, or, of a couple leaving, "He didn't
even know that girl when they came in." He was just being
a small-town boy. But with Mayfred he must have been different; she laughed so much. "What do they talk about?"
Ben asked me, perplexed. "Ask them," I advised. "You
think they'd tell me?" "I doubt it," I said. "They wouldn't
know what to say," I added. "They would just tell you the
last things they said." "You mean like, why do they call it
the Seine if they don't seine for fish in it? Real funny."
    Jamie got worried about Mayfred in Paris because the son
of the hotel owner, a young Frenchman so charming he
looked like somebody had made him up whole cloth, wanted
to take her out. She finally consented with some trepidation
on our part, especially from Ben, who in this case posed as
her uncle, with strict orders from her father. The Frenchman, named Paul something, was not disturbed in the least:
Ben fitted right in with his ideas of how things ought to be.
So Mayfred went out with him, looking, except for her
sunny hair, more French than the natives — we all had to
admit being proud of her. I, also, had invitations, but none
so elegant. "What happened?" we all asked, the next day.
"Nothing," she insisted. "We just went to this little night-
club place near some school . . . begins with an 'S.' "
"The Sorbonne," said Ben, whose bemusement, at that
moment, peaked. "Then what?" Eric asked. "Well,
nothing. You just eat something, then talk and have some
wine and get up and dance. They dance different. Like
this." She locked her hands together in air. "He thought he
couldn't talk good enough for me in English, but it was

OK.'' Paul sent her some *marrons glacés*, which she opened on the train south, and Jamie munched one with happy jaws. Paul had not suited him. It was soon after that, he and Mayfred began their pairing off. In Jamie's mind we were moving on to Monte Carlo, and had been ever since London. The first thing he did was find out how to get to the Casino.

He got dressed for dinner better than he had since the Savoy. Mayfred seemed to know a lot about the gambling places, but her attitude was different from his. Jamie was bird-dogging toward the moment; she was just curious. ''I've got to trail along,'' Eric said after dinner, ''just to see the show.'' ''Not only that,'' said Ben, ''we might have to stop him in case he gets too carried away. We might have to bail him out.'' When we three, following up the rear (this was Jamie's night), entered the discreetly glittering rotunda, stepped on thick carpets beneath the giant, multiprismed chandeliers, heard the low chant of the croupier, the click of roulette, the rustle of money at the bank, and saw the bright rhythmic movements of dealers and wheels and stacks of chips, it was still Jamie's face that was the sight worth watching. All was mirrored there. Straight from the bank, he visited card tables and wheels, played the blind dealing machine — chemin-de-fer — and finally turned, a small sum to the good, to his real goal: roulette. Eric had by then lost a hundred francs or so, but I had about made up for it, and Ben wouldn't play at all. ''It's my Presbyterian side,'' he told us. His mother had been one of those. ''It's known as 'riotous living,' '' he added.

It wasn't riotous at first, but it was before we left, because Jamie, once he advanced on the roulette, with Mayfred beside him — she was wearing some sort of gold blouse with long peasant sleeves and a low-cut neck she had picked up cheap in a shop that afternoon, and was not speaking to him but instead, with a gesture so European you'd think she'd been born there, slipping her arm through his just at the wrist and leaning her head back a little — was giving off the glow of somebody so magically aided by a presence every inch his own that he could not and would not lose. Jamie, in fact, looked suddenly aristocratic, overbred, like a Russian greyhound or a Rumanian prince. Both Eric and I suspended our own operations to watch. The little ball went clicking around as the wheel spun. Black. Red. And red. Back to black. All wins. People stopped to look on. Two losses, then the wins again, continuing. Mayfred had a look of curious bliss around her mouth — she looked like a cat in process of a good purr. The take mounted.

Ben called Eric and me aside. "It's going on all night," he said. We all sat down at the little gold and white marble bar and ordered Perriers.

"Well," said Eric, "what did he start with?"

"Couldn't have been much," said Ben, "if I didn't miss anything. He didn't change more than a couple of hundred at the desk."

"That sounds like a lot to me," said Eric.

"I mean," said Ben, "it won't ruin him to lose it all."

"You got us into this," said Eric to me.

"Oh, gosh, I know it. But look. He's having the time of his life."

Everybody in the room had stopped to watch Jamie's luck. Some people were laughing. He had a way of stopping everybody and saying, "What's *that* mean?" as if only English could or ought to be spoken in the entire world. Some man near us said, *"Le cavalier de l'Okla-hum,"* and another answered, *"Du Texas, plutôt."* Then he took three more in a row and they were silent.

It was Mayfred who made him stop. It seemed like she had an adding machine in her head. All of a sudden she told him something, whispered in his ear. When he shook his head, she caught his hand. When he pulled away, she grabbed his arm. When he lifted his arm, she came up with it, right off the floor. For a minute I thought they were both going to fall over into the roulette wheel.

"You got to stop, Jamie!" Mayfred said in the loudest Alabama voice I guess they'd ever be liable to hear that side of the ocean. It was curdling, like cheering for 'Bama against Ole Miss in the Sugar Bowl. "I don't have to stop!" he yelled right back. "If you don't stop," Mayfred shouted, "I'll never speak to you again, Jamie Marshall, as long as I live!"

The croupier looked helpless, and everybody in the room was turning away like they didn't see us, while through a thin door at the end of the room, a man in black tie was approaching who could only be called the "management." Ben was already pulling Jamie toward the bank. "Cash it in now. We'll go along to another one . . . maybe tomorrow we can . . ." It was like pulling a stubborn calf across the lot, but he finally made it with some help from Mayfred, who stood over Jamie while he counted everything to the last sou. She made us all take a taxi back to the hotel because she said it was common knowledge when you won a lot they sent somebody out to rob you, first thing. Next day she couldn't rest till she got Jamie to change the francs into traveler's checks, U.S. He had won well over two thousand dollars, all told.

The next thing, as they saw it, was to keep Jamie out of the Casino. Ben haggled a long time over lunch, and Eric, who was good at scheming, figured out a way to get up to a village in the hills where there was a Matisse chapel he couldn't live longer without seeing. And Mayfred took to handholding and even gave Jamie on the sly (I caught her at it) a little nibbling kiss or two. What did they care? I wondered. I thought he should get to go back and lose it all.

It was up in the mountain village that afternoon that I blundered in where I'd rather not have gone. I had come out of the chapel where Ben and Eric were deep in discussion of whether Matisse could ever place in the front rank of French art, and had climbed part of the slope nearby where a narrow stair ran up to a small square with a dry stone fountain.

Beyond that, in the French manner, was a small café with a striped awning and a few tables. From somewhere I heard Jamie's voice, saying, "I know, but what'd you do it for?" "Well, what does anybody do anything for? I wanted to." "But what would you want to *for*, Mayfred?" "Same reason you'd want to sometime." "I wouldn't want to except to be with you." "Well, I'm right here, aren't I? You got your wish." "What I wish is you hadn't done it." It was bound to be marrying Donald that he meant. He had a frown that would come at times between his light eyebrows. I came to associate it with Mayfred. How she was running him. When they stepped around the corner of the path, holding hands (immediately dropped), I saw that frown. Did I have to dislike Mayfred, the way she was acting? The funny thing was, I didn't even know.

We lingered around the village and ate there, and the bus was late, so we never made it back to the Casino. By then all Jamie seemed to like was being with Mayfred, and the frown disappeared.

Walking back to the apartment, passing darkened doorways, picking up pieces of Eric's past like fragments in the street.

". . . And then you did or didn't marry her, and she died and left you the legacy. . . ."

"Oh, we did get married, all right, the anticlimax of a number of years. I wish you could have known her. The marriage was civil. She was afraid the family would cause a row if she wanted to leave me anything. That was when she knew she hadn't had long to live. Not that it was any great fortune. She had some property out near Pasquallo, a little town near here. I sold it. I had to fight them in court for a while, but it did eventually clear up."

"You've worked, too, for this other family? . . ."

"The Rinaldi. You must have got all this from Ben, though maybe I wrote you, too. They were friends of hers. It's all connections here, like anywhere else. Right now they're all at the sea below Genoa. I'd be there, too, but I'd some business in town, and you were coming. It's the export side I've helped them with. I do know English, and a little law, in spite of all.''

"So it's a regular Italian life," I mused, climbing stairs, entering his *salotto*, where I saw again the woman's picture in a silver frame. Was that her, the one who had died? "Was she blond?" I asked, moving as curiously through his life as a child through a new room.

"Giana, you mean? No, part Sardinian, dark as they come. Oh, you mean her. No, that's Lisa, one of the Rinaldi, Paolo's sister . . . that's him up there."

I saw then, over a bookshelf, a man's enlarged photo: tweed jacket, pipe, all in the English style.

"So what else, Ella Mason?" His voice was amused at me.

"She's pretty," I said.

"Very pretty," he agreed.

We drifted out to the terrace once more.

It is time I talked about Ben and Eric, about how it was with me and with them and with the three of us.

When I look back on pictures of myself in those days, I see a girl in shorts, weighing a few pounds more than she thought she should, low-set, with a womanly cast to her body, chopped-off reddish hair and a wide, freckled, almost boyish grin, happy to be posing between two tall boys, who happened to be her cousins, smiling their white tentative smiles. Ben and Eric. They were smart. They were fun. They did everything right. And most of all, they admitted me. I was the audience they needed.

I had to run to keep up. I read Poe because of Ben's thesis, and Wallace Stevens because Eric liked his poetry. I even, finding him referred to at times, tried to read Plato. (Ben studied Greek.) But what I did was not of much interest to them. Still, they wanted me around. Sometimes Ben made a point of "conversing" with me — what courses, what books, et cetera — but he made me feel like a high-school student. Eric, seldom bothering with me, was more on my level when he did. To each other, they talked at a gallop. Literature turned them on; their ideas flowed, ran back and forth like a current. I loved hearing them.

I think of little things they did. Such as Ben coming back from Sewanee with a small Roman statue, copy of something Greek — Apollo, I think — just a fragment, a head, turned aside, shoulders and a part of a back. His professor had given it to him as a special mark of favor. He set it on his favorite pigeonhole desk, to stay there, it would seem, for always, to be seen always by the rest of us — by me.

Such as Eric ordering his "secondhand but good condition" set of Henry James's novels with prefaces, saying, "I know this is corny, but it's what I wanted," making space in his Mama's old upright secretary with glass-front bookshelves above, and my feeling that they'd always be there. I strummed my fingers across the spines lettered in gold. Someday I would draw down one or another to read them. No hurry.

Such as the three of us packing Mama's picnic basket (it seems my folks were the ones with the practical things — tennis court, croquet set; though Jamie's set up a badminton court at one time, it didn't take) to take to a place called Beulah Woods for a spring day in the sun near a creek where water ran clear over white limestone, then plunged off into a swimming hole. Ben sat on a bedspread reading Ransom's poetry aloud and we gossiped about the latest town scandal, involving a druggist, a real-estate deal where some property went cheap to him, though it seemed now that his wife had been part of the bargain, being lent out on a regular basis to the man who sold him the property. The druggist was a newcomer. A man we all knew in town had been after the property and was now threatening to sue. "Do you think it was written in the deed, so many nights a week she goes off to work the property out," Ben speculated. "Do you think they calculated the interest?" It wasn't the first time our talk had run toward sexual things; in a small town, secrets didn't often get kept for long.

More than once I'd dreamed that someday Ben or Eric one would ask me somewhere alone. A few years before the picnic, romping through our big old rambling house at twilight with Jamie, who loved playing hide-and-seek, I had run into the guest room, where Ben was standing in the half dark by the bed. He was looking at something he'd found there in the twilight, some book or ornament, and I mistook him for Jamie and threw my arms around him crying, "Caught you!" We fell over the bed together and rolled for a moment before I knew then it was Ben, but knew I'd wanted it to be; or didn't I really know all along it was Ben, but pretended I didn't? Without a doubt when his weight came down over me, I knew I wanted it to be there. I felt his body, for a moment so entirely present, draw back and up. Then he stood, turning away, leaving. "You better grow up," was what I think he said. Lingering feelings made me want to seek him out the next day or so. Sulky, I wanted to say, "I *am* growing up." But another time he said, "We're cousins, you know."

Eric for a while dated a girl from one of the next towns. She used to ask him over to parties and they would drive to Birmingham sometimes, but he never had her over to Martinsville. Ben, that summer we went to Europe, let it be known he was writing and getting letters from a girl at Sewanee. She was a pianist named Sylvia. "You want to hear music played softly in the 'drawing room,' " I clowned at him. " 'Just a song at twilight.' " "Now, Ella Mason, you behave," he said.

I had boys to take me places. I could flirt and I got a rush at dances and I could go off the next to the highest diving board and was good in doubles. Once I went on strike from Ben and Eric for over a week. I was going with that boy from Tuscaloosa and I had begun to think he was the right one and get ideas. Why fool around with my cousins? But I missed them. I went around one afternoon. They were talking out on the porch. The record player was going inside, something of Berlioz's that Ben was onto. They waited till it finished before they'd speak to me. Then Eric, smiling from the depths of a chair, said, "Hey, Ella Mason," and Ben, getting up to unlatch the screen, said, "Ella Mason, where on earth have you been?" I'd have to think they were glad.

Ben was dark. He had straight, dark-brown hair, dry-looking in the sun, growing thick at the brow, but flat at night when he put a damp comb through it, and darker. It fitted close to his head like a monk's hood. He wore large glasses with lucite rims. Eric had sandy hair, softly appealing and always mussed. He didn't bother much with his looks. In the day they scuffed around in open-throated shirts and loafers, crinkled seersucker pants, or shorts; tennis shoes when they played were always dirty white. At night, when they cleaned up, it was still casual but fresh laundered. But when they dressed, in shirts and ties with an inch of white cuff laid crisp against their brown hands: they were splendid!

"Ella Mason," Eric said, "if that boy doesn't like you, he's not worth worrying about." He had put his arm around me coming out of the picture show. I ought to drop it, a tired romance, but couldn't quite. Not till that moment. Then I did.

"Those boys," said Mr Felix Gresham from across the street. "Getting time they started earning something 'stead of all time settin' around." He used to come over and tell Mama everything he thought, though no kin to anybody. "I reckon there's time enough for that," Mama said. "Now going off to France," said Mr Gresham, as though that spoke for itself. "Not just France," Mama said, "England, too, and Italy." "Ain't nothing in France," said Mr Gresham. "I don't know if there is or not," said Mama. "I never have been." She meant that to hush him up, but the truth is, Mr Gresham might have been to France in World War I. I never thought to ask. Now he's dead.

Eric and Ben. I guess I was in love with both of them.

Wouldn't it be nice, I used to think, if one were my brother and the other my brother's best friend, and then I could just quietly and without so much as thinking about it find myself marrying the friend (now which would I choose for which?) and so we could go on forever? At other times, frustrated, I suppose, by their never changing toward me, I would plan on doing something spectacular, finding a Yankee, for instance, so impressive and brilliant and established in some important career that they'd have to listen to him, learn what he was doing and what he thought and what he knew, while I sat silent and poised throughout the conversation, the cat that ate the cream, though of course too polite to show satisfaction. Fantasies, one by one, would sing to me for a little while.

At Christmas vacation before our summer abroad, just before Ben got accepted to Yale and just while Eric was getting bored with law school, there was a quarrel. I didn't know the details, but they went back to school with things still unsettled among us. I got friendly with Jamie then, more than before. He was down at Tuscaloosa, like me. It's when I got to know Mayfred better, on weekends at home. Why bother with Eric and Ben? It had been a poor season. One letter came from Ben and I answered it, saying that I had come to like Jamie and Mayfred so much; their parents were always giving parties and we were having a grand time. In answer I got a long, serious letter about time passing and what it did, how we must remember that what we had was always going to be a part of ourselves. That he thought of jonquils coming up now and how they always looked like jonquils, just absent for a time, and how the roots stayed the same. He was looking forward, he said, to spring and coming home.

Just for fun I sat down and wrote him a love letter. I said he was a fool and a dunce and didn't he know while he was writing out all these ideas that I was a live young woman and only a second cousin and that through the years while he was talking about Yeats, Proust and Edgar Allan Poe that I was longing to have my arms around him the way they were when we fell over in the bed that twilight romping with Jamie and why in the ever-loving world couldn't he see me as I was, a live girl, instead of a cousin-spinster, listening to him and Eric make brilliant conversation? Was he trying to turn me into an old maid? Wasn't he supposed, at least, to be intelligent? So why couldn't he see what I was really like? But I didn't mail it. I didn't because for one thing, I doubted that I meant it. Suppose, by a miracle, Ben said, "You're right, every word." What about Eric? I started dating somebody new at school. I tore the letter up.

Eric called soon after. He just thought it would do him good to say hello. Studying for long hours wasn't his favorite sport. He'd heard from Ben; the hard feelings were over; he was ready for spring holidays already. I said, "I hope to be in town, but I'm really not sure." A week later I forgot a date with the boy I thought I liked. The earlier one showed up again. Hadn't I liked him, after all? How to be sure? I bought a new straw hat, white-and-navy for Easter, with a ribbon down the back, and came home.

Just before Easter, Jamie's parents gave a party for us all. There had been a cold snap and we were all inside, with purplish-red punch and a buffet laid out. Jamie's folks had this relatively new house, with new carpets and furnishings, and the family dismay ran to what a big mortgage they were carrying and how it would never be paid out. Meantime his mother (no kin) looked completely unworried as she arranged tables that seemed to have been copied from magazines. I came alone, having had to help Papa with some typing, and so saw Ben and Eric for the first time, though we'd talked on the phone.

Eric looked older, a little worn. I saw something drawn in the way he laughed, a sort of restraint about him. He was standing aside and looking at a point where no one and nothing were. But he came to when I spoke and gave that laugh and then a hug. Ben was busy "conversing" with a couple in town who had somebody at Sewanee, too. He

smoked a pipe now, I noticed, smelly when we hugged. He
had soon come to join Eric and me, and it was at that
moment, the three of us standing together for the first time
since Christmas, and change having been mentioned at least
once by way of Ben's letter, that I knew some tension was
mounting, bringing obscure moments with it. We turned to
one another but did not speak readily about anything. I had
thought I was the only one, sensitive to something imagined
— having "vapors," as somebody called it — but I could
tell we were all at a loss for some reason none of us knew.
Because if Ben and Eric knew, articulate as they were, they
would have said so. In the silence so suddenly fallen, something was ticking.

Maybe, I thought, they just don't like Martinsville anymore. They always said that parties were dull and squirmed
out of them when they could. I lay awake thinking, They'll
move on soon; I won't see them again.

It was the next morning Eric called and we all grasped for
Europe like the drowning, clinging to what we could.

After Monte Carlo, we left France by train and came down
to Florence. The streets were narrow there and we joked
about going single file like Indians. "What I need is mocca-
sins," said Jamie, who was always blundering over the
uneven paving stones. At the Uffizi, the second day, Eric, in
a trance before Botticelli, fell silent. Could we ever get him
to speak again? Hardly a word. Five in number, we leaned
over the balustrades along the Arno, all silent then from the
weariness of sight-seeing, and the heat, and there I heard it
once more, the ticking of something hidden among us. Was
it to deny it we decided to take the photograph? We had
taken a lot, but this one, I think, was special. I have it still. It
was in the Piazza Signoria.

"Which monument?" we kept asking. Ben wanted Donatello's lion, and Eric the steps of the Old Palace. Jamie
wanted Cosimo I on his horse. I wanted the *Perseus* of
Cellini, and Mayfred the *Rape of the Sabines*. So Ben made

straws out of toothpicks and we drew and Mayfred won. We got lined up and Ben framed us. Then we had to find somebody, a slim Italian boy as it turned out, to snap us for a few hundred lire. It seemed we were proving something serious and good, and smiled with our straight family smiles, Jamie with his arm around Mayfred, and she with her smart new straw sun hat held to the back of her head, and me between Ben and Eric, arms entwined. A photo outlasts everybody, and this one with the frantic scene behind us, the moving torso of the warrior holding high the prey while we smiled our ordinary smiles — it was a period, the end of a phase.

Not that the photograph itself caused the end of anything. Donald Bailey caused it. He telephoned the pensione that night from Atlanta to say he was in the hospital, gravely ill, something they might have to operate for any day, some sort of brain tumor was what they were afraid of. Mayfred said she'd come.

We all got stunned. Ben and Eric and I straggled off together while she and Jamie went to the upstairs sitting room and sat in the corner. "Honest to God," said Eric, "I just didn't know Donald Bailey had a brain." "He had headaches," said Ben. "Oh, I knew he had a head," said Eric. "We could see that."

By night it was settled. Mayfred would fly back from Rome. Once again she got us to promise secrecy — how she did that I don't know, the youngest one and yet not even Ben could prevail on her one way or the other. By now she had spent most of her money. Donald, we knew, was rich; he came of a rich family and had, furthermore, money of his own. So if she wanted to fly back from Rome, the ticket, already purchased, would be waiting for her. Mayfred got to be privileged, in my opinion, because none of us knew her family too well. Her father was a blood cousin but not too highly regarded — he was thought to be a rather silly man who "traveled" and dealt with "all sorts of people" — and her mother was from "off," a Georgia girl, fluttery. If it had been my folks and if I had started all this wild marrying and flying off, Ben would have been on the phone to Martinsville by sundown.

One thing in the Mayfred departure that went without question: Jamie would go to Rome to see her off. We couldn't have sealed him in or held him with ropes. He had got on to something new in Italy, or so I felt, because where before then had we seen in gallery after gallery, strong men, young and old, with enraptured eyes, enthralled before a woman's painted image, wanting nothing? What he had got was an idea of devotion. It fitted him. It suited. He would do anything for Mayfred and want nothing. If she had got pregnant and told him she was a virgin, he would have sworn to it before the Inquisition. It could positively alarm you for him to see him satisfied with the feelings he had found. Long after I went to bed, he was at the door or in the corridor with Mayfred, discussing baggage and calling a hotel in Rome to get a reservation for when he saw her off.

Mayfred had bought a lot of things. She had an eye for what she could wear with what, and she would pick up pieces of this and that for putting costumes and accessories together. She had to get some extra luggage and it was Jamie, of course, who promised to see it sent safely to her, through a shipping company in Rome. His two thousand dollars was coming in handy, was all I could think.

Hot, I couldn't sleep, so I went out in the sitting room to find a magazine. Ben was up. The three men usually took a large room together, taking turns for the extra cot. Ever since we got the news, Ben had had what Eric called his "family mood." Now he called me over. "I can't let those kids go down there alone," he said. "They seem like children to me — and Jamie . . . about all he can say is *grazie* and *quanto*." "Then let's all go," I said, "I've given up sleeping for tonight, anyway." "Eric's hooked on Florence," said Ben. "Can't you tell? He counts the cypresses on every knoll. He can spot a Della Robbia a block off. If I make him leave three days early, he'll never forgive me. Besides, our reservations in that hotel can't be changed.

We called for Jamie and they're full. He's staying third-class somewhere till we all come. I don't mind doing that. Then we'll all meet up just the way we planned, have our week in Rome and go catch the boat from Naples." "I think they could make it on their own," I said. "It's just that you'd worry every minute." He grinned; "Our father for the duration," was what Eric called him. "I know I'm that way," he said.

Another thing was that Ben had been getting little caches of letters at various points along our trek from his girl friend Sylvia, the one he'd been dating up at Sewanee. She was getting a job in New York that fall that would be convenient to Yale. She wrote a spidery hand on thick rippled stationery, cream colored, and had promised in her last dispatch, received in Paris, to write to Rome. Ben could have had an itch for that. But mainly he was that way, careful and concerned. He had in mind what we all felt, that just as absolutely anything could be done by Mayfred, so could absolutely anything happen to her. He also knew what we all knew: that if the Colosseum started falling on her, Jamie would leap bodily under the rocks.

At 2 A.M. it was too much for me to think about. I went to bed and was so exhausted, I didn't even hear Mayfred leave.

I woke up about ten with a low tapping on my door. It was Eric. "Is this the sleep of the just?" he asked me as I opened the door. The air in the corridor was fresh; it must have rained in the night. No one was about. All the guests, I supposed, were well out into the day's routine, seeing what next tour was on the list. On a trip you were always planning something. Ben planned for us. He kept a little notebook.

Standing in my doorway alone with Eric, in a loose robe with a cool morning breeze and my hair not even combed, I suddenly laughed. Eric laughed, too. "I'm glad they're gone," he said, and looked past my shoulder.

I dressed and went out with him for some breakfast, cappuccino and croissants at a café in the Signoria. We didn't talk much. It was terrible, in the sense of the Mason Skinner Marshall and Phillips sense of family, even to think you were glad they were gone, let alone say it. I took Eric's silence as one of his ironies, what he was best at. He would say, for instance, if you were discussing somebody's problem that wouldn't ever have any solution, "It's time somebody died." There wasn't much to say after that. Another time, when his daddy got into a rage with a next-door neighbor over their property line, Eric said, "You'd better marry her." Once he put things in an extreme light, nobody could talk about them anymore. Saying "I'm glad they're gone" was like that.

But it was a break. I thought of the way I'd been seeing them. How Jamie's becoming had been impressing me, every day more. How Mayfred was a kind of spirit, grown bigger than life. How Ben's dominance now seemed not worrisome, but princely, his heritage. We were into a Renaissance of ourselves, I wanted to say, but was afraid they wouldn't see it the way I did. Only Eric had eluded me. What was he becoming? For once he didn't have to discuss Poe's idea of women, or the Southern code of honor, or Henry James's views of France and England.

As for me, I was, at least, sure that my style had changed. I had bought my little linen blouses and loose skirts, my sandals and braided silver bracelets. "That's great on you!" Mayfred had cried. "Now try this one!" On the streets, Italians passed me too close not to be noticed; they murmured musically in my ear, saying I didn't know just what; waiters leaned on my shoulder to describe dishes of the day.

Eric and I wandered across the river, following narrow streets lined with great stone palaces, seeing them open into small piazzas whose names were not well-known. We had lunch in a friendly place with a curtain of thin twisted metal sticks in the open door, an amber-colored dog lying on the marble floor near the serving table. We ordered favorite things without looking at the menu. We drank white wine. "This is fun," I suddenly said. He turned to me. Out of his private distance, he seemed to be looking down at me. "I think so, too."

He suddenly switched on to me, like somebody searching

and finding with the lens of a camera. He began to ask me things. What did you think of that, Ella Mason? What about this, Ella Mason? Ella Mason, did you think Ben was right when he said? . . . I could hardly swing on to what was being asked of me, thick and fast. But he seemed to like my answers, actually to listen. Not that all those years I'd been dumb as a stone. I had prattled quite a lot. It's just that they never treated me one to one, the way Eric was doing now. We talked for nearly an hour, then, with no one left in the restaurant but us, stopped as suddenly as we'd started. Eric said, "That's a pretty dress."

The sun was strong outside. The dog was asleep near the door. Even the one remaining waiter was drowsing on his feet. It was the shutting-up time for everything and we went out into streets blanked out with metal shutters. We hugged the shady side and went single file back to home base, as we'd come to call it, wherever we stayed.

A Vespa snarled by and I stepped into a cool courtyard to avoid it. I found myself in a large yawning mouth, mysterious as a cave, shadowy, with the trickling sound of a fountain and the glimmer in the depths of water running through ferns and moss. Along the interior of the street wall, fragments of ancient sculpture, found, I guess, when they'd built the palazzo, had been set into the masonry. One was a horse, neck and shoulder, another an arm holding a shield and a third at about my height the profile of a woman, a nymph or some such. Eric stopped to look at each, for, as Ben had said, Eric loved everything there, and then he said, "Come here, Ella Mason." I stood where he wanted, by the little sculptured relief, and he took my face and turned it to look at it closer. Then with a strong hand (I remembered tennis), he pressed my face against the stone face and held it for a moment. The stone bit into my flesh and that was the first time that Eric, bending deliberately to do so, kissed me on the mouth. He had held one side of me against the wall, so that I couldn't raise my arm to him, and the other arm was pinned down by his elbow; the hand that pressed my face into the stone was that one, so that I couldn't move closer to him, as I wanted to do, and when he dropped away suddenly, turned on his heel and walked rapidly away, I could only hasten to follow, my voice gone, my pulses all throbbing together. I remember my anger, the old dreams about him and Ben stirred to life again, thinking, *If he thinks he can just walk away*, and knowing with anger, too, *It's got to be now*, as if in the walled land of kinship, thicker in our illustrious connection than any fortress in Europe, a door had creaked open at last. Eric, Eric, Eric. I'm always seeing your retreating heels, how they looked angry. But why? It was worth coming for, after thirty years, to ask that. . . .

"That day you kissed me in the street, the first time," I asked him. Night on the terrace, a bottle of Chianti between our chairs. "You walked away. Were you angry? Your heels looked angry. I can see them still."

"The trip in the first place," he said, "it had to do with you partly. Maybe you didn't understand that. We were outward bound, leaving you, a sister in a sense. We'd talked about it."

"I adored you so," I said. "I think I was less than a sister, more like a dog."

"For a little while you weren't either one." He found my hand in the dark. "It was a wonderful little while."

Memories: Eric in the empty corridor of the pensione. How Italy folds up and goes to sleep from two to four. His not looking back for me, going straight to his door. The door closing, but no key turning and me turning the door handle and stepping in. And he at the window already with his back to me and how he heard the sliding latch on the door — I slid it with my hands behind me — heard it click shut and turned. His face and mine, what we knew. Betraying Ben.

: Walking by the Arno, watching a white-and-green scull stroking by into the twilight, the rower a boy or girl in white and green, growing dimmer to the rhythm of the long oars, vanishing into arrow shape, then pencil thickness, then movement without substance, on. . . .

: A trek the next afternoon through twisted streets to a famous chape. Sitting quiet in a cloister, drinking in the symmetry, the silence. Holding hands. " 'D' for Donatello," said Eric. " 'D' for Della Robbia," I said. " 'M' for Michelangelo," he continued. " M' for Medici." " 'L' for Leonardo." "I can't think of an 'L,' " I gave up. "Lumbago. There's an old master." "Worse than Jamie." We were always going home again.

: Running into the manager of the pensione one morning in the corridor. He'd solemnly bowed to us and kissed my hand. *"Bella ragazza,"* he remarked. "The way life ought to be," said Eric. I thought we might be free forever, but from what?

At the train station waiting the departure we were supposed to take for Rome, "Why do we have to go?" I pleaded. "Why can't we just stay here?"

"Use your common sense, Ella Mason."

"I don't have any."

He squeezed my shoulder. "We'll get by all right," he said. "That is, if you don't let on."

I promised not to. Rather languidly I watched the landscape slide past as we glided south. I would obey Eric, I thought, for always. "Once I wrote a love letter to you," I said. "I wrote it at night by candlelight at home one summer. I tore it up."

"You told me that," he recalled, "but you said you couldn't remember if it was to me or Ben."

"I just remembered," I said. "It was you. . . ."

"Why did we ever leave?" I asked Eric in the dead of the night, a blackness now. "Why did we ever decide we had to go to Rome?"

"I didn't think of it as even a choice," he said. "But at that point, how could I know what was there, ahead?"

We got off the train feeling small — at least, I did. Ben was standing there, looking around him, tall, searching for us, then seeing. But no Jamie. Something to ask. I wondered if he'd gone back with Mayfred. "No, he's running around Rome." The big smooth station, echoing, open to the warm day. "Hundreds of churches," Ben went on. "Millions. He's checking them off." He helped us in a taxi with the skill of somebody who'd lived in Rome for ten years, and gave the address. "He's got to do something now that Mayfred's gone. It's getting like something he might take seriously, is all. Finding out what Catholics believe. He's either losing all his money, or falling in love, or getting religion."

"He didn't lose any money," said Eric. "He made some."

"Well, it's the same thing," said Ben, always right and not wanting to argue with us. He seemed a lot older than the two of us, at least to me. Ben was tall.

We had mail in Rome; Ben brought it to the table that night. I read Mama's aloud to them: " 'When I think of you children over there, I count you all like my own chickens out in the yard, thinking I've got to go out in the dark and make sure the gate's locked because not a one ought to get out of there. To me, you're all my own, and thinking of chickens is my way of saying prayers for you to be safe at home again.' "

"You'd think we were off in a war," said Eric.

"It's a bold metaphor," said Ben, pouring wine for us, "but that never stopped Cousin Charlotte."

I wanted to giggle at Mama, as I usually did, but instead my eyes filled with tears, surprising me, and a minute more and I would have dared to snap at Ben. But, Eric, who had got some mail, too, abruptly got up and left the table. I almost ran after him, but intent on what I'd promised about not letting on to Ben, I stayed and finished dinner. He had been pale, white. Ben thought he might be sick. He didn't return. We didn't know.

Jamie and Ben finally went to bed. "He'll come back when he wants to," said Ben.

I waited till their door had closed, and then, possessed, I

204 ELIZABETH SPENCER

crept out to the front desk. "Signor Mason," I said, "the one with the *capelli leggero* —" My Italian came from the dictionary straight to the listener. I found out later I had said that Eric's hair didn't weigh much. Still, they understood. He had taken a room, someone who spoke English explained. He wanted to be alone. I said he might be sick, and I guess they could read my face, because I was guided by a porter in a blue working jacket and cloth shoes, into a labyrinth. Italian buildings, I knew by now, are constructed like dreams. There are passages departing from central hallways, stairs that twist back upon themselves, dark silent doors. My guide stopped before one. *"Ecco,"* he said, and left. I knocked softly, and the door eventually cracked open. "Oh, it's you." "Eric. Are you all right? I didn't know . . ."

He opened the door a little wider. "Ella Mason —" he began. Maybe he was sick. I caught his arm. The whole intensity of my young life in that moment shook free of everything but Eric. It was as though I'd traveled miles to find him. I came inside and we kissed, and then I was sitting apart from him on the edge of the bed and he in a chair, and a letter, official-looking, the top of the envelope torn open in a ragged line, lay on a high black-marble-topped table with bowed legs, between us. He said to read it and I did, and put it back where I found it.

It said that Eric had failed his law exams. That in view of the family connection with the university (his father had gone there and some cousin was head of the board of trustees), a special meeting had been held to grant his repeating the term's work so as to graduate in the fall, but the evidences of his negligence were too numerous and the vote had gone against it. I remember saying something like, "Anybody can fail exams —" as I knew people who had, but knew, also, that those people weren't "us," not one of our class or connection, not kin to the brilliant Ben, or nephew of a governor, or descended from a great Civil War general.

"All year long," he said, "I've been acting like a fool, as if I expected to get by. This last semester especially. It all seemed too easy. It is easy. It's easy and boring. I was fencing blindfold with somebody so far beneath me it wasn't worth the trouble to look at him. The only way to keep the interest up was to see how close I could come without damage. Well, I ran right into it, head on. God, does it serve me right. I'd read books Ben was reading, follow his interests, instead of boning over law. But I wanted the degree. Hot damn, I wanted it!"

"Another school," I said. "You can transfer credits and start over."

"This won't go away."

"Everybody loves you," I faltered, adding, "Especially me."

He almost laughed, at my youngness, I guess, but then said, "Ella Mason," as gently as feathers falling, and came to hold me a while, but not like before, the way we'd been. We sat down on the bed and then fell back on it and I could hear his heart's steady thumping under his shirt. But it wasn't the beat of a lover's heart just then; it was more like the echo of a distant bell or the near march of a clock, and I fell to looking over his shoulder.

It was a curious room, one I guess they wouldn't have rented to anybody if Rome hadn't been, as they told us, so full. The shutters were closed on something that suggested more of a courtyard than the outside as no streak or glimmer of light came through, and the bed was huge, with a great dark tall rectangle of a headboard and a footboard only slightly lower. There were brass sconces set ornamentally around the moldings, looking down, cupids and fawns and smiling goat faces, with bulbs concealed in them, though the only light came from the one dim lamp on the bedside table. There were heavy, dark engravings of Rome — by Piranesi or somebody like that — the avenues, the monuments, the river. And one panel of small pictures in a series showed some familiar scenes in Florence.

My thoughts, unable to reach Eric's, kept wandering off tourist fashion among the myth faces peeking from the sconces, laughing down, among the walks of Rome — the arched bridge over the Tiber where life-size angels stood poised; the rise of the Palatine, mysterious among trees; the horseman on the Campidoglio, his hand outstretched; and Florence, beckoning still. I couldn't keep my mind at any one set with all such around me, and Eric, besides, had gone back to the table and was writing a letter on hotel stationery. When my caught breath turned to a little cry, he looked up and said, "It's my problem, Ella Mason. Just let me handle it." He came to stand by me, and pressed my head against him, then lifted my face by the chin. "Don't go talking about it. Promise." I promised.

I wandered back through the labyrinth, thinking I'd be lost in there forever like a Poe lady. Damn Ben, I thought, he's too above it all for anybody to fall in love or fail an examination. I'm better off lost, at this rate. So thinking, I turned a corner and stepped out into the hotel lobby.

It was Jamie's and Ben's assumption that Eric had picked up some girl and gone home with her. I never told them better. Let them think that.

"Your Mama wrote you a letter about some chickens once, how she counted children like counting chickens," Eric said, thirty years later. "Do you remember that?"

We fell to remembering Mama. "There's nobody like her," I said. "She has long talks with Papa. They started a year or so after he died. I wish I could talk to him."

"What would you say?"

"I'd ask him to look up Howard. See'f he's doing all right."

"Your husband?" Eric wasn't sure of the name.

I guess joking about your husband's death isn't quite the thing. I met Howard on a trip to Texas after we got home from abroad. I was visiting my roommate. Whatever else Eric did for me, our time together had made me ready for

more. I pined for him alone, but what I looked was ripe and
ready for practically anybody. So Howard said. He was a
widower with a Texas-size fortune. When he said I looked
like a good breeder, I didn't even get mad. That's how he
knew I'd do. Still, it took a while. I kept wanting Eric, wanting my old dream: my brilliant cousins, princely, cavalier.

Howard and I had two sons, in their twenties now.
Howard got killed in a jeep accident out on his cattle ranch.
Don't think I didn't get married again, to a wild California
boy ten years younger. It lasted six months exactly.

"What about that other one?" Eric asked me. "Number
two."

I had got the divorce papers the same day they called to
say Howard's tombstone had arrived. "Well, you know,
Eric, I always was a little bit crazy."

"You thought he was cute."

"I guess so."

"You and I," said Eric, smooth as silk into the deep silent
darkness that now was ours — even the towers seemed to
have folded up and gone home — "we never worked it out,
did we?"

"I never knew if you really wanted to. I did, God knows. I
wouldn't marry Howard for over a year because of you."

"I stayed undecided about everything. One thing that's
not is a marrying frame of mind."

"Then you left for Europe."

"I felt I'd missed the boat for everywhere else. War service, then that law school thing. It was too late for me. And
nothing was of interest. I could move but not with much
conviction. I felt for you — maybe more than you know —
but you were moving on already. You know, Ella Mason,
you never are still."

"But you could have told me that!"

"I think I did, one way or another. You sat still and
fidgeted." He laughed.

It's true that energy is my middle name.

The lights along the river were dim and so little was moving past by now they seemed fixed and distant, stars from some long-dead galaxy, maybe. I think I slept. Then I heard Eric.

"I think back so often to the five of us — you and Ben, Jamie and Mayfred and me. There was something I could never get out of mind. You remember when we were planning everything about Europe, Europe, Europe before we left, and you'd all come over to my house and we'd sit out on the side porch, listening to Ben mainly, but with Jamie asking some questions like, 'Do they have bathtubs like us?' Remember that? You would snuggle down in one of those canvas chairs like a sling, and Ben was in the big armchair — Daddy's — and Jamie sort of sprawled around on the couch among the travel folders, when we heard the front gate scrape on the sidewalk and heard the way it would clatter when it closed. A warm night and the streetlight filtering in patterns through the trees and shrubs and a smell of honeysuckle from where it was all baled up on the yard fence and a cape jessamine outside, I remember that, too — white flowers in among the leaves. And steps on the walk. They stopped, then they walked again, and Ben got up (I should have) and unlatched the screen. If you didn't latch the screen it wouldn't shut. Mayfred came in. Jamie said, 'Why'd you stop on the walk, Mayfred?' She said, 'There was this toadfrog. I almost stepped on him.' Then she was among us, walking in, one of us. I was sitting back in the corner, watching, and I felt, If I live to be a thousand, I'll never feel more love than I do this minute. Love of these, my blood, and this place, here. I could close my eyes for years and hear the gate scrape, the steps pause, the door latch and unlatch, hear her say, 'There was this toadfrog . . .' I would want literally to embrace that one minute, hold it forever."

"But you're not there," I said into the dark. "You're here. Where we were. You chose it."

"There's no denying that," was all he answered.

We had sailed from Naples, a sad day under mist, with Vesuvius hardly visible and damp clinging to everything —

the end of summer. We couldn't even make out the outlines
of the ship, an Italian-line monster from those days called
the *Independence*. It towered white over us and we tunneled
in. The crossing was rainy and drab. Crossed emotions
played around among us, while Ben, noble and aware, tried
to be our mast. He read aloud to us, discussed, joked, tried
to get our attention.

Jamie wanted to argue about Catholicism. It didn't suit
Ben for him to drift that way. Ben was headed toward
Anglican belief: that's what his Sylvia was, not to mention
T.S. Eliot. But Jamie had met an American Jesuit from In-
diana in Rome and chummed around with him; they'd even
gone to the beach. "You're wrong about that," I heard him
tell Ben. "I'm going to prove it by Father Rogers when we
get home."

I worried about Eric; I longed for Eric; I strolled the decks
and stood by Eric at the rail. He looked with gray eyes out at
the gray sea. He said, "You know, Ella Mason, I don't give
a damn if Jamie joins the Catholic Church or not." "Me,
either," I agreed. We kissed in the dark beneath the life-
boats, and made love once in the cabin while Ben and Jamie
were at the movies, but in a furtive way, as if the grown people were at church. Ben read aloud to us from a book on
Hadrian's Villa, where we'd all been. There was a half day
of sun.

I went to the pool to swim, and up came Jamie, out of the
water. He was skinny, string beans and spaghetti. "Ella
Mason," he said in his dark croak of a voice, "I'll never be
the same again." I was tired of all of them, even Jamie.
"Then gain some weight," I snapped, and went pretty off
the diving board.

Ben knew about the law-school thing. The first day out,
coming from the writing lounge, I saw Eric and Ben standing together in a corner of an enclosed deck. Ben had a letter
in his hand, and just from one glance I recognized the stationery of the hotel where we'd stayed in Rome and knew it
was the letter Eric had been writing. I heard Ben. "You say
it's not important, but I know it is — I knew that last

Christmas.'' And Eric, ''Think what you like, it's not to me.'' And Ben, ''What you feel about it, that's not what matters. There's a right way of looking at it. Only to make you see it.'' And Eric, ''You'd better give up. You never will.''

What kept me in my tracks was something multiple, yet single, the way a number can contain powers and elements that have gone into its making and can be unfolded, opened up, nearly forever. Ambition and why some had it, success and failure and what the difference was and why you had to notice it at all. These matters, back and forth across the net, were what was going on.

What had stopped me in the first place, though, and chilled me, was that they sounded angry. I knew they had quarreled last Christmas; was this why? It must have been. Ben's anger was attack and Eric's self-defense, defiance. Hadn't they always been like brothers? Yes, and they were standing so, intent, a little apart, in hot debate, like two officers locked in different plans of attack at dawn, stubbornly held to the point of fury. Ben's position, based on rightness, classical and firm. Enforced by what he was. And Eric's wrong, except in and for himself, for holding on to himself. How to defend that? He couldn't, but he did. And equally. They were just looking up and seeing me, and nervous at my intrusion I stepped across the high shipboard sill to the deck, missed clearing it and fell sprawling. ''Oh, Ella Mason!'' they cried at once, and picked me up, the way they always had.

One more thing I remember from that ship. It was Ben, finding me one night after dinner alone in the lounge. Everyone was below: we were docking in the morning. He sat down and lighted his pipe. ''It's all passed so fast, don't you think?'' he said. There was such a jumble in my mind still, I didn't answer. All I could hear was Eric saying, after we'd made love, ''It's got to stop now. I've got to find some shape to things. There was promise, promises. You've got to see we're saying they're worthless, that nothing matters.''

What did matter to me, except Eric? "I wish I'd never come," I burst out at Ben, childish, hurting him, I guess. How much did Ben know? He never said. He came close and put his arm around me. "You're the sister I never had," he said. "I hope you change your mind about it." I said I was sorry and snuffled awhile into his shoulder. When I looked up, I saw his love. So maybe he did know, and forgave us. He kissed my forehead.

At the New York pier, who should show up but Mayfred.

She was crisp in black and white, her long blond hair wind shaken, her laughter a wholesome joy. "Y'all look just terrible," she told us with a friendly giggle, and as usual made us straighten up, tuck our tummies in and look like quality. Jamie forgot religion, and Eric quit worrying over a missing bag, and Ben said, "Well, look who's here!" "How's Donald?" I asked her. I figured he was either all right or dead. The first was true. They didn't have to do a brain-tumor operation; all he'd had was a pinched nerve at the base of his cortex. "What's a cortex?" Jamie asked. "It sounds too personal to inquire," said Eric, and right then they brought him his bag.

On the train home, Mayfred rode backward in our large drawing-room compartment (courtesy of Donald Bailey) and the landscape, getting more southern every minute, went rocketing past. "You can't guess how I spent my time when Donald was in the hospital. Nothing to do but sit."

"Working crossword puzzles," said Jamie.

"Crocheting," said Eric, provoking a laugh.

"Reading *Vogue*," said Ben.

"All wrong! I read Edgar Allan Poe! What's more, I memorized that poem! That one Ben wrote on. You know? That 'Ulalume'!"

Everybody laughed but Ben, and Mayfred was laughing, too, her grand girlish sputters, innocent as sun and water, her beautiful large white teeth, even as a cover girl's. Ben,

courteously at the end of the sofa, smiled faintly. It was best
not to believe this was true.

> " 'The skies they were ashen and sober;
>   The leaves they were crisped and sere —
>   The leaves they were withering and sere:
> It was the night in the lonesome October
>   Of my most immemorial year. . . .' "

"By God, she's done it," said Ben.

At that point Jamie and I began to laugh, and Eric, who
had at first looked quizzical, started laughing, too. Ben said,
"Oh, cut it out, Mayfred." But she said, "No, sir, I'm not!
I *did* all that. I know *every* word! Just wait, I'll show you."
She went right on, full speed, to the "ghoul-haunted wood-
land of Weir."

Back as straight as a ramrod, Ben left the compartment.
Mayfred stopped. An hour later, when he came back, she
started again. But it wasn't till she got to Psyche "uplifting
her finger" (Mayfred lifted hers) saying, " 'Ah, fly! — let
us fly! — for we must,' " and all that about the "tremulous
light, the crystalline light," et cetera, that Ben gave up and
joined in the general merriment. She actually did know it,
every word. He followed along open-mouthed through
"Astarte" and "Sybillic," and murmured, "Oh, my
God," when she got to:

> " 'Ulalume — Ulalume —
> 'Tis the vault of thy lost Ulalume!' "

because she let go in a wail like a hound's bugle and the con-
ductor, who was passing, looked in to see if we were all
right.

We rolled into Chattanooga in the best of humor and filed
off the train into the waiting arms of my parents, Eric's
parents and selected members from Ben's and Jamie's
families. There was nobody from Mayfred's, but they'd sent

word. They all kept checking us over, as though we might need washing or might have got scarred some way. "Just promise me one thing!" Mama kept saying, just about to cry. "Don't y'all ever go away again, you hear? Not all of you! Just promise you won't do it! Promise me right now!"

I guess we must have promised, the way she was begging us to.

Ben married his Sylvia, with her pedigree and family estate in Connecticut. He's a big professor, lecturing in literature, up East. Jamie married a Catholic girl from West Virginia. He works in her father's firm and has sired a happy lot of kids. Mayfred went to New York after she left Donald and works for a big fashion house. She's been in and out of marriages, from time to time.

And Eric and I are sitting holding hands on a terrace in far off Italy. Midnight struck long ago, and we know it. We are sitting there, talking, in the pitch-black dark.

PENGUIN · SHORT · FICTION

Other Titles In This Series